Other Books by Lee Winter

The Villains Series:
Book 1

The
Fixer

LEE WINTER

Acknowledgments

I never intended to write one story told over two books, but it turns out some ice queens take quite a bit longer to melt than others. Clearly redeeming someone as complex as Michelle Hastings cannot be rushed! As a result, it was no small favor asking my beta readers to pore over two books not one.

I am so appreciative to my friend, Ylva CEO Astrid Ohletz, who always seems to magically know when there's a scene missing.

Sandy Unger was my wonderful Jewish sensitivity reader once more, offering her knowledge of the inner workings of amusing, meddling saftas and their uptight granddaughters.

Órla Smith was my expert on my Irish characters—and I now have considerably more Irish sayings and slang in my vocabulary!

My eternally entertaining friend Charlotte Loudermilt offered comments that ranged from insightful and observant to hilariously insulting, as always. Thanks, mate!

Ann Etter earns my undying appreciation for helping me invent a company that doesn't exist and yet does. Working out the accounting and financial nuances for bringing The Fixers into being was no easy feat. So, if anyone wants to create a top-secret DC corporation that flies under the radar but also pays all its taxes (to avoid attention), feel free to use our Fixers' template!

Huge thanks, once more, go to my exemplary content editor Alissa McGowan, who always sharpens and improves my books so much.

Gratitude as well goes to my copy editor Michelle Aguilar.

Lastly, thank you to my readers for taking a chance on a book with a protagonist I know everyone hated. I heard a lot: "But HOW can Michelle be redeemed?"

Good question. I used to think it was impossible too, given she was so awful to Catherine Ayers in *The Red Files* and *Under Your Skin*. I hated her so much. Now I see who she really is—and nothing is as it seems.

I hope you enjoy her journey to redemption as much as I did writing it.

Dedication

The Fixer and *Chaos Agent* would not exist if not for Angela Dawe. Angela's voicing of Michelle Hastings in "First-Class Villains", a short story from my *Sliced Ice* anthology, was stunning. Her suppressed longing, icy competence, and sharp, no-nonsense take on my villain floored me so much that I immediately wanted to write Michelle's story.

So, this book is dedicated to my inspiration, friend, and narrator—the legendary Angela Dawe.

Chapter 1
Office With No Name

THE FIRST TIME EDEN ACQUIRED an archnemesis, she had just turned twenty and was not exactly in the market for one. Although with a surname like Lawless, she supposed acquiring enemies might be more of a design feature than a bug.

Given Eden's main expertise lay in disrupting the status quo and organizing protests for good causes, perhaps it was almost inevitable.

Fun fact: Eden's first protest was in utero. Her mother, River, then eight months pregnant, fist punching the skies, hair whipping around her face, had been glowing when a photographer snapped her at a Save the Whales demonstration off the coast of Japan.

By age nine, Eden had done more sit-ins, night reclaimings, tree chainings, and placard waving than most children her age had scraped knees. So, by twenty, Eden had become adept at both the art of shaking up society and clinging to building faces, protesting her way to a college expulsion and one extremely cranky nemesis.

That event turned out to be highly relevant to why she was now sitting here, sixteen years later, in the fancy end of Washington DC, outside an office that had no name.

She'd pulled in here around midnight the previous night instead of stopping at her best friend's place as she normally would. Eden had wanted to be all set first thing this morning with a good parking spot out front for Gloria—her tastefully rainbow-painted 2008 Dodge Sprinter 3500 van.

She never minded sleeping in Gloria, which was fitted out for that purpose. Eden's DIY reno work over the years had seen her add a sweet double bed, cute oven, compact high-end shower, toilet, and wall-mounted TV. But the outside was another matter.

Gloria looked vastly out of place in DC, tapestried as she was with faded stickers marking protest movements over the decades—championing rainforests, rights for women, POC, and the LGBT+, and... snow leopards. Eden really liked snow leopards.

Goddess, she was being distracted. Eden raked her fingers through her unruly hair, hoping it would behave for once, then peered back up at the building she had to visit in a few minutes.

So the big question was: Why did this office have no name? Wasn't that weird? Eden yanked her phone out of her corduroy jacket to read the email yet again.

Dear Ms. Lawless

My name is Arnold Clemmons. I'm a researcher for a consultancy firm.

Your name and skill set came up when I was investigating a project for my employer. We are seeking to recruit for a short-term assignment an individual who is both creative and clever, media savvy, IT literate, and able to disrupt the status quo through any legal means necessary.

The pay is generous and you would set your own hours. However, a nondisclosure agreement would need to be signed before any specifics are revealed as to this project or my employer's name.

I can say that the work would involve you being based in Wingapo, Maryland—your hometown, I believe. And it involves a person from your past who was fundamental in your career shift.

If this interests you, I can set up a meeting with my employer at their office in Washington DC. A plane ticket and accommodation can be provided if you are out of the area. A street parking pass will be supplied if you require it.

Yours sincerely,

Arnold Clemmons

This job was about someone who'd been "fundamental in her career shift"? That could mean only one person: Francine Wilson. Now *Mayor* Francine Wilson, a.k.a. Eden's archnemesis.

But what did Francine have to do with some mysterious, secretive organization based in a glass tower in DC? And speaking of mysteries, what was its name?

Eden had assumed when she'd pulled up outside its address on M Street that she'd learn the name from simply looking at the door.

No such luck. It had no sign. Just an odd black symbol, like a stemless five-leaf clover. The tinted glass was too dark to see inside the foyer. A speaker sat next to the door. That was it.

Eden suddenly felt self-conscious. What was she even doing here? What skills could she possibly possess that fit in around here?

One way to find out. She leaped out of Gloria and strode up to the building.

She tugged the door. *Locked.* Then she pressed the speaker button.

A deep male voice replied: "Yes?"

"Um, hi? I'm Eden Lawless? I have an appointment—"

"Yes." The door clicked open.

The foyer was marble and the lighting dim, thanks to all those tinted windows. A black leather couch sat before a glass coffee table, a security counter, and two elevators. It was devoid of anything else.

An enormous guard who'd triple-dipped on his muscle allocation beckoned her to his desk. "I need some ID, Ms. Lawless."

Eden dug out her Maryland driver's license.

The guard pulled out a tablet, snapped a photo of the license, and then tapped some notes into his device. He pushed her license back along with a blank, white plastic card.

"Elevator pass," he said. "Enter it into the slot inside the elevator. You will be met upon exiting. Good day, Ms. Lawless."

Eden shortly found herself in a sleek metal cube, whisking up fast. There were no numbers, only double letters occasionally lighting up, indicating the passage of floors: MM, CE, CS, among others.

Before long, the doors opened at PS, and she stepped out onto a floor filled with wide windows and a stunning view. Okay, they were *really* high up. Was this the top floor? Maybe PS stood for Penthouse Suite?

A mid-twenties dark-skinned woman with the most exquisite eyebrows led Eden to another black leather couch. She oozed class with her stylish short Afro, manicured nails, and tailored gray skirt suit—definitely expensive.

She offered no name. "Your phone, Ms. Lawless? And any other recording devices." The woman held out her hand.

Eden coughed up her battered phone.

The confiscation was "temporary," the receptionist assured her while gingerly placing Eden's device in a steel box beside her desk. She locked it with a soft *snick* sound.

Eden inhaled deeply. *What the hell have I gotten myself into?*

It reminded her of the time some oil executives had wanted to fly her to their headquarters in Texas for a "pleasant chat over lunch" about the way she'd made a campaign reporting unleaded gas's possible links to cancer go viral. And she'd gone because why not? If she changed just one executive's view, she'd be delighted.

The next day had been a shocking reality check when several oil corporations had released publicity photos of her lunching in style with their executives—living the high life, being a sellout, or so the material implied. Compromised. Even though she'd spent every minute arguing with them between bites of food she was too anxious to taste. Her environmentalist client had dumped her immediately.

Lesson learned.

Or was it? What did this nameless organization want with her? Had she just walked right into a complicated trap or a con—all because they'd dangled Francine Wilson in front of her?

If it was a con, it was an expensive one. Even the billionaire oil execs didn't have an office like this. Her gaze drifted from the stylized chrome door handles to the elegant matching light switches and the beautiful floor lamps in each corner curling over like metallic dancers touching their knees.

At the end of the room, taller than Eden, sat some sort of bronze Renaissance sculpture. It was of a female nude, shrouded in sculpted windswept cloth, face angled away, hair blown behind her. Astonishing how the cloth looked real and soft not metallic. Beautiful. And expensive. As in museum-exhibit expensive.

"You like it?" the receptionist asked, following her gaze.

"Um, sure? What is it?"

The woman's dark brown eyes leveled Eden with a long look. "*Vol Haut.* That's French. It means fly high."

Fly high. That about summed up this whole place. "Is it…um, classic? Some dead white Italian dude from the Renaissance era?" She could picture him already.

"*Chinese* sculptor Luo Li Rong made it, and *she* was born in 1980."

Eden gave a sheepish grin. Wrong on all counts, then. "Ah."

"But the sculpture is a classic," the receptionist conceded with a tiny sniff. "In my opinion, at least. Our CEO bought it from a gallery in France at the artist's last showing. There was a fierce bidding war for it."

So, the CEO had a ton of splash cash to blow on bronze nudes? Interesting. Eden wondered if he was some self-indulgent collector or simply a lech.

Her ears pricked up at the faintest noise. At first, Eden had thought she was hearing things, but, no, it was there: a faint, untidy hum. After ten more minutes of hearing it, she cleared her throat and glanced at the other woman.

The receptionist looked up pointedly at the latest interruption, an eyebrow high and arched. "*Yes,* Ms. Lawless?"

"Do you hear that noise?"

"Yes, Ms. Lawless," came the cultured reply without any further explanation.

Oh, for Christ's sake. "What on earth is it?"

"White noise," the woman replied. "It is to facilitate higher productivity by muting sounds of others working and talking. Further," she paused, as if for effect, "our particular white noise technology has a dampening field in it that will prevent any audio recording devices from working."

Eden's jaw dropped. "Is that even a thing?" She was quite well up on most tech thanks to IT once having been her field of study. This was new.

"I can assure you, Ms. Lawless, it is most definitely a...*thing*." She returned to work.

Right, well, that shut Eden up—as intended, she had no doubt.

Time ticked on. What was taking so long? Was this some intimidation tactic? Show the minion who was boss? But why? They had actively sought her out, not the other way around.

She ran her hands down her good jeans, the black ones that didn't obviously look like denim unless you touched them. Eden had no doubt she was wildly out of place here, which might explain the receptionist's attitude. Probably didn't see too many social agitators or Earth justice warriors around here.

Eden toyed with the thin chain at her neck. It had a round symbol representing Gaia—a flat tree in a circle, with curling, interconnected branches to signify Mother Earth. Her mom had given it to her before disappearing off to her latest protest, harassing supertrawlers overfishing in the North Sea. That had been over eighteen months ago. She'd kept extending her mission. Eden missed River every day.

She shifted her polished black boots and hunched further back into her jacket. It probably wasn't the usual posh office interview look, but if they wanted Eden, this was what they got.

A door opened down the hall and a sixty-ish woman with graying blond hair made a beeline toward her. She was pleasantly plump and beautifully presented in a champagne-colored skirt and chiffon ivory blouse. Her confident walk and attitude were commanding. Eden was transfixed. She must be high up the company ladder, surely?

Then she smiled at Eden, which transformed her from imperious to maternal. Gone instantly was any hint of power, like a switch had flipped off.

What an unusual effect. Eden stared in surprise.

"If you'll come this way, please, Ms. Lawless," she said. "Our CEO is ready to see you now."

CEO? She'd scored an interview with the CEO? "Sure." Eden shot to her feet. "Sure," she said again to the woman's now retreating back.

A few moments later, her escort knocked on a polished oak door, eased it open, and announced, "Ms. Lawless is here for her interview." She turned to Eden expectantly.

With a "thanks," Eden stepped through the door.

———⟐———

Eden looked around. The CEO's office was spacious, with yet another black leather couch by the window. Gray carpet felt plush and thick beneath her boots. The off-white walls were broken up by art prints; probably something bidding-war worthy too, but Eden knew even less about abstract art than she did bronze nudes.

Despite the art, everything seemed so…soulless.

The strange, soft, white-noise hiss was louder in here. Prickles went up Eden's neck.

She spun around to find a minimalist glass desk tucked away on one side of the room. It was not a remotely logical place to put a desk unless you needed your back to a solid wall. The office's rear was entirely wall-to-wall windows.

Behind the desk sat a woman in an immaculate navy blazer with a blindingly white shirt collar jutting high up her neck. Her dark-chestnut hair had been corralled into a tight ball low against her neck. That neck was hard to miss. Long and tapered, it came to a strong, firm jaw and proud chin. All her features were angular, like a goddess from a Grecian urn, especially her pointy chin and classically elegant, longer nose. Her high cheekbones, free of any makeup, were sharp as a blade. As was her impatient expression.

Eden's heart jumped, and her palms slicked at being caught gawking.

The woman shifted her hands from her keyboard to her desk, interlacing long fingers in front of herself; she regarded Eden as one might an insect that required assessment for pinning in a display case.

Those penetrating hazel eyes were so dark and intense that Eden indeed felt pinned in place.

She stopped in front of the desk.

The woman gestured for Eden to sit in an overstuffed black chair opposite, and she obeyed instantly.

Up close, the CEO was beyond intimidating. Her posture was fixed and straight, and there was so much stillness. Unusual. Eden was used to acquaintances and friends being loud, making themselves larger to fill spaces not typically designed for them. But this woman, lean and compact though she was, seemed to effortlessly fill her whole office. So much authority.

"Thank you, Tilly," the woman suddenly said. Her voice was low, no-nonsense, and almost curt.

Eden's escort merely nodded, exiting with an effortless grace.

Okay, so the possibly personal assistant was Tilly. Eden was relieved someone around here had a name. She hoped the intimidating CEO would introduce herself now too.

"I trust you found us okay," the woman said instead, voice soft and almost faintly amused. "Not everyone does."

There was something so cool about how she spoke, as if she barely bothered speaking much at all and the listener should feel fortunate to be graced with an audience.

"Well, I'm not surprised," Eden said, settling back a little in the chair. "Your office has no name. You just have some weird, squishy, little round logo."

"It's a pentalobe. And no, there's little point having a secret organization and then emblazoning our name across the office."

"Why not just use a fake name?" Eden asked, warming to the topic. She leaned forward. "Like Humboldt Industries."

"Humboldt…" the woman's look became perplexed. "What on earth is that?"

"Exactly." Eden spread her hands out as if sharing her genius idea with the world. "Nothing. But it sounds like something. Right? Maybe you make cheese? Maybe you don't. Who can say?"

The other woman stared at her for long enough that Eden began to squirm. "Cheese," she finally muttered.

"Yeah." Eden trailed off at the woman's pinched expression. "Never mind, then."

The woman apparently gave up on any pretense at interest in the topic and leaned back. "I'm curious about something. You were offered free accommodation in a top hotel and a flight here if you needed it. You declined both and only accepted the parking pass. Why?"

"Maybe I was in the neighborhood," she said lightly.

"You weren't. My researcher said you were doing work in Ohio campaigning for nurses this week. So, you drove seven hours to attend an interview when you could have arrived in style and well-rested. I ask again, why?"

How could the researcher know that? Eden didn't advertise her clients or her whereabouts. Maybe one of the nurses had tagged her in something on social media? It was creepy how knowledgeable these people were about her, especially given how little she knew in return.

Eden eyeballed the woman watching her impassively. "Because I like to know who I'm dealing with before I take favors. That way I don't end up beholden to someone down the track that I'd rather not be." Lesson learned from those Texan oil execs. *Fool me once...*

The woman gave a faint nod of what looked a lot like approval. "Understandable." She smiled. "Tell me, what did you think of the bronze in the main office?"

"The nude?" Eden clarified.

"*Was* she nude?" The woman tilted her head.

Good question. Did having sculpted transparent gauze all over you make you naked or not? "Yes."

The CEO regarded her impassively. "Interesting. See, I'd argue no. She has a covering of the cloth, even if one can see through it."

"It's irrelevant as a covering if it's of no use."

"It's of use to her. *She* might find it useful in some way. Maybe it gives her confidence. Or it's her mask? Or distracts us from something else she hides?"

The hell? Eden blinked at her. "She's *nude*," she enunciated, then stared at her incredulously.

The other woman gave a soft snicker and glanced down at a folder, as if about to ask another question, but Eden was over these weird games.

"Look, can we cut to the chase? Why am I here? What's the job, please? And, most especially, what's your name?"

"Ms. Lawless, I'm sure you have many questions," she began, her voice a mesmerizing, low, almost derisive tone.

"Of *course* I have many questions." Was she kidding?

"And I'm afraid I won't be able to answer most of them. Our clients pay top dollar for secrecy. Our entire consultancy firm runs on the premise their identities will be protected. That is our number-one priority: keeping secrets. So, I cannot tell you who hired us for this project or why."

"But…"

"No." One cold, firm word stopped Eden's protest dead. "What I can tell you is this: a person who ruined your life once in your hometown is about to have a *very* bad time of her reelection campaign for mayor. Is that something you're interested in hearing more about?"

Francine Wilson having a bad time for once in her life? "Yeah," Eden said hoarsely. "Big yeah."

"All right." The woman slid some papers across the desk. "Our standard nondisclosure agreement. It says you can't talk about me, our organization, the job you're doing for us, or anything else associated with us."

"Well, I don't *know* anything, so it'll be hard to blab."

"Now, maybe. You will acquire more information as time goes on. The price to hear what we have in mind is your signature." She pushed a pen across the desk. "Well, two of them. The forms are in duplicate."

Eden picked up the paperwork, reading carefully. It seemed pretty straightforward. Don't spill the beans and her sorry ass wouldn't be sued into the Stone Age. "If I sign this, will you tell me your name?"

"Since my name will be right beneath yours as witness, that's a given."

"Good. Because it'd be weird having a boss without a name." She signed her blocky solid scribble, then pushed the page back. "Otherwise, what would I call you? M?"

"M?" The woman's expression turned puzzled. "Because our building is on M Street?"

"No, as in James Bond? His boss?"

The CEO reviewed Eden's signatures, then signed her own name twice with acutely slanted, mashed letters that Eden couldn't read upside down. Then she lifted an eyebrow. "You feel you are James Bond?"

"Um. No."

The CEO shot her a withering look that made her feel a foot tall as she pushed one document over to Eden. "Your copy. I encourage you to study it in detail."

Eden immediately tried to decipher the woman's squishy signature and turn it into a name.

"My name is Michelle Hastings." She paused, and her mouth made the tiniest uptick at the sides. "To save you the eye strain."

Eden immediately looked up from the scrawl in relief. "Okay. Great. Hi!" she said a little too brightly.

"*Hi*," Michelle drawled back.

Eden plowed on to hide how ridiculous she felt. "Well, I like Michelle better than M. Although Judi Dench's M was *the* best. And I guess it's not *bad* to be compared to Dame Judi."

Michelle stared at her as if Eden had lost her damned mind.

Well, okay, she *might* be overcompensating for her nervousness by babbling. "Right. So, Michelle—"

The other woman twitched.

What? She was supposed to call her *Ms. Hastings*? She wasn't Eden's boss. Not yet, anyway. She didn't know her. Certainly not enough to confer some sort of floor-scraping deference. Respect was earned.

"*Michelle*," Eden repeated, kind of enjoying the way the other woman seemed to be biting back a reprimand—probably hard for her, not controlling everything. "Francine Wilson is the most corrupt person my hometown's ever seen."

"Do tell."

Eden gave a frustrated huff. "When I locked horns with her, I was a twenty-year-old college kid and she was a big-deal property developer. She owns most of the real estate in Wingapo County, all the off-campus student accommodation for my local college there and most of it around Hood College in neighboring Frederick."

"Yes," Michelle said briskly. "And Francine Wilson has acquired vastly more property since you tangled with her. She's also grown more powerful since becoming mayor. Apparently, she counts the Maryland Attorney General as her closest friend."

Eden scowled. "Closest bribe recipient, you mean."

"And you know this for a fact?"

"I know *her*. Look, Francine's not some successful businesswoman who just happens to be a property developer. My beef with her is not about jealousy or hating the rich or her ambition to own half the world. Francine's a dirty slumlord. And *that* is a fact."

"Mm." Michelle watched her through hooded eyes.

"Don't believe me?" Eden clenched her fists as the injustices of long ago rose up into her throat. "She gets away with murder. She's untouchable! Anyone who says anything negative about her is portrayed as a bitter nutjob by the media and cops. She has them in her back pocket. She cuts corners on maintenance on her properties, but when tenants, like, oh I dunno, poor college kids, complain to the attorney general, Wingapo Police, or the media, it gets buried. Everyone in any position of power is either intimidated or compromised. If that's not bad enough, now she's the mayor! I'm glad I wasn't there to see that. She has so much power, it's disgusting."

"Well," Michelle said evenly. "I happen to agree."

"You do?" Surprise stole through Eden. She unlocked her fists and surreptitiously wiped her sweaty palms down her pants. Usually no one believed her. It sounded so outlandish, as though Eden was some crazy conspiracy theorist.

"Of course." Michelle drew a page out of her folder and read. "My researcher has concluded Francine Wilson is 'corrupt, cocky, loaded with cash, and about to run for her third mayoral term even though it is thoroughly undeserved.' And she *will* win. So…" She cocked her head. "Want to help us prevent that?"

Eden blinked. Her mouth went dry. "Why now? And why me?"

"I have no idea why a client reached out to us now, not two terms ago, to prevent Wilson's win. But your second question is simple:

Mr. Clemmons spent months in Wingapo assessing what was needed to accomplish the client's request. He came to the same conclusion you did: the media and police have been paid off; the attorney general too."

"No kidding." Eden hunched over at the painful reminder. "She hurts anyone who gets in her way." She inhaled sharply. "I got in her way."

"Yes, you did. Memorably so. In fact, according to Mr. Clemmons, you remain the only person to stand up to her in any meaningful way. You got under her skin in a way no one has before or since. So that makes you the ideal candidate to do it again."

"But I LOST!" Eden cried out before mortification flooded her. "Hell! Sorry."

"Yes, you lost." Michelle said calmly, as if Eden hadn't lost her composure. "She had your father fired to get back at you. Additionally, she managed to get you expelled and run out of town. That's power."

"Yeah," Eden said sullenly.

Michelle's eyes left her notes and met Eden's. "She was a mere property developer at the time. She's on your old college's board and had a wing named after her at your father's now former workplace thanks to all her donations. That tells me she has no qualms about using her power and influence to punish her enemies."

Eden ground her teeth.

"Well, enemy, singular," Michelle corrected. "Since you appear to be her only one—officially, anyway." She pulled another page out of her folder. "Our researcher says you were expelled from Wingapo State University for making threats against a public figure. Namely, Francine Wilson."

Eden sighed.

Michelle cocked her head. "No argument then?"

"What's the point? She claims it's true, got the media to print it, the college to act on it. What's the real story—my side—got to do with anything?"

"As it turns out, we trade on the truth here. And secrets. And lies. We especially love the *real story*." Michelle flipped through her folder and drew out a photocopy of a news article. "Very creative," she noted. "It's impressive you managed to finally get a negative story into your local paper about the mayor."

Eden stared mulishly at the photograph of her infamous anti-Francine protest. The whole facade of the Wilson Properties building, all three stories of Francine's precious headquarters, was covered in computer paper to create an optical illusion.

A dozen of Eden's college friends, as fed up as she'd been with the substandard accommodation, had helped her stick up the paper for hours in the middle of the night. They'd swayed from abseiling ropes, affixing fifteen long reams of computer paper side by side to the windows.

From a distance, it showed the image of Francine Wilson's head, smiling benevolently like a giant Communist propaganda banner. But up close, passersby discovered the photo was made up of typed words...thousands and thousands of anonymous complaints from Wilson Properties tenants about unfixed issues. Low water pressure. Cracks in walls. Mold growth. No heat. Roach infestations.

Eden's eyes slid to the headline: *Vandals target property company office; make threats*

"Sure, I got a negative story into print...but it was negative about *me*," Eden said with a growl. Because when the local paper had printed its story, there hadn't been a single word about the tenants' complaints in the entire article. Just a rant about how Eden and her "juvenile delinquent accomplices" had misused college resources and threatened to harm Francine and her employees.

Okay, the misusing college resources part had been true. It was also how police had worked out it was her. She'd used the college computer lab to print her protest materials. And amidst all the printed complaints had been a few goading comments. Lines that Francine had twisted and called threats and demanded the university act on.

We won't let you get away with this!
You should be punished for treating tenants like scum!
This isn't over. We've only just begun!
YOU should pay this time! You and ALL your nasty-assed staff who ignore us!

It was the last comment that did it. Threatening more than five people with violence in Maryland turned out to be a felony. The frustrating part was that Eden hadn't even written those comments, but that didn't matter to her college. She'd been the ringleader; the protest materials were her responsibility. And Francine had threatened the college with all manner of serious police charges, bad publicity, donation-pulling, and general wrath until Eden was expelled.

"Wilson is a powerful, vindictive woman with no obvious chinks in her armor," Michelle concluded, dropping the article back into her folder.

"No kidding," Eden said under her breath.

"Except one." Michelle looked at her. And kept looking.

"Me?" Eden had surely misheard. If she was a chink in Francine Wilson's armor, it had to be the smallest chink in history.

"My researcher is adamant. In all the years Wilson has been throwing her weight around Wingapo County, you're the only person to have unsettled her. You even enraged her to the point that she showed her anger in public. She dropped her facade long enough for the people to glimpse who she really was. You're the reason she didn't get elected the first year she ran. Of course, she later made massive PR strides and the early incidents were forgotten. But in that brief window that you two were at war, you, Ms. Lawless, remain the only person to have ever seriously rattled Francine Wilson. So, naturally, we want you for this assignment."

"But she still won," Eden said quietly. "She always wins."

"You rattle her, Ms. Lawless," Michelle repeated. "You drive her crazy and throw her off her game. When you can make someone angry, they make mistakes, and *that's* what I'm counting on. Remember that you last encountered her when you were a student of limited means and connections. This time, you'll have us behind you, highly connected experts, as well as access to money and clout."

"So send one of your highly connected experts!"

"I can't send just anyone. *You're* the one who has her number. You're the one who distracts her. You *know* her. You are uniquely qualified for this assignment. Not to mention, you have a creative mind. You are *ideal.*"

Well, she made a good argument. But still. Facing Francine again? Her gut churned in dismay. "She's…a lot. Going home is a big deal for me. I couldn't finish my IT degree because of her. My dad still doesn't talk to me. Everyone I grew up with thinks I threatened Francine and her staff! Gah! She's the devil!" Eden sagged. "And honestly? I'm afraid she's unstoppable."

"She *lost* that first election," Michelle reminded her, eyes sharp. "Because of *you*. You ensured everyone saw the real woman. Even if they forgot later, for one moment in time *you* won, and that's why she retaliated savagely. Ms. Lawless, you already destroyed her once; I simply want you to do it again."

"How?" Eden croaked out. "I mean, specifically? What can I do?"

"You know the players. They're all still there. You know what *not* to do and who to avoid. I'll need all your creativity to get around the blackouts on any negative media reporting of her. So: Find a way to make the public remember what she's like and do it in such a way that even the media will have to cover it. Can you do that?"

"I…maybe?" Eden said slowly. "But just because I can doesn't mean I should."

"You said it yourself: She's the devil. Shouldn't devils be defeated?" Michelle's tone was taunting.

"Devils burn you, Michelle. Everyone and everything she touches—if she doesn't like you, you're crispy. Look, I've moved on. I don't see what I'd get from this aside from revenge, which, sure, might be a blast for five seconds, but it's not really me. In fact, there's nothing in this for me but pain. Wingapo has some depressing memories for me. Why would I do this to myself again?"

Michelle smiled slightly. "To *win*. And besides, you will get a very generous payment if Wilson loses the election. That should keep your little…protest endeavors in funding for years. So why not have Wilson fund your future as the ultimate 'screw you' to her?" She slid a packet across the table. "The remuneration details are all in there."

Eden reached for it.

"But the CliffsNotes are that it includes a contract stating that your pay is two hundred thousand if Wilson loses her election. Plus fifty thousand for expenses on a debit card supplied to you. The con-

THE FIXER

tract further stipulates that everything you do must be done legally and nothing can ever be linked to us. It must appear that you decided to do this yourself out of the blue."

Eden swallowed in shock. Two *hundred* thousand... "Holy..." she whispered. "That is *not* chump change."

A smirk darted across Michelle's face. "What did you expect from us?"

"I'm not sure," Eden said honestly. "I don't know who 'us' is. I mean, I was half convinced this was a sex-slave kidnapping scam thing."

This time, Michelle's perfect mask dropped, replaced with astonishment. "A...what?"

"Well, only *half* convinced. I was also open to this being some classy, upscale con. Though I'm not sure I have much of anything you could scam from me. Maybe Gloria. That's my van. She's named after Gloria Steinem and she used to be a FedEx van but I've tricked her up now," Eden rambled on, feeling a little dazed. She paused for a breath. "I'm *still* open to considering that this could be a con. Just so you know."

Michelle's look turned startled. "Well," she said slowly, as if not sure quite how to take this turn of events. "We have no interest in acquiring your...Gloria." Her eyes tightened. "I can assure you we're more in the business of political climate change than wallowing about in filth such as sexual slavery."

"An argument could be made they're the same. Politics and filth." Eden shrugged.

That seemed to stymie Michelle.

"Look, I'm interested, I am," Eden said, before this snowballed into anything weirder. "Can I think about it? Take a day or two? This is a lot to take in, you know? I'm just a liberal-leftie protest organizer who loves a good cause. You're asking me to go back to where my life fell apart and poke at those old wounds again." Eden gave a slow headshake. "My brain is overwhelmed. I don't think I can force any decisions right now. Can I take some time?"

"You have twenty-four hours, and then I need your answer. If you wish to proceed, reply to the secured email we will send you with a Yes, and that will be considered agreement to our contract here." She tapped the envelope. "We will get you to digitally sign off on it properly within days. My PA, Tilly—Ottilie Zimmermann—will liaise with you if we need anything further. Her number is in the envelope too."

"Sure. Okay." Eden nodded. "Twenty-four hours. Right." She reached for the envelope in front of her.

"Wait." Michelle put her hand out for it and Eden slid it back.

Michelle's fountain pen had a glossy tortoiseshell grip. She scribbled on the envelope. "I'm going to assume, once you've dealt with your *overwhelmed brain*, that you will take this offer. If so, you will be expected to Skype in your progress reports each evening. These are the Skype details for that video call. Eight sharp each night that you're in Wingapo. Do not be late."

"Skype? Nightly?" Eden blinked. "You don't trust me?"

"It's *standard operating procedure*." Michelle's eyes tightened. "It's surely not too much to ask given how much you'll be paid? I like to be sure we've invested wisely. Do not ask for special treatment."

"Uh. Okay. No problem." Eden nodded. The CEO wasn't wrong. This *was* a lot of money. So it'd make sense a handler had been assigned to find out what she was up to on the ground.

"Good," Michelle said. "Any further questions?"

Eden shook her head mutely.

"Tilly will show you out." She pressed a buzzer, and her assistant reappeared at the door. "Ms. Lawless is leaving now," Michelle told her.

Eden scrambled to her feet.

"Oh, and Ms. Lawless," Michelle added sharply, "you will address me as Ms. Hastings going forward in any interactions or correspondence."

Eden paused and said quietly, "I'm sorry, I won't be doing that."

"Excuse me?"

"Don't take it personally, but I find the demand to use honorifics classist. We're all humans, right? All spinning on this big ol' marble, just trying to survive, put our pants on one leg at a time like everyone else. Historically, they slapped pretentious labels on those with money or power to keep the little guy in their place. To push them down. They call it respect, but they never return it. I'm not about that. Equality, Michelle. I'm only ever about equality."

Michelle's lips pressed together.

"Only exception," Eden continued, "is if it's someone changing the whole world in some amazing way. Then they'd have earned it. Like, if you were curing cancer on the side." She paused. "Wait, since I don't know what else you do around here, I can't assume anything. You aren't, are you? Curing cancer?"

Michelle snorted. "Not that I'm aware of."

Eden grinned. "Okay, then. Well, I'll go and let you return to… whatever the heck it is all you secret squirrels do around here."

"Secret. Squirrels?" Michelle's expression was incredulous.

With a shrug, Eden said, "Well, without a name, that's what I'm calling you people in my head."

"Not just in your head, it seems," Michelle muttered.

"I guess not." Eden grinned. "Oops."

"If it helps, outside our office, many of our contractors call it 'The Club' to avoid questions."

"The…*club*." Eden peered around. "Seriously? *Is* there a club around here? Like a floor down or something? Blackjack? Lounge? Sultry singers, maybe?"

"No." Michelle bit off the word and glanced at her watch.

Eden took the hint and headed to the door. "Okay, right. I'll get back to you ASAP. Bye, Michelle."

She didn't have to look back to know the other woman had reacted at being called that.

Eden's phone was firmly pushed back into her hand by the snooty, art-loving receptionist. She glanced back at the bronze sculpture—*still freaking nude*. Then she was being inserted into the elevator by the ever-efficient Tilly.

Outside once more, Eden stared back up at the building's towering facade, feeling like she'd just been hit by something powerful, strange, and overwhelming. Hard to like or dislike yet, too soon to say, but really mysterious. A bit like Michelle Hastings. Although she was un-forgettable in another way too.

Not that Eden was going to focus on something so shallow as looks. She had to weigh up the offer dispassionately and not for a moment think of those beautiful, sardonic lips, that intense expression, or the powerful presence that filled her whole office.

She unlocked her van and tossed "The Club's" envelope on her passenger seat.

Instead of starting her engine, she glanced back up to the top floor of the building. She couldn't see anything, of course, but she had the strangest sensation she was being watched.

———⊷⟡⟞———

"*Standard operating procedure.*"

"You heard that?" Michelle looked up as her assistant returned after showing Lawless out.

Tilly merely looked back at her.

"Of course you did," Michelle added dryly.

What was the point of using white noise if private conversations could be overheard?

Through *closed* doors.

Oh. Tilly had to have listened in through her desk phone. She pursed her lips. "I'd suggest eavesdropping is inappropriate, but it *is* a central tenet of our business model."

Tilly smiled her agreement. Her usually stern face softened, transforming itself in a way that always impressed Michelle. No wonder she'd been an effective field agent back in the day.

"On this particular candidate, I was too curious not to find out how the meeting was going," Tilly said. "So...are we going to talk about our new standard operating procedure?"

"Yes, well, she's new." Michelle hated the tinge of defensiveness in her voice. "How do I know if she'll be any good?"

"You never asked to Skype any of the other new hires on their first assignments."

"They aren't rampaging, idealistic social justice warriors with the potential to go off piste."

"You worry that Ms. Lawless is a loose cannon?" Tilly asked.

This time, Michelle did lift her gaze. "I'm not sure *what* she is." Well, not exactly. "But she bears watching."

Her assistant snorted. "She is different, isn't she? That nonsense about rebranding ourselves as makers of Humboldt cheese?"

"That was the exact moment I wondered if Clemmons was playing a joke on me. He sent us a panda," Michelle said with a wry smile. "You know—all innocent, cute, and hapless, means well, but without a single conniving bone in her body."

"You think she's cute?" Tilly asked neutrally.

Michelle wasn't fooled by the innocent question. Her PA was wily and observant and could fish like a pro. "Only if you like pandas—especially guileless ones. There's a reason they're endangered." She frowned. "Do you think Clemmons lost his mind recommending her? All I see is someone raw and naïve and hopelessly out of her depth here. She's clever enough in the shallow end, I'll grant you, but we're bottomless."

"Well, I'd guarantee we don't have any other contractors on our books like her."

"Given that our contractors are all sharks and snakes, no, it's safe to say we have no pandas. Her face when I told her the pay?" Michelle said with faint amusement. "I thought you'd have to administer her CPR."

"Me?" Tilly's eyebrow lifted slightly. "Not you?"

Again with the fishing. But only fools laid bare their necks, especially around here, even to generally harmless sixty-four-year-old assistants named Ottilie Zimmermann.

"No, thank you," Michelle said lightly. "I might catch that Girl Scout idealism of hers. Next thing, I'd be saving endangered species in my downtime."

"No chance of that." Tilly bit off a half-laugh. "I can't help but notice she passed your little sculpture test."

"Yes. That was interesting, wasn't it?"

The sculpture question was a personality test Michelle gave all potential hires. It was irrelevant whether Lawless said the figure was nude or not. Michelle would argue either side depending on a candidate's answer. The idea was to test whether Lawless would change her answer to match Michelle's. Whether she would ingratiate herself to a potential boss by changing her opinion on a frivolous matter that she had no investment in.

The staff who worked here knew diplomacy. Most had slid high up government or security agencies before joining The Fixers. They knew the value of manipulation and of having bosses like you. No one had ever dug their heels in and stuck to their original answer on the test, knowing it could cost them a potential job.

Except Lawless.

Michelle regarded her assistant thoughtfully. Tilly had been with The Fixers from the beginning and had held her CEO assistant job long before Michelle had arrived. "Tell me honestly, Tilly: how would you have answered if I'd given you that test in your interview?"

Tilly supplied one of her completely disarming smiles that made her look like a kindly grandmother. She affected a sweet, down-home voice and answered, "Why, Ms. Hastings, I'm sure you know more about art than I do. I've never seen *anything* like that before where I come from. Are you an art expert then? Is that an interest of yours?"

Michelle laughed at the insincerity and clever pivot. "Remind me never to cross you."

"Wise." Tilly looked pleased. "So...*is* Lawless the only one to stick to her guns on the test?"

"The only one to do it directly. O'Brian came close." She adjusted her voice to the man's accent—New York City with a solid dollop of Irish he'd never lost despite twenty-five years in the US. "He said: 'Shame I got the answer wrong, but it's feckin' *art*. I do guns, knives, lockpickin', tracin', stakeouts, and all that. So: when do I start my *actual* job?'"

"That sounds like him. Interesting that you promoted him straight to head of security. Was his answer a factor?"

"It was." Michelle admitted. "I prefer honest people who aren't afraid of speaking their mind even if it's uncomfortable, especially given the truth is a rare commodity around here." Being honest was an absurd concept in DC. "I know our entire company depends on us skulking around, being slippery and clever, so it's refreshing knowing where I stand. Of course I chose him."

Tilly studied her for a moment. "Well, then, I imagine you'll enjoy Ms. Lawless a great deal. She is nothing if not frank. Even when she's not speaking, she can be read like an open book."

Enjoy Ms. Lawless? Hardly. The candidate struck Michelle as a somewhat strange individual who'd dressed as if she were heading to a rave in those chunky boots, trucker jacket, and pants that were barely disguised jeans. She *was* forthright, interesting, and unpolished, and she held the rare distinction of being the only one to pass Michelle's honesty test. But she was also decidedly odd, like the squarest of pegs. So, no, there would be no enjoying Lawless. She glared at Tilly for even making the suggestion.

Unperturbed, her PA wandered over to the sweeping rear office windows and then stopped, looking down. She spoke into the glass: "Ms. Hastings, have you seen what she drives?"

"You mean the infamous Gloria?"

"Your eyeballs may never recover. It's a hippie's dream ride, complete with solar panels."

Solar panels? Did she live in that thing, then? Michelle shuddered at the idea. "I'll leave it to my imagination and presume it's the most appalling-looking revamped FedEx van in human existence."

Tilly turned from the window, her eyebrow cocked. "Isn't it ridiculous that that naïve, sweet summer child has somehow managed to make an arch enemy?" Incredulity laced her tone.

"That may speak more about Wilson than Lawless. I admit I'm rather curious as to what that 'naïve, sweet summer child' will come up with to get a powerful mayor on the outs with the public."

"You're assuming Lawless will take the job."

"She will. Even professional crusaders need funding. Think how many doomed critters she can save from extinction," Michelle drawled. "We might actually be putting money into a worthy pocket for once."

"That'll be a first." Tilly's tone was dry.

Wasn't that the truth? For the briefest second, Michelle's heart gave a bitter clench at the reminder. The Fixers was the antithesis of everything Eden Lawless stood for. For the right price, they either made the weak powerful or crushed the enemies of the powerful. They mainly fulfilled the whims and dreams of people who didn't deserve it.

Rare was the day they helped bleeding-heart causes. Even then, it was usually an unintended side effect from some larger, dirtier deed.

And because they were mere consultants—making suggestions, calling in favors from their extensive network, scratching mutual backs, being helpful to a point, it was all entirely legal. Mostly. As long as you didn't count all the bribes and computer hacks.

The Fixers didn't exist on paper anywhere. A Washington DC accountancy firm paid all their expenses, wages, equipment, and building rent under a file they called The Club. The Fixers' Hong Kong-based headquarters, in turn, paid the accountancy firm. The five Americans behind the offshore headquarters made up The Fixers' board. It was one perfect, neat circle.

All parties were scrupulous to ensure there were no tax or filing irregularities that could cause any officials to sniff around. For decades, that had kept The Fixers invisible and safe: two things Michelle prized a great deal as CEO. It was the reason for their ongoing success.

"Lawless is trying to take on the system," Tilly mused.

"Yes," Michelle said quietly. "She'll never win."

"No. That's not how the world works. But am I wrong or does Lawless actually seem to think *we're* doing the greater good? Her cancer question, for instance? She has no idea who she's throwing her lot in with."

"No," Michelle said, wondering why she'd clenched her jaw. "She doesn't have a clue."

"Would she even have stepped foot in our building if she knew who we are?"

"No chance at all." Michelle gave Tilly a serious look. "It goes without saying, but I'll say it anyway: it's best for everyone involved that Lawless never finds out what we do here. Specifically, how... open...we can be to dealing with grayer areas of morality. Don't you agree?"

Tilly inclined her head in acceptance.

Good. Message received.

Chapter 2

Celebration Nachos

THE DOWNSIDE OF BEING A minor revolutionary was the fact Eden spent most of her life living out of her van. Gloria smelled of dirt collected from across America no matter how often she cleaned her. Not that she didn't adore her baby, which she'd tricked out to be almost fancy. Still, living and working in the same twenty-foot-long space 24/7 could get stale.

The upside of being a minor revolutionary, though, was she had multiple home bases, thanks to a friendship network that spread from coast to coast. And no greater friend existed in the world than Aggie Teo, owner of a warm heart and a one-bedroom slice of adorableness in Marshall Heights, DC. Eden had decided the moment she'd left her interview this morning that what she needed was some chill and processing time with her best friend.

Aggie—short for Agatha, thanks to her crime-novel loving mom—had been Eden's college roommate in Wingapo and these days could be counted on for a pull-out sofa bed, mockery for Eden's "super-lez" outfits, and enthusiastic commentary on the state of her dating life. Eden's dating life, of course; never Aggie's.

Aggie didn't need any commentary on her own love life because she'd been mooning over the same man for fifteen years. The *not*-couple were still navigating how or whether to go from friends to more. Apparently, that was not something to rush.

The moment Eden pulled up in front of Aggie's townhouse, a skinny, two-story, sky-blue building, a sense of peace and warmth settled over her. It was shattered in two seconds when her phone rang.

She answered: "Eden."

"Oh, thank God you're there."

"Helen?" She frowned and checked her phone for the time. Eden was helping this client gain public support for nurses facing a staff shortage and pay crisis in Ohio. At this very minute, Helen was supposed to be mid-protest, at the center of a media photo op. "What's wrong?"

"The governor didn't turn up." There was a panicked wheeze down the line. "And when he didn't show, the media packed up and left." She huffed. "I practiced my sound bites, just like you said too. No more than ten seconds."

Damn. Eden rubbed her temple. No media, no coverage. No awareness of their cause. She'd thought the governor wanted to look sympathetic to a bunch of nurses, with his election coming up. On the other hand, he had been seen dining with the biggest hospital's administrator two days ago. Someone had changed his mind.

"So we've taken to the streets," Helen said uncertainly. "We couldn't think what else to do to get the media to notice us. We're blocking traffic now, waving our signs. I think when the traffic starts backing up, we'll make the news anyway."

Goddammit. *Amateurs.* "No," Eden said instantly. "Get everyone off the road immediately. I mean it. Not one person should have a toe in front of a vehicle."

"What? Why?"

"Are you *trying* to turn public sentiment against you? Instead of people wanting better conditions for you, all you're doing is creating a bunch of angry drivers who'll be late to meetings, jobs, appointments, whatever and who'll never support you after this."

"But it's a common tactic!" Helen sputtered. "Everyone does it."

"Organized, well-advertised street marches are one thing, sure. Bedlam like this is not a sound tactic. You've paid for my expert guidance, so listen when I give it: Get your people off the street before you make headlines for being hauled off to jail. While you're doing that, put Melissa on."

"Ah, okay." A rustling noise sounded.

While her client found her second-in-charge, the woman who ran their nursing union's social media, Eden quickly jumped to Google and tapped in a query, studying the results.

"Hi?"

"Melissa, it's Eden. I need you to get everyone some new protest signs or write over what they have with: *honk if you support nurses. Honk harder if you love Steve Carrell.*"

"What?" She paused. "Why some random actor?"

"His mother was a psychiatric nurse. Do the same for Tina Turner—she worked as a nurse's aide. Repeat for Jenny McCarthy, Julie Walters, Paul Brandt, and anyone else you can find with a link to nursing. You get the idea. Now here's the important bit. Wave the signs—from the *side* of the road. Do *not* get in the way of traffic—and get lots of photos and videos of the nurses doing it."

"Okay," Melissa said. "Can do."

"Upload the photos to social media and tag the relevant star named in that sign. You only need one star to retweet the protest pic, but the more who do, the better for us. When one celebrity retweets it, post that tweet to the governor, the hospital execs, and anyone else in power. Ask them why they don't think helping Ohioan nurses is worth their time. Ask the Governor especially why he snubbed nurses today. Get *everyone* to retweet that to him. Drown him in tweets."

"I don't think the governor will care. He only reluctantly agreed to attend our meeting and pulled the plug at the first opportunity. Besides, it's only social media. He doesn't even run his account."

Eden snorted. "He might care when the media pick up the story after a celebrity makes journalists give a crap about nurses' issues. On that note, I'll email you a list of sympathetic reporters to alert to the celebrity tweets when they start coming in. They'll follow up, don't worry. Nothing like combining sympathy for nurses, apathy from a politician, and the concerns of a popular celebrity to get the media excited."

"How do you know all this?" Melissa asked, sounding a little dazed.

"It's my job." Eden fished her battered media contacts book out of her glove box and scanned it for Ohioans. "Try Jennifer Richards first at WJW-TV. Both her kids work in healthcare, if I remember correctly. Send her a video she can air of people honking at the signs, especially footage related to whichever celebrity has retweeted."

"What makes you so sure one will?"

"Most celebrities remember where they come from, especially ones from a working-class background. They'd feel like they're turning their backs on their roots not to share this. Okay?"

"Right. Helen's back." More rustling sounded.

"Hi." Helen sounded breathless. "I got everyone off the street. Now what?"

"Talk to Melissa. Let me know how it goes. Just stick to the game plan and you should get the media exposure you want."

"Thanks, Eden. You're a legend."

Eden snorted. "I do my best. You stay safe. Don't let the governor, the hospital execs, or the police take over your story. Remember, *you* control the narrative."

"Yes, right."

"Good. Gotta go. Bye!"

She pocketed her phone just as Aggie's door flew open with a thud.

A tiny human blur topped with shaggy white-blond hair launched itself from the top step with a shriek of delight and grew larger until it filled Eden's side window. Aggie was always a bundle of excitement.

Her small but solid body was squeezed into dog pajamas. That was her standard "office" wear, given she worked from home as a supervisor for a help line for teens.

"Edie!" Aggie knocked on her window before Eden could roll it down. "Don't you make me wait, now!"

Eden slid down the window and grinned. "Woman, you know your neighbors don't need a street-wide announcement every time I'm in town."

"They'll live," Aggie declared, her expression unrepentant. "Everyone around here knows I hang with the strangest people." Her arm made a great looping motion toward herself. "Come in, come in. I need your gossip like air. Life's way too dull since you abandoned me."

Eden snorted but hauled ass outside, slamming the door behind her. "You make it sound like we're tragic exes, when I know you only have eyes for Colin. Is it okay if I crash here tonight? And, well, today?"

Aggie huffed. "No Colin talk. You make me sound boring and indecisive. Which I am. Of course you can crash. I keep that sofa bed just for you, you know. It's got divots in exactly your shape." She led Eden up to her house.

As soon as they were inside, Aggie flung her arms around Eden with abandon and squeezed like an anaconda—if anacondas were uns-cary little rib-crackers who wore dog pajamas in the middle of the day.

"I like your new color." Eden nodded at Aggie's hair as she finally extracted herself from the hug. "You were a redhead last time."

"That was three whole months ago," Aggie protested. "Don't you ever look at my Insta? I've been working out if I'm having more fun as a blond. I'll report back my findings."

"Which does Colin prefer?" Eden asked slyly.

"No, no, we're not doing this again. You know the rules: I have no *official* love life but live vicariously through yours while we sort our shit out."

"Uh huh. And you know I haven't dated anyone since that intense no-nukes girl. Pretty sure she only wanted me for a green card." Eden made her ass at home on Aggie's couch and then inspected the palm tree prints on the new cushions. Well, not *new*, new. "Oh hey, the eighties called; they want your cushions back."

"I got them for free." Aggie's eyes lit up. "Don't you love them? Someone dumped them on the curb. Can you believe that?"

"All too easily." Eden gave one a ginger poke. No plume of dust emerged.

"Want a drink?"

"Goddess, yes. I've had a wild, weird-ass morning."

"I'll get your usual." Aggie shot over to the fridge, pulled out a light-beer bottle, called "head's up," and tossed it to her.

Eden snatched it out of the air with ease. Fast reflexes came with her job—you never knew who was going to almost clobber you with a wayward sign.

Aggie joined her on the couch, holding her one true love, Bacchus-F, the energy drink her cousins in South Korea had hooked her on.

"How are your folks?" Eden asked. "Still scandalized by the fact you associate with me—or worse, that you sneak in an occasional protest?"

A few years back, Aggie had left her social worker job and hit the protest circuit with Eden. The absolute highlight had been their rescuing Kevin—a one-eyed, tan-and-white guinea pig—from a cosmetics testing lab. The old boy (Kev had to be six by now) lived the high life in a huge enclosure that ran all around, up, down, and through Aggie's house.

She always claimed that the best part of protesting with Eden had been meeting Kevin, but the truth was Aggie loved fighting for a cause. She'd only quit the protest circuit when her parents finally wore her down.

The Teos were mild-mannered and adorable but tended to get a collective round of indigestion whenever their only daughter broke the rules. *Any* rules. Especially ones in their adopted country of America. But Eden still loved Aggie's whole huge, enthusiastic clan to bits and pieces—and it was mutual.

"My folks are same as ever," Aggie said with a long-suffering sigh. "Worried about me, my career, my scandalously single status at my age."

"Same old, same old, then." Eden cracked the beer and took a deep sip. "Oh *yes*. I needed this to numb the weird of today."

Aggie twisted sideways to take her in. "You know it's only eleven, right? And that sounded way too heartfelt. Fill me in. What's the weirdness? Not the nurses' protest, right?"

Eden shook her head and peered at her beer.

"So, the weird is what?"

"I've signed an NDA, so I can't say much. But I have a job offer that would see me going back home for a bit. It'd stir up the old shit again. Not sure I'm up for it."

"The old shit?" Aggie's eyes slowly widened. "Francine? That massively vindictive cow?"

"I'd like it on the record that I named no names." Eden gave her a coy look.

"Right, sure. We're absolutely not talking about anyone we know."

"Anyway, I don't know if I'm up for poking over old bones again. You know how much that messed with my head."

"Yeah, girl. I do. I really do." Aggie gave her a long look.

Eden stared back morosely. "She made my life hell. And turned Dad against me. He's still giving me radio silence."

Aggie's expression radiated concern. "Why would you ever want to go back? Wingapo's so small—what, forty thousand people? Odds are high you'd bump into him somewhere."

Eden chewed her bottom lip. "Maybe I'll get lucky, though."

"Maybe." Aggie's frowned deepened. "Can we circle back to the why? It'd have to be good."

"A lot of money. And a job that might make a certain person squirm a lot."

"I know you don't care about the money." Aggie tilted her head. "So, *are* you planning on making Francine squirm?"

"I can't answer that. Legally, I mean. But hypothetically speaking, wouldn't it be nice if the woman who drummed me out of town got shown up for who she is? Well, I mean again? A better-executed job this time?"

"Better-executed..." Aggie drew in a breath. "You get that the cops and media are still hers? If you go after her, you'll still be painted as the bitter jerk attacking a decent businesswoman. I'm all for a bit of vengeance, but Francine is untouchable."

"Right." Wasn't that what she'd tried to explain to Michelle? Aggie knew. She'd been right beside her. Watched as Eden's ass got hauled over hot coals. She'd been the one to hold Eden as she cried when her father told her he was done with her. That she wasn't his kid.

"So why do this to yourself?" Aggie asked.

Good question.

"She's up for reelection, and she's even more powerful than she was." Eden tried to think positive. "But I'll be better resourced than before. I just need a good plan. Something subtle. That was my mistake last time."

"Mmm," Aggie said. "Well, I suppose she can't trash your reputation any worse. What's she going to do? Turn your dad against you? Make people hate you? It's already done."

Now, that was an excellent point. Eden nodded. "True."

"I just worry about how it'll hurt you. You were so young when she shredded you last time. That stuff scars."

It did. "But I'm not the idealistic kid I was," Eden tried. "I'm smarter. Stronger, I hope."

"Yes. We're all different. It's been what, fifteen, sixteen years? She'll be different too. She'll know even more vicious ways to fight back. You'll have to be ready."

"I will be."

"Sounds like you've decided," Aggie said and slapped Eden's thigh. "Well, you know what this means." She jumped up. "Celebration nachos."

"That's a new one." Eden chuckled. "A variation, no doubt, on Comfort nachos, Hangover nachos, Monday nachos…"

"Hey, no badmouthing the nachos, or I'll eat them all myself." Aggie dumped a bag of corn chips onto a plate, added a gloopy half bottle of spicy bean sauce and followed it with an excessive amount of shredded cheese. She slid it into the microwave and mashed some buttons until it came on with a loud whirring noise.

"Does your mom know you do that to food?" Eden asked.

"She must never know," Aggie said grimly. "I never could convince her that Western junk food has its merits when she can whip up her kimchi-jjigae in the same amount of time."

That was a wild exaggeration, but Eden knew what she meant. "I miss your mom." She stared at the noisy microwave with its obscene cargo. "And her cooking."

Mrs. Teo's signature spicy vegetable stew was to die for, Korean soul food at its finest. Unfortunately, Aggie had entirely failed to inherit the cooking gene.

"I'll tell her," Aggie said. "She'll be sorry to miss you. I mean, unless you're staying a few days this time?" Aggie's look was hopeful.

"I can't. If I take this new job, I'll need to get to Wingapo ASAP."

"Please tell me you're not tangled up in some shit for the CIA," Aggie said, side-eying her. "Remember, you're Eden Lawless, Force for Good, not Occasional Regime Overthrower."

The microwave dinged.

"The CIA works *outside* of America, and I know you know that," Eden said with an eye roll. "And before you start, I'm not working for the FBI, either. Everything in the skyscraper of an office I interviewed at was bronze or chrome and cost a mint. And do not get me started on the multimillion-dollar view or fancy French sculpture. It's private enterprise. And honestly, that's all I know. The office had no name."

"Are you sure you want to get in bed with them, knowing jack-all about them?" Aggie retrieved the gooey, nuke-blasted plate of possibly-food and placed it in front of Eden along with some paper napkins.

Eden took a cheesy corn chip and bit in. After chewing savagely and trying not to wince at its weird texture, she declared, "This isn't the worst thing you've ever pulled out of your microwave."

"High praise." Aggie grinned. "Now, stop dodging the question."

"Okay, sure, I have reservations. But, equally, my cause aligns with theirs on this project."

"Francine really does deserve to go down," Aggie agreed.

"I never said that's what I'm doing," Eden protested. "But as an abstract thought? Hell. Yeah."

"It still bugs me how quickly everyone forgot all the stuff you brought to light," Aggie said. "I did not imagine our rental having a crack wide enough to put my hand through. But within a few months of your protest, it all faded away into nothing."

"I'm pretty sure the tenants haven't forgotten." Eden took another swig of beer. "The people who can't do a damned thing about the condition of their properties and can't afford to leave."

Aggie reached for a gooey nacho chip. "Girl, if anyone can do this, it's you."

"That's just what my new boss said."

"But I know it'll probably hurt. If you need me there, you say the word, and I'll come. I'll bring reinforcements too. Allies, beer, Victory nachos, whatever you need." She shot Eden a genuine look of support before cramming the goopy chip into her mouth.

Gratitude filled her. "Thanks for the offer, but I think I'll be fine."

"Okay." Aggie's steady gaze held hers as she chewed slowly. She was so rarely serious for this long; it was a little unnerving. "If you're sure you know what you're doing."

Not a clue, Eden wanted to say. But it was decided. She pulled out her phone before she lost her nerve and emailed the address she'd been given, sending one word: *yes*.

Two minutes later, her phone pinged. Except it wasn't a reply from her new company.

Tina Turner bit! Look!

That was from Melissa. Eden clicked a link to find the singer's tweet, already liked by twelve thousand fans, with a photo of a nurse holding a sign asking motorists to *Honk if you like nurses or Tina Turner*. The tweet read:

Nurses are simply the best! I should know! I support the nurses protest-ing in Ohio!

Two other celebrities had also retweeted the protest, their messages also quoted and sent to the governor and media.

Excellent. This might just work out better than her original plans for the protest.

An email from Helen said the governor had already agreed to a new meeting, one he promised to attend this time. And two reporters had reached out, seeking more information on the nurses' dispute. *Excellent work*, she emailed them both back.

All due to you, Helen wrote, including a bunch of star emojis.

Eden grinned. Happy clients made her happy too.

Her phone pinged again, but this time from an unknown number.

Welcome to The Fixers, Ms. Lawless

The Fixers? That was their name? Interesting. And for some reason, Eden just knew it had been Michelle behind that message. Unbidden, even as her heart raced with anxiety for what lay ahead, she smiled.

Then, just for shits and giggles, she texted back on a whim.

Thanks. Btw she's definitely nude.

Chapter 3
Edgar Degas and the Meaning of Life

Cheeky. Michelle put down her phone with a smirk, deciding that, if nothing else, Lawless might be marginally entertaining. As long as she didn't cross any lines or disrespect Michelle, she would allow it. She leaned back in her chair and gazed out at her view as she mentally ran through her task list. Something unsavory floated to the top of the pile.

Michelle punched the intercom button and said, "Tilly? Get me Cavaner's file. Time we squeezed the senator. Send that hacker to see me. What's his name?"

"Which one?"

"The one we hired from LA after the SmartPay job went south."

"Snakepit."

"Yes." She sighed at the name, but his talent was undeniable. They'd tried to hire the young man's IT partner in crime too, but he'd opted to stay in LA.

Five minutes later, a rumpled young man in a Nuka Cola T-shirt stood before her nervously. He ran his fingers through an attempt at three-day beard growth.

Tilly pointed him to the visitor's chair and exited.

"Mr...Snakepit." Michelle eyed him.

"Yes?" he said, his voice breaking, a blush sliding up his cheeks.

"I'm in need of your...special skills."

"Which ones? Uh…Miss, Ms…um, ma'am. Specifically?"

Michelle pushed Senator Cavaner's file across the table. "This man has incurred the wrath of The Fixers. He needs to be reminded we're not to be messed with."

"Oh-kay?" He nodded hard and repeatedly, then reached for the folder, flicking it open, and scanned the bio file on the top.

"Today, cut off his heating," Michelle said, ticking off her fingers. "Tomorrow, his power. Next day, his credit cards and those of his wife."

"Um…ma'am, it's uh, the middle of winter," Snakepit stammered out. His eyes darted to the page in front of him. "He lives in an effin' cold place, pardon my French. Snow and stuff. Cutting off his heat and power…" He faded out.

"I'm aware. The harsher the lesson, the faster it is learned."

"Oh. Right."

"So you can do it?"

"Yes." Snakepit appeared to rally. "Want me to remotely disable his cell phone and his wife's?"

"No." Michelle leaned back in her chair and regarded him impassively.

"Okay," Snakepit said, chewing on his lip. "Is that everything?"

"For now."

"What'd he do, anyway?"

"Crossed us. That is unacceptable."

"Right." His head bobbed up and down.

"Email me a report of your progress each day, confirming you've enacted the task on your worklist."

He scrambled to his feet, clutching the folder to his concave chest.

"Before you go…" She paused, wondering why she cared. "Your friend in LA, the one who said no to joining us here…"

"Duppy."

Do they have to have such ridiculous names? "Yes. Why did he say no? I'd have thought shoving bundles of cash into the bank accounts of teen hackers would be a dream gig."

His cheeks reddened.

"What is it?"

"Uh, I don't think you want me to tell you 'zactly what Duppy said."

Michelle made an impatient *go on* gesture.

Snakepit scratched his ear and then looked down at his scuffed sneakers. "He said, 'I won't work for any piece of shit who screws over Catherine Ayers. She's a fuckin' legend.'"

Michelle's breath stilled, and she went very, very cold at a name she was trying extremely hard not to be reminded of. She did not—could not—speak.

He shuffled a little, then rushed on, apparently misunderstanding the chill in her expression. "I wouldn't take it personal, him sayin' no. See, he had the hots for her. Not just coz she's such a sick journalist. I mean *her*."

"She's sick?" Horror rose. How had her sources not told her—

"Uh, no," he cut into her thoughts. "Like...*lit*? *Dope*?" His eyebrows scrunched together. "Uhhh. *Cool*?"

"Oh."

"Even though she's *wayyy* too old for him. Like, in her forties and everything." He gave a chuckle as if the mere idea of finding Catherine Ayers attractive was ridiculous.

Stupid boy. Ayers was utterly breathtaking, inside and out. Only a complete fool would fail to see that or—far more inexcusably—know it, have her, and toss her away.

Michelle was obviously a complete fool. She set her jaw hard.

Snakepit fell silent when Michelle still hadn't so much as twitched.

"You may go," she said sharply. "Remember: daily updates."

He bolted out like his pants were on fire.

Michelle's emotions darkened and swirled. Not again. She despised the waves of guilt and regret she'd had to contend with ever since she'd lost Catherine Ayers nine years ago.

No, not lost, for pity's sake. *Broken*. Michelle had broken Ayers. For a job.

That little drip of a kid...Duppy...turned out to have far more integrity than Michelle. He'd been smart enough to know when to say no.

The familiar stir of self-loathing rose, and she forced it back down. Well, she'd just *had* to ask. She always had to tug the loose threads and satisfy her curiosity. Served her right.

Tilly stuck her head in the office, murmuring something about filing. It was a weak excuse even to Michelle's see-sawing brain.

Indeed, her PA made no move toward the filing cabinet in the corner.

"You heard," Michelle accused.

"Yes."

"I don't want to discuss it."

Tilly rocked back a little on her sensible heels. "All right, then, I'll change the topic," she said briskly. "Snakepit has a point about how cold it is where Cavaner lives. Are you aware they have a newborn?"

"Of course." She waited a beat, then added, "I let him keep his phone to find accommodation. The point isn't to be cruel, it's to frustrate him into compliance."

"He won't be able to check into a hotel without credit cards."

"I'm aware. But the man has hundreds of friends with mansions; staffers too. Someone will put them up. He will detest asking for help. He'll feel vulnerable."

"He'll be furious," Tilly said.

"And helpless." Michelle felt a gleam of triumph. "Fury and helplessness should get his attention."

"So how do you see it playing out?" Tilly asked, eyes hooded.

"When he calls, outraged and vowing retribution, tell him I'm in a meeting. Keep informing him of that until he stops shouting and starts begging. *Then* you can put him through."

"Of course, Ms. Hastings," came the professional reply. "And *then* we restore all his services?"

"No." Michelle gave her a menacing smile. "Then we wait one more day to test his penitence. He will never challenge us again after this."

"Or he lashes out." Tilly shot her a warning look. "Exposes us. It's a risk."

"I know men like him," Michelle said, unmoved. "He's all bluster. The risk is negligible. He'll be crawling on his belly for forgiveness within two weeks."

"And if he isn't?"

"I'll send in O'Brian for a little one-on-one chat. Even his shadow's intimidating."

"And when the senator backs down?" Tilly asked.

"Then I'll make him really suffer. I hear he collects art. French impressionists. I'm wondering how he feels about being parted with a few of them in penance."

Tilly's eyebrows went up.

Michelle tapped her lip. "I've always thought my office could use a Degas."

"Really? I had no idea you liked ballet."

"Of course I don't like ballet," Michelle said with a snort. "Little girls painted in fluffy pink tutus? I think not." Michelle gave her a wide smile. "I like *winning*."

And just like that, her dark mood evaporated.

<hr/>

That evening, Michelle let herself into her apartment, dropped her keys into a small glazed ceramic dish by the door, and hung up her coat.

"Safta?" she called, turning on the lights. Why hadn't her grandmother done so? It was late, and the living room was shrouded in darkness. She hurried to her grandmother's bedroom, wondering if maybe she'd simply turned in early. Or not. Alarm filled her. "Safta?"

"Out here," came a thin voice from an unexpected location.

Michelle stopped mid-stride and pivoted. She slid open the door of the balcony and instantly shivered. Hannah was stretched out on a deck chair, legs covered in a tartan blanket, and sipping her usual Four Roses bourbon.

"It's cold," Michelle scolded her. "Your chest…"

"Is fine, child. Stop fretting." She gave a soft cluck.

"What are you doing out here?" Michelle asked, concern snaking into her tone again.

"You worry too much, bubbeleh. I caught sight of the sunset earlier and was entranced. Then I decided to stay for Mother Nature's floor show." She waved at the heavens. "It's not often we don't have cloud cover. Isn't it beautiful?"

Michelle relaxed marginally. "Are you warm enough?"

"You didn't answer my question." Hannah's tone was teasing and gentle.

Michelle dutifully flicked her gaze up, noted yes, indeed, stars were present, same as every other night. "Beautiful," she muttered dryly.

"Cynic. Now, sit," her grandmother said, patting the deck chair beside her. "Tell me about your day while we soak up the wonders of the universe."

"The wonders? How much bourbon have you been drinking?" she teased. Still, she sat.

"Are *you* warm enough?" Hannah waved at Michelle's business suit. "You could move your chair closer and share my blanket."

"I'm fine," Michelle said. Even though it was cold and the hairs on her arms were forming goose bumps, she was used to the cold. She preferred it to being petted like a small child, which her grandmother was guilty of whenever within range. "Work was…"

Michelle paused. Her grandmother knew little about what she did, even though they'd lived together for nine years now, ever since her grandmother had experienced one fall too many. Michelle had spun it as being of mutual benefit—that since her divorce, she wasn't used to so much space in her huge apartment.

The truth was, Michelle loved her solitude. So, about twice a year, Hannah took an extended stay at a friend's home in Florida, which enabled Michelle the distance she needed to recharge her mental batteries. It was incredibly thoughtful, but her safta was smart like that.

"Work was what?" Hannah asked. "You didn't finish your sentence."

"I hired a new employee." A flash of Eden Lawless's quirking mouth, blunt exhortations, and honest eyes filled her head. "A temporary employee," she felt the sudden urge to clarify. "She's only with us for ten weeks."

Why had she added that?

"Ten weeks? I see." The old woman's green eyes crinkled. "Well, she's obviously made an impression."

Michelle's head snapped sharply to the side to look at her. "Why do you say that?"

"Because you bothered to mention her, even if she's only with you for a little while. You've never mentioned any other employees. I was starting to think you ran that consultancy firm of yours all on your own." Her eyes sparkled. "Tell me about her?"

"You know I run an organization where clients highly value their secrecy," Michelle began. How many times had she reminded her nosy grandmother of this?

"Your employee isn't a client. So, no secrets to share there. Just humor an old woman who doesn't get out anymore. Who can't walk far enough to even go to the park and meet new people without everyone being terrified she'll fall." She waved at her ailing hip and knee. "Talk to me about someone new or my poor, fragile mind will wither away."

Okay, that was just plain manipulative. Rather impressed, Michelle gave her a gentle poke in the side. "I know what you're doing."

"Do you, now?" Hannah smiled serenely. "Are you going to refuse an old woman her dying wish?"

"You are aware your dying wish changes every other hour?"

Hannah shot her a dramatically aggrieved look. "Well, won't you feel bad if this *is* my last one and you just ignored it?"

Michelle laughed. It was an odd sound to her own ears. She'd not found much to laugh about in a long, long time. "Fine, you manipulative old woman," Michelle said lightly. "Her name is Eden. Eden Lawless, if you can believe it."

"Oh, I like the sound of her already. Does she lean more to Biblical gardens or ladies in leather skirts who throw men around a lot?"

"Ex-cuse me?"

"How can *I* know about Lucy Lawless at my age and you don't?"

Michelle peered at her, utterly lost.

"*Xena? Warrior Princess?*" Hannah tried.

"Oh. That." Michelle side-eyed her grandmother, who clearly loved her schlocky TV shows far too much. "So sue me if I've been focused on my career. But, fine. Between Eden and Lawless, she definitely leans to the latter name. She's someone who stirs up trouble."

"And you like that."

"It's...useful." Michelle nestled back further into her chair, forgetting about the cold now. "Once upon a time, she made trouble for someone in authority. It didn't end well for her."

"Ah." Her safta looked entranced. "But she didn't take that lying down?"

"No. I mean, she went away and licked her wounds. But then she rebuilt her life. In fact, she made a whole career out of her particular brand of trouble."

"Same as you did," the old woman said firmly, pride in her voice. "When you had your...upset...with the FBI. And with your parents. You made your own path."

Not the same at all, Michelle wanted to say but absolutely couldn't. This was not a safe topic. With effort, she pushed the memories away and buried them next to the other not-safe topics.

"Where will you send your new employee?" Her grandmother's voice cut into her thoughts. "Or will she work in your office?"

Michelle didn't answer; her safta knew better than this.

Following the silence, Hannah gave a mournful wave and said in Hebrew with an enormous, long-suffering sigh, "*S'iz nisht dayn bobes eysek.*"

It's none of your grandmother's business.

The silence dragged out. Michelle debated telling her. After all, who was Hannah going to disclose her secrets to, anyway? The woman never left their apartment, thanks to her poor health and balance issues. She had no contact with her son anymore. And her few friends had no interest in political affairs, preferring to swap recipes and ailments over the phone.

"She's off to Wingapo," Michelle said finally.

"Ah," Hannah said, delight in her tone. "Beautiful place. Shame about the mayor."

"How do you know about Wingapo? And how have you heard of its mayor?" Michelle asked in surprise. "The place is tiny. Unremarkable in every way."

"I know its primary industry is soybean," Hannah replied earnestly. "Or it was until the Chinese markets dried up."

At Michelle's astonished stare, her safta relented and laughed hard. "All right, I admit, Wingapo came up on one of the news channels a few days ago. Because it's election season, they ran a story on all Maryland's female mayors. Francine Wilson's segment was framed as the 'brilliant property developer turned mayor who can do no wrong.'" Her grandmother waved her hand. "Oh, it was so much baloney. She's shady, that one."

"How can you tell?" Michelle asked, even more astonished.

"Bubbeleh, if you ever want to see who's up to tricks, take a look at where all the honey's being flung."

"The honey?"

"When you try to catch flies, you put out honey. Well, now, that news report put out so much honey, absolutely covered that mayor in it, all this fawning and carry-on, and it made me wonder why they were trying so hard."

"Or it could just be a puff piece?" Michelle said.

"None of the other mayor stories were like that. Wilson's piece was *so* ingratiating! As if she'd *invented* women in politics! I finally decided the mayor had to have paid someone to run the story that way. Or forced them to."

"Mmm." Well, Wilson certainly had form. "Maybe."

"Your maybe is my definitely. Goodness me, it was *such* nonsense." Hannah tapped Michelle's arm gently. "So, what's your troublemaker friend going to do with the mayor?"

"Who said she was going to do anything with her?" *Also, not a friend.*

"The *honey*, bubbeleh. Far too much of it. If you're sending Eden Lawless to Wingapo, I assume it has to be about that mayor." She leaned closer in. "Are you going to expose her?" A childlike delight at the idea sparkled in her grandmother's eyes.

"How do you know I'm not the one *supplying* the honey?" Michelle arched an eyebrow.

"Are you?" Hannah looked at her with genuine interest. "You're the one making Mayor Wilson look good? I thought you'd be more subtle than that."

Michelle smiled at the compliment. "I couldn't tell you either way."

44

"Well then, I guess I'll just have to pay attention to the news out of Wingapo, and I'll see for myself. But you know what else is interesting? The mayor's election is in *ten weeks*."

Michelle shook her head. Her grandmother was far too sharp for her own good. "Have you eaten? Shall we order in?"

"No, I'm fine. I'm still full from kugel at lunch. I just want to look at the stars some more. Will you stay and watch with me?"

Michelle had so much work to catch up on. So many emails to reply to. And since Lawless had confirmed she would be doing the Wingapo project, she had to action quite a few job requests to ensure...

"Just a few minutes more, child. Then you can go back to reshaping the world."

Reshaping the world?

Michelle wondered how and when her grandmother had worked out what her day job was. Or was she just fishing for clues again? "Just a few minutes more."

"Wonderful." She sounded delighted. "Now, then, tell me more about this delightful Eden."

She's hardly delightful, Michelle wanted to object. But her safta's expression was too blissful.

"There's nothing really to say. She does drive the most awful van, though." As soon as Tilly had left her office, Michelle had sneaked a peek at it from the window. Simple curiosity, of course.

Michelle smiled. "It's yellow," she began. "And red and green and blue. A rainbow of colors. It's covered all over in protest stickers. She calls it Gloria."

"How unusual! She sounds *so* interesting. That reminds me of my VW bus back in the sixties. Took it to Woodstock and all over California, but I'm sure you don't want to hear about that." Her eyes twinkled.

Michelle tried very much not to picture her sweet grandmother getting up to mischief at Woodstock.

Instead, she slid a little closer to the other woman—allowing her to tuck that old tartan blanket over both their legs, patting it exactly so—and lost herself in the stars.

Chapter 4

The Power of Peacocks

Nothing could have prepared Eden for the eccentric delights of the Spruce Treesort Bed and Breakfast, Wingapo, which sat just outside of town, hidden in a pocket of lush, green wilderness.

This place hadn't been around when she was growing up; she was quite sure she'd remember hearing about this.

Because seriously? Red-tiled turrets?

She'd looked up the website before she'd driven here, and her eyes had scarcely known what to focus on. The bronze clawfoot bathtub? The electric blue walls with stenciled peacocks? Four-poster beds draped in hanging silks? The round "contemplation room" with window seats overlooking a courtyard crammed with potted plants and fruit trees?

Obviously, Michelle Hastings had not been the one who'd selected Eden's accommodation. This was way too quirky and fun, and Michelle was wound up tighter than a military snare drum.

Eden was greeted at the door as if she were a long-lost daughter—engulfing hugs and cheek-smacking kisses—by a forty-something, Rubenesque Black woman adorned in a colorful head scarf, fat clinking bangles, and lemon-colored yoga gear.

"Melba C. Lotus," she introduced herself. "C stands for whatever you want it to be. My momma never got around to deciding so left it at C. She's passed now, so I can't ask her if that's really what happened or just some tall tale our family tells."

"Great to meet you. I'm Eden. And, hey, my middle name's Celeste if you ever want to borrow it."

"Maybe I will," Melba replied with a thoughtful look. She dug a jangling hand into her headscarf and retrieved a pen, then wrote on her hand. "Reminding myself of things I remember while I still remember 'em," she explained. Her palm was covered in smudged scribbles. An inky *Celeste* was now added to them. "Then the fun of it is tryin' to work out what it all says at the end of the day."

Melba suddenly burst out laughing, which made her belly jiggle cheerfully. Her joy was infectious. "Lord, I probably have more fun trying to decode my smudges than anything else." She thrust the pen back under her headscarf.

"Let's do a tour." The host strode off, calling over her shoulder, "Sorry about my wardrobe. I'm not being disrespectful in wearing my leggings and go-go gear meeting you. It's just it's my running day today."

Melba stopped so suddenly, Eden almost walked into her. Seemingly oblivious to this, Melba added, "And by running, I mean more like walking. And by walking, I mean…giving a new guest the tour and hoping that counts as burnin' up enough calories to try my baby boy's black forest cake at lunch." Her eyes glazed over. "Jimmy's tryin' out a new recipe. I always like to be obliging and build up his confidence. But those calories will dog you like a shadow unless you can cancel 'em out some way."

"Calories don't count when made with love." Eden gave her a grin that said she highly endorsed enabling.

Melba laughed long and hard at that. "Lord, that's gonna be my new motto. I'll be quoting that to be sure." She eyed her. "Do you like music, Ms. Lawless? Or may I call you Eden? What a lovely name Eden is. My momma gave me my name after Melba Moore, the R&B singer. Is R&B something you like?"

She didn't wait for an answer and headed into a lounge room wallpapered in a salmon pink design and crammed in every nook with knick-knacks, from wooden clocks to stuffed birds.

It smelled of incense and second-hand books and the nice dusty aroma of an antique shop—old wood varnishes and ancient crumbling tomes.

Melba bustled over to the oldest record player Eden had ever seen. "Here's Melba's 'This Is It.'" A toe-tapping tune filled the air. "So good."

"Definitely." Eden swayed a bit. "It's lovely."

Melba chuckled. "We're gonna get along just fine. And two and a half months will pass mighty slow if we're not getting on. You're my longest booking ever. Most people only ever stay for a weekend. A week if they're on their honeymoon."

The unspoken question hung in the air.

Melba dropped onto a green velvet couch with golden brocade. "You sit right down here," she patted the plush cushion beside her, "and tell me what brings you here."

Eden eased onto the couch and wondered how much she could say. She was a naturally honest person, but she'd signed an NDA. However, there was no way she could pass her stay off as a tourist having some R&R. Alone. For months. Melba was right. The length of stay stood out as odd. And Eden's activities, nosing around Francine Wilson's business, would be hard to hide in a small town. Gossips loved fresh meat, and there was none fresher than Eden. Melba would inevitably hear about her movements one way or another.

"I'm interested in the mayoral election." Eden decided a half-truth would be a good cover. "I'm following it. For work. Which I can't say too much about."

"You're a reporter?" Melba guessed, eyes lighting up with interest. "And you're covering our little mayor's race? But why?"

Eden didn't correct her assumption. "Mayor Wilson is an...unusual person."

Melba studied Eden more closely. "You say *unusual* the way I say *maggoty flesh wound.*"

Oops. "I meant no disrespect."

"Do you know the mayor personally? Have you two met?" Melba asked curiously.

"Years ago. I actually grew up around here."

"How interesting. I only moved here with my son about ten years ago. I needed a break. Teaching special-needs kids is rewarding, but it drains you, especially when you don't get much respect from Admin. I wanted a change. So when Momma passed and left me some money, I decided to just pick a spot on the map and make some magic."

"And you really did." Eden glanced around the room again, stopping on a spray of plumage. "You have a lot of birds. Feathers. Art..." She stopped as she caught sight of an *actual stuffed peacock.*

"Oh, they're not mine!" Melba cackled. "Momma loved them. Called peacocks her good-luck charm. She grew up with people trying to hide her light under a bushel. They told her not to be too smart or loud or bright and show others up. Jealous folks will make trouble and push you down to punish you."

Melba waved at the beautiful stuffed bird in the corner. "Momma would always remind us kids about peacocks. No one tells them to be less impressive than they are. They're like, 'I know I'm fabulous! Don't believe me? Look!'" She splayed her hands out wide as if imitating a peacock showing its feathers. "I think that's a good philosophy to adopt."

"It really is." Eden decided she liked Melba.

A polite knock sounded on the open living room door, and a young Black man entered. His gentle brown eyes darted to Eden and back to Melba.

"Ma, the cake's in the oven." He worried his hands in front of himself and seemed to shrink a little under Eden's curious gaze. His words were a little slow, and his fidgeting increased.

"Thank you, my beautiful baby boy."

He rolled his eyes at that. "Ma, I'm nineteen!"

"You'll always be my baby to me. Now, then, this is our guest for the next few months, Eden. Eden, hon, this is Jimmy. He's our cook. Self-taught and so skilled. But you'll see that come mealtime. There's a meal schedule in your room, and you just join us if you want, or ask for a plate to go to your room."

Eden blinked. "Um, I thought only breakfasts were included?"

"Usually. Your company paid us to cater every meal and said no expenses spared. We are to treat you like royalty."

They what? Eden would have to email Tilly a thanks.

"I appreciate the income, I must say. Guests are a bit thin on the ground this time of year, so this booking alone will really help us out. Your employer also paid extra to ensure discretion. Didn't have to do that, of course. I won't be telling anyone who's staying with us. Jimmy knows not to as well, don't you, Jimmy?"

He nodded. "I know not talk to about our guests or anything happening here." His words were slow and carefully formed. "Not that I want to anyways." He fidgeted again.

Eden smiled warmly at him, trying to show she didn't bite. "Thank you," she said. It was obvious Jimmy wasn't someone who fit in easily. Her heart went out to him. "I think you'd be lovely to talk to, though, if you ever wanted to. If you're bored and I'm not working, you can talk to me anytime. And if you don't want to, that's fine too. I don't mind either way."

Jimmy gave an uncertain little nod. "I'll go check I put the timer on the cake now. Um, ma'am."

"Good idea," Melba said. "We don't want it extra crispy."

Jimmy left and Melba said, "Thank you." Her tone was soft.

"What for?"

"Understanding. I know you do; I see it in your eyes. My boy was born with some developmental delays. For some reason, and the doctors never could explain to me exactly why, he didn't get enough oxygen into him when he was born. He was blue as death. So, he's just a bit slower than the other kids. He got bullied for it so bad that he's self-conscious and avoids people now. But I love you offered to talk with him if he's in the mood for it. Sometimes he does open up a little, if he feels safe."

"He seems sweet. And I love talking to people from all walks of life, so it's no hardship," Eden said earnestly. "I find everyone's interesting in their own way. Some you have to dig a bit under the surface to get to who they really are, but everyone has something that makes them fascinating. Not always *good*-fascinating, of course," she added with a dry chuckle as Francine Wilson's face floated into mind. "But everyone's got something that's unique. Something that's just them. More than anything, I love finding what that is."

Melba was quiet for a moment. "I can see you're a kind person. Thoughtful too. What I can't understand is how someone like you is mixed up in politics."

"I was assigned the job by my boss." That much was true. "I wasn't even sure I wanted to do it. Coming back home; there's a lot of painful memories for me in Wingapo. But I guess doing something that makes us afraid is good for us, right?"

"To an extent," Melba said after a moment's thought. "But frightening ourselves for no good reason can be a bit silly too."

At Eden's uncertain look, she patted her arm and added, "But you don't strike me as the silly type. I'm betting you'll be fine, and it won't be as bad as you remember it. Don't worry about a thing. And if anyone gives you a hard time, you come to me and I'll see how I can help."

"I appreciate the offer," Eden said, touched. "But I'm sure I'll be fine." Besides, what could a small-town B&B owner possibly do to protect her from Mayor Wilson?

"Y'know, I hear a lot of things around Wingapo," Melba said. "It's amazing how much people say when they forget I'm even there. More fool them." She grinned.

Eden shook her head. "They must be blind. I don't think you'd be very easy to overlook. In fact, you may be one of the most memorable people I've ever met."

Melba beamed. "How wonderful you think so. Momma'd be proud to hear that." She spread both her hands wide again. "Peacocks! Am I right?"

"Right." Eden chuckled.

———◆———

Eden spent the day reacquainting herself as to where everything was in town. Little had changed. Stores here or there were different, of course, but they were fundamentally the same streets she'd walked as a student. Occasionally she'd catch sight of people she thought she knew, and it was a little shocking to see they'd aged sixteen years. More stoop in the older people. More lines in younger faces.

No one recognized her, though. That was probably a blessing because it meant no one would warn Francine she was back in town. It probably wouldn't really matter if Francine knew—it's not like she'd divine Eden's purpose for being home again. But her being aware just brought them one step closer to a showdown Eden wasn't looking forward to. She'd happily go for the rest of her life never seeing the vindictive woman again.

That evening, after a largely unproductive day, she sat down to dinner with Melba and Jimmy. The feast was enormous. As the B&B's only guest, it seemed all their energies were focused on pleasing her.

A golden, crunchy, deep-fried crab cake appeared with a vast array of sides, including macaroni salad and coleslaw. It was delicious, as Eden had announced repeatedly between swooning, causing Jimmy's cheeks to darken in delight.

And then came dessert.

"Jimmy's saved you some of his black forest cake," Melba said proudly. "I think it might be his finest creation yet, and that's sayin' something."

Eden was by then already stuffed to the gills, but she couldn't turn down Jimmy and his hopeful expression.

And it was magnificent—a glistening, dark-chocolate layered cake with an oozing dollop of creamy homemade vanilla ice cream. Eden was going to die of gluttony if she ate like this for ten weeks.

Finally, after assuring them both she was quite full and second helpings weren't needed, she made her escape to her room.

Her bedroom was pale indigo. It came with the most enormous bed with a curving wrought-iron headboard and a small table by the window overlooking lime-green potted trees that were festooned with golden, winking string lights. Peacock artwork was on the wall over the bed; a framed girl danced on the facing wall, her beautiful dark-skinned body contrasted by a flowing white gown. On the bedside table was a round retro clock and an essential oil diffuser. Despite not being on, it smelled of cinnamon and spices.

Eden's eye caught the time on the clock. Eight o'clock! She was supposed to Skype with the office now, not that she had much to report.

She dug up the Skype name Michelle had scrawled on her envelope and typed it into the app's search window on her laptop.

Briefly, Eden wondered which poor minion had been assigned the job of keeping an eye on her to make sure she was trustworthy. She hoped it wasn't the condescending receptionist/art lover. All snooty attitude and perfect eyebrows, she made Eden feel like a bumbling hick.

Maybe that assistant was stuck with overseeing her? She'd seemed nice, but then again, she'd be pretty busy as Michelle's PA. As if Tilly would have time to personally bother with...

Michelle Hastings was staring back at her.

Michelle. Hastings.

Eden's brain did a weird little dance of confusion and then fritzed.

"Oh," Eden said. "I mean hi. I didn't expect to see you here."

Michelle frowned. "*You* Skyped *me*. I answered. What were you expecting?"

"A lackey?" Eden said, her voice rising in embarrassment. "Someone pretty low down the ladder to check that I'm not absconding with your money?"

Michelle's lips thinned. "Well, you're stuck with me. I'm here. So, report."

Report?

Oh no! Eden would have prepared something formal and official sounding if she'd realized it was the boss she'd be talking to. She tried furiously to think. What had she been doing all day?

"Okay, um, so I checked into the B&B. It's, ah...certainly *out there.*" Eden's gaze darted around the room, pausing on butterfly-shaped pendant lights she hadn't noticed before.

At Michelle's narrowing eyes, she added hastily: "But nice. *Really* nice. Melba, who runs the place, is wonderful. Her son too. Please thank Tilly for choosing it."

"I have no intention of thanking my PA for simply doing her job. Ms. Lawless, get to the point, please. A report should be about the *assignment* not the quality of the mints on your pillow."

"Okay, of course." *Shit, shit, shit!* "Right, well, it's only me booked in here, so it's not like I'll be spotted by other guests who can gossip about anything I'm up to on this, er, assignment."

"Of course it's just you." Michelle gave her a long-suffering sigh. "The entire B&B was booked out by us to ensure our security protocols would be met."

"The whole..." That was nuts! The place had five guest rooms. It had to have cost a fortune. "For all two and a half months?"

"Obviously. We don't want leaks, mess, chaos, indiscretions, rogue elements, or anything that could complicate things. It's why you're in a B&B and not a hotel. Smaller establishments are far easier to contain."

Contain? That sounded like spy talk. "I feel like I'm in a special op," Eden muttered.

"You are. How have you not grasped this yet?" Michelle asked. "Look, we pay you well and ensure an environment for success. And in turn, we expect you to deliver. On that score, what have you achieved so far?"

Achieved? In just one day? "I refamiliarized myself with the layout of Wingapo. It's been a long time. I don't want to get lost..." She faded out. Goddess. That sounded lame. Eden tried to think of something professional-sounding. "I don't want to get lost at a mission-critical moment." *There now.*

The faintest twitch ticked up the edge of Michelle's mouth. "Mission. Critical. Moment," she repeated. "Oh no, we wouldn't want that."

Eden felt her cheeks flare like molten lava. *Dying now.*

She looked away to disguise her embarrassment and mashed a few buttons on her laptop to distract herself or at least make it look like she was busy working on something *mission-y*. Accidentally, she took a screen grab. *Oops.* She blinked at the frozen Michelle image, then quickly minimized it when her boss resumed speaking.

"Have you come up with a plan yet to torpedo your target's campaign?"

In *one* day? Her incredulity must have shown, because Michelle continued, "I'm not saying I expect you to have an idea this soon. I was just asking if you *had* already thought of something. You seem to have a creative mind."

Surprise briefly flickered across Michelle's face before it returned to neutral—as if she hadn't intended to say that out loud.

"Creative, huh?" Eden said with a grin. "Why *thank you*, Michelle. I'm going to print that out as a motivational quote and stick it up somewhere because I suspect you don't compliment people often, especially us lowly minions." She chuckled.

Astonishment flooded Michelle's features. Followed by disapproval so strong, her eyes flashed. Then came a curt: "There is a *line*, Ms. Lawless. Do not be presumptuous. That was disrespectful. Now, work on your plan. I expect results from you soon. We'll talk tomorrow night."

And then the screen went blank.

Okay, what on earth just happened?

Eden stared at the blank screen for a second, then swallowed.

Had she crossed a line? She hadn't meant to. Or was Michelle super touchy about etiquette?

She grabbed her phone and texted Aggie.

If I jokingly suggested my boss doesn't compliment people, especially her lowly minions, would that be crossing a line? Presumptuous and disrespectful? AITA? Or is she being a ridiculous precious petal who can't see I was kidding?

The reply came back in a minute.

Oh girl! "Am I the asshole," you ask ever so innocently? Yes, you idiot. You totally are. And hey, don't get fired; you just got there!

But I was only teasing! Eden protested.

You basically told her she was a crap manager. You barely know her. She doesn't know you! Can you remember that fancy uptown DC businesses are diff to us laid-back protest types? She's a professional. She expects you to be too.

That sounds boring. Eden pouted at her screen as she hit send.

You expect your boss to entertain you? Edie, wtf? That's for friends, not her.

Oh. Well, when she put it like that. Embarrassment filled her at her misstep. *Should I apologize?*

Maybe just don't mention it again, get on with your job, and it'll blow over.

But no teasing or jokes with her ever? Ever????

God, woman, seriously? If you can't restrain yourself, call me instead and I'll let you attempt your wit on me. Yes, I know. I'm the best. Gotta go. C's over for dinner.

Ooh! Before she could offer a teasing reply about her and Colin's fine nonromance, Aggie texted again.

If you say anything double entendre-y, I will water down your beer in my fridge.

But…

I mean it.

Give my love to Colin.

Eden tossed in a heart symbol and left them to their night of platonic friendship and mutual pining. Clueless idiots.

Not that she could talk. Idiocy was apparently her forte too. But she was still figuring out the parameters with Michelle. It was hard not to want to get to know people. As she'd explained to Melba, everyone was fascinating in their own way. She loved connecting with new people and finding out what made them tick. And, yes, making them laugh too. Of course she could be professional when it was needed. She would!

But there was just something about Michelle, something about her stern, prickly exterior, that made Eden itch to find out what lay under her mask. And teasing came so naturally as a way to draw out someone's true self.

It wasn't just simple curiosity, though, was it? Eden nudged that thought around with a frown. *What else can it be? What is it about Michelle Hastings specifically?*

She maximized the accidental screen grab. Michelle's burning eyes stared back at her as if trying to reach through the video feed to give her a shake.

Eden bit her nail as she stared at the image. Quite clearly no one *ever* teased the CEO because her reaction had been so instant. Shock. Then disdain. Rejection. Then gone.

She crawled under the fat, puffy duvet and tried to read a little before sleep.

Two hours later, she sat up.

It *wasn't* just curiosity that made her want to understand everything about Michelle. It wasn't curiosity that made her tease her powerful boss. It was *attraction*.

Ugh. She was an idiot, all right. Such a total idiot. No wonder Michelle had told her she'd crossed a line. Had she known?

Oh Goddess. She really hoped not.

With cheeks burning in humiliation, Eden thumped her pillow and tried to sleep, visions of her icy, sexy, totally uninterested boss dancing through her head.

⁕

Michelle's jaw worked in fury as she shut down her Skype. She snapped shut the laptop lid with more vigor than it deserved and left her home office in darkness.

Damn Eden Lawless. Presumptuous little... The rudeness!

"Bubbeleh?"

She turned toward her grandmother's voice and tamped her annoyance down. "Yes?"

"Why are you muttering at your little computer?"

She was? Michelle scowled. She was half inclined to retort: *because that undisciplined underling you were so intrigued by last night thinks she has a right to judge me. She laughed at me. Mocked me right to my face!*

"I'm not muttering," she lied with little conviction.

Who cares what some temp employee thinks of me or how I run my office? Michelle thought with a snarl. Besides, Lawless was accurate in that Michelle never gave out compliments. So that wasn't the issue. What was?

I just hated her for saying it.

Why?

"Well, dear, it sure did sound like muttering to me. Anything you want to talk about?"

"No, thanks." Michelle picked over her reaction.

She thought she had a right to talk to me that way. Realization dawned. *Like we're equals. No, worse. Like a friend.*

Michelle's jaw tightened. She had spent a very long time ensuring her professionalism at the office was a thick, protective cloak no one could penetrate. No one dared. Tilly, when bored, occasionally made the attempt, but Michelle kept her at arm's length too.

In the past nine years, no one in her circle had poked at her casually as Lawless had. No one had even attempted to since Alberto Baldoni had worked at The Fixers. That asshole was her ex-husband for good reason. She hadn't been blameless, of course. But he'd made such a science of airing her dirty laundry at work. He wanted her punished, broken, and humiliated in front of her colleagues.

She'd fought back, but the cost had been terrible. She would never get over what she'd done to silence them all. Nor did she deserve to.

No wonder she was furious at Lawless. The woman's casual teasing had stirred up the old business again. Alberto and his mockery. The nightmare reminder that kept tapping furiously at her brain like some taunting Edgar Allen Poe poem. The knowledge she could not escape: that, inside, she was not good.

It was fine, though. Michelle gritted her teeth. Well, it *would* be fine. She'd simply rebury those memories yet again. And she'd already handled Lawless. Sure, Michelle's reaction tonight had been…strong. Too sharp, especially for someone reputed for being aloof and above it all. But shutting down Lawless now would have the desired effect. The impertinent woman needed to learn. Michelle was not a *friend* to playfully tease. She was Lawless's *boss*.

And the sooner Lawless got that through her sweet panda skull, the better for everyone.

Well, not *sweet*. She ground her jaw. Absolutely not sweet.

She checked the time and made a call. "I need a Room Four Special in an hour."

It wasn't a request.

"Of course, Ms. Hastings," came the smooth reply. "It'll be ready."

Chapter 5

The Candidates

EDEN DECIDED HER PLAN OF attack for a new day would be to not dwell on Michelle's abrupt Skype exit the previous night and to assess the political lay of the land.

Although, to be fair, it was tempting to dwell on Michelle. She was so dark and secretive; two things Eden truly did not understand. It was fascinating being in her orbit. Even if apparently you shouldn't get too close or you got burned for your temerity.

Nope. Not going to think about that. Her brain pouted in dismay. She had decided, though, on this one topic she would ignore Aggie's usually good advice.

She'd tone her teasing down a little, but she wasn't going to pretend to be someone else for ten long weeks. Michelle could get huffy every time or just accept it. For both their sakes, Eden hoped it was the latter.

For now, though, she decided to focus on the mayoral race rather than her attractive moody boss. Maybe she'd work out who hired The Fixers to put a political hit on Francine. Obviously a campaign rival had the most to gain.

Beyond Francine, there were only two other candidates. One, retired pediatrician, Dr. Ronald Boone. Eden knew him vaguely from childhood doctor visits, a gentle soul who kept lime lollipops in his desk drawer. Not a natural fit for any political office, but a thoroughly decent man.

Two, Bubba Nevada (his actual name), a used-car salesman who filled the local airwaves with shouty, obnoxious TV ads.

Visiting Bubba had stolen minutes off her life she'd never get back.

The man was as solid and dense as a manhole cover. Within moments of entering his used-car lot, he swaggered over to her, his bright red suspenders pinning down his lumberjack shirt while he holler-talked faster than a country auctioneer.

He tried to convince her to buy a new truck or a used car, then vote for him. Then, with a complete lack of concern or guile, he admitted that his entire mayoral run was to get publicity for his company. Finally, he'd pushed a business card into her hand in case she changed her mind about a new vehicle. The logo was just a photo of Bubba shooting finger guns.

She left feeling as though she needed a delousing.

<hr />

Her next stop was Doctor Ronald Boone's campaign headquarters, which turned out to be a small office space wedged between a shoe store and a Middle Eastern takeout place. The smell of kebabs and gyros was driving her crazy before she'd even entered the office, a reminder that she probably shouldn't have skipped breakfast. But she'd woken up still full from the feast last night.

"Hello!" came a bright voice from a young woman at the desk. She paused in folding brochures and wedging them into envelopes. "Welcome to Dr. Ron's office."

Eden glanced around at the signs. The slogan read: *The Doctor Is In!* Beside that were a lot of check boxes with big ticks in them.

"I'm Gail. You looking to volunteer?" the woman asked, sounding hopeful.

"Um, no, just curious about the candidate. What he stands for and all that."

"Oh, right!" Gail jumped up. "So much." Her enthusiasm filled her face, and she rushed over to Eden, holding out one of the brochures she'd been folding. "Here, read all about the doc." She pushed it into Eden's hands.

VOTE FOR DR. RON!
He's for FAMILY
He's for KIDS
He's for COMMUNITY
He's for LIBRARIES
He's DR. RON

Well that certainly said very little. That was it? Not *He's for destroying corrupt mayors*? How disappointing.

"So...he's the family values candidate?" Eden said dryly. Didn't they all say that? Well, not Bubba. He was the consumerism candidate and proud of being an obnoxious boor.

"Oh yes, of course. He loves kids. And families," Gail gushed. "I mean he'd have to, being a pediatrician all these years. Well, former. He's retired now."

"When did he retire?"

"Last year, but he's full of excitement about a new stage in life. He'd be such a wonderful mayor."

"What about your current mayor?" Eden asked neutrally. "Is she wonderful?"

"Oh, well, er..." Gail's enthusiasm petered out. "Always room for improvement, isn't there?"

Was the entire town brainwashed? How could even an opposition candidate's staff be unwilling to admit in public that their mayor was a toxic, corrupt mess? Or totally unsuitable at the bare minimum?

Wait, did they even know? It had been sixteen years since Eden had pulled her stunt. People forgot. Or if they didn't forget, they conveniently chose not to dwell on it to get along. Or maybe they knew that payback was a bitch when crossing Francine.

Before Eden could work out which it was with perky Gail, the door opened and an elderly gentleman stepped inside, holding the door open for a stooped woman clutching a pretty bunch of flowers in her gnarled hands.

"Dr. Ron" still had the kindest, twinkling eyes, and his hair was as white as ever. The woman was his wife, she knew, but Eden couldn't recall her name.

It was jarring how her former doctor wore such a vacant expression. It was the look that often came with aging: eyes ringed red and a little too wet. The capillaries in his cheeks were too pronounced. He had to be…what, seventy-plus, now?

She doubted he'd remember her, but it might be awkward if he did since she was attempting to fly under the radar. It wouldn't take long for Francine to work out she was back in town if she heard an unusual name like Eden being circulated.

"Hullo, hullo, hullo," Dr. Ron said jovially, casting his gaze around the almost empty room. "I got a call you wanted me to approve the brochures." He looked at Eden, then at her hands. "Is this one here? I don't think we've met. Are you one of my volunteers?"

"No," Eden said, handing over the brochure anyway. "I'm just passing through."

"Of course, of course," he said garrulously. He studied the words for a moment, squinting, as if he needed reading glasses, then his eyes shifted to Gail. "That looks wonderful, my dear. Wonderful!"

Gail beamed. "Thank you, Dr. Ron. I worked really hard on them all yesterday. And the printers said they could print off ten thousand by tomorrow if—"

"Wonderful, wonderful," Dr. Ron repeated, cutting her off, the details clearly of little interest. He turned to his wife, then glanced back at Gail. "Have you met my wife, Sophia?"

"Oh, we've met," Mrs. Boone said, giving Gail a loaded look.

A cloud crossed the volunteer's eyes.

"Married forty years and my Sophie's still as gorgeous as the day we met," Dr. Ron said.

Mrs. Boone murmured, "Forty-*six* years, but he likes to round down." She handed Gail the flowers she was clasping. "Picked them from my garden this morning. I hope they'll brighten up the office."

"They always do," Gail said with great enthusiasm, and set about replacing them with similar but drooping flowers in the vase on her desk. "Thanks. You always choose the most gorgeous colors."

"They've won awards, Sophia's gardens," Dr. Ron announced, looking delighted by the thought. "She's spent so much time on them. Her flowers are as beautiful as she is."

Mrs. Boone smiled indulgently, then turned to Eden. "Passing through, dear? Are you a tourist?"

"Yes," Eden said. "I saw the signs for your husband and wondered about him. I mean, I've heard all about the current mayor, so I thought I'd stick my head in."

Mrs. Boone's gaze grew speculative. "I can't say it ever occurred to me to sight-see an election office when I was a young tourist."

"Oh, I'm weird like that." Eden gave a shrug. "I love elections and politics. It's a thing."

"Is that so?" Mrs. Boone's tone was faintly incredulous. "I must say I'm not so fond of them, but I'd do anything to support Ronald." She slipped her hand through her husband's arm and shot him an adoring smile.

He met it with one of his own.

"On that note, Gail, dear," Mrs. Boone continued, "I'll be holding another fundraiser at the house on Sunday. Please spread the word to the usual suspects. I'll be cooking all my best dishes, if that's any incentive." She gave a modest chuckle.

"Wonderful," Dr. Ron said. "I suppose we should get going, then. Oh, did the printers say when they'll have the next batch of brochures done? And how many?"

Mrs. Boone patted his arm and slid the brochure from his fingers. "Tomorrow, darling, ten thousand. Gail said that already." She gave it the once over, then nodded to Gail.

The volunteer exhaled and smiled. "Great."

"Of course. Yes." Dr. Ron smiled back. "You did say that. All right. Let's seize the day, then."

He exited in a slow but steady shuffle.

On Mrs. Boone's way out, she passed the brochure back to Eden, which seemed fair since it had been hers to start with. "Souvenir. For your 'politics thing.'" Mrs. Boone smiled, then closed the door behind them.

A beat passed. Gail and Eden looked at each other.

"So," Gail said, attempting to inject some brightness back in her voice. "That was Dr. Ron. Isn't he sweet? And his wife's a real whirlwind. She's amazing too—all those fundraisers? She's so organized. We're in with a real shot." The tone was upbeat, but her anxious eyes told another story.

Eden drew in a breath. "Dr. Ron's the leading candidate, then?"

"Oh yes. He's our best chance at unseating the mayor."

"Why is he running? Why not enjoy his retirement? Surely he's earned it?"

"He's very excited to do something new," Gail parroted her earlier words once more. "Something fresh."

"How long have you been volunteering for his campaign?"

"About six months."

Eden's eyebrows rose. "He didn't remember you," she said quietly. "And he didn't remember how many brochures were printed."

Silence fell once more.

Suspicion sharpened Gail's features. "Do you work for the mayor? Going to spread lies about Dr. Ron?"

Lies that the man was barely with it? That was no lie.

Gail's expression hardened.

Eden sighed. "Look, your candidate's secret is safe with me, okay? I'd sooner crawl over broken glass than work for Francine. Or Bubba Nevada, for that matter."

"Okay. Sorry," Gail said, shoulders relaxing. "Dr. Ron can't help he's getting on a bit. He tries hard to remember, and he's such a good, good man. His wife is a great support for him. Although once she told me after a really long night of fundraising that she really wished he didn't have to run at all."

"Then why is he?"

"I'm honestly not sure," Gail admitted. "But I'm glad someone decent is." A wistful look overtook her. "Honestly, some days I wish Sophia Boone was the one running. Not only is she smart and all that, but she's old money—refined, you know? Elegant. Classy. The complete opposite of Bubba in every way. She's amazing. I told her that once, that she could have run instead, and she laughed and said even if she didn't hate politics personally, she was all about supporting her man in whatever he does, not taking the limelight."

"A pity. You need someone sharp to beat Francine. The sharper the better. And that's not Bubba."

"That idiot? Of course not." Gail's nostrils flared. "Like I said, Dr. Ron's our best chance and I'm going to do my best to see it happens."

"Why?" Eden asked. "Why do you care?"

"Because Mayor Wilson shouldn't run again."

"I agree," Eden said. "But why do you think that?"

"I'm a student at Wingapo College."

"Are you renting terrible accommodation nearby, by any chance?" Eden asked, with a knowing look. "Holes in the plasterwork? Or the floor?"

"Something like that. But I'm not saying that on the record to anyone. So, if anyone asks me, I'll deny it."

"As if that'd be reported around here. You've seen Wingapo's media, right?" Eden snorted.

"Oh." Gail laughed then and relaxed. "Yeah. True. Sorry. You get paranoid. You never know if one of her people is listening. The chief of police has been known to have a friendly chat with 'troublemakers.'"

"How charmingly totalitarian of him. It is on brand for Francine, though."

Gail shifted from foot to foot. "I really don't want to keep talking about this, okay? Look, bottom line is, best we can all hope for is the sweetest man ever beats her in a fair and open election."

"I'm all in favor of that." On the way to the door, Eden added, "I wish you the best of luck."

"Hey?" Gail called. "Please don't tell anyone about Dr. Ron. It's not common knowledge he struggles with his memory."

"Promise I won't hurt him." She opened the door and turned. "The world needs more good guys."

"It does." Gail's sunny enthusiasm returned. "It really does."

"But I think you should be aware that if I've noticed, a lot of other people have too. It's a testament to how well-liked Dr. Ron is that you haven't heard it, but small towns are a hotbed of gossip."

Gail slumped and shot her a miserable look. "I guess."

"Just be prepared, okay?" Eden left.

Over lunch of a cheap 7-11 egg salad sandwich out by the local creek, Eden studied the brochure for Ronald Boone. It was thin on policy. Most of his ideas could be swapped in for the talking points of any political campaign for any candidate in any state; hell, probably any country.

Of course people wanted safer parks and more libraries and happier kids and nicer schools. Who didn't?

It was only on the back page, right down at the bottom, that she saw something of interest.

As mayor, Dr. Ron would stop the excessive expansion of Mayor Wilson's solar plants. How many of these do we need? We need to be able to see our beautiful Wingapo countryside without rows and rows of solar panels.

Okay, that was different. Campaigning *against* solar power? While she knew plenty of politicians who argued for coal or even nuclear power due to job numbers or lobbyist reach, Dr. Boone didn't seem interested in those options. It was purely anti-solar-plant aesthetics by the sound of things.

Eden finished her sandwich and grabbed her phone. She browsed the mayor's policies page and tried not to feel sick when she saw the woman's photo for the first time in years.

She stopped scrolling and forced herself to look at her nemesis. Eden firmly believed you could tell anything you ever wanted to know about someone just from their eyes and mouth.

Francine's full, crimson-lipsticked mouth was forced into a knowing, professional smile that seemed to say, "Vote for me and you *will* thank me." Those dark, endless obsidian eyes were still cruel. Oh, they seemed harmless in this photo, but Eden knew better.

Francine's outfit was a jet-black business suit with a crimson scarf, matching her lipstick, and discreet gold pendant earrings, all conveying a highly efficient business executive.

To Eden, she seemed more like a highly efficient contract killer. She had never met anyone more dangerous—and with all the entitled money- and power-hungry executives she'd encountered in her life, that was saying something.

Eden continued scrolling until she reached the section on Jobs and Business Opportunities.

Solar Plants
With the loss of overseas demand for soybean production, Wingapo has looked for other opportunities for local farmers and businesspeople to explore. Solar production—both the panels, and the power it produces—is a cheap, environmentally friendly option that creates jobs and can open up vast markets.

Underneath was a list of the two solar facilities in Wingapo, as well as a much longer list of proposed plants that would get approval after the election.

It was a *very* long list.

Eden frowned. She'd never seen anything like this. Most counties had one or two energy supply creators—usually coal-based, but every now and then, some enterprising local government would try its hand at renewable power.

This, though, was something else. It was as if someone had passionately fallen in love with a growth opportunity using solar and decided to use every single spare inch of land to do so.

A lot of local farmers likely would have sold to one of the area's three private solar companies to allow this to happen. Their soybean market was gone when China stopped buying. So, when a developer had knocked and asked to use their land for solar facilities, they'd said yes.

There was opportunistic, though, and then there was excessive.

Eden called up a mapping app and began cross-referencing where the approved new facilities would be. Everywhere farming used to be was the short answer.

Half an hour later, she put down her phone, stunned. She'd just discovered a blinding chink in Mayor Wilson's black, perfectly tailored armor. And she had an idea to destroy her.

Chapter 6

Temptations

MICHELLE STALKED FROM THE ELEVATOR doors to the penthouse suite of Hotel Duxton DC. She rapped sharply twice and waited.

Her irritation magnified when a slim young man with sunken cheeks answered the door. She disliked Aaron Bolt for his rat-like tendencies. He sniveled and was as shifty as a plastic bag in a breeze.

"Mr. Bolt," she said curtly. "I was due to have a meeting with the senator." She glanced at her watch though it was unnecessary. "Right now, in fact."

"Ms. Hastings," the political toady said, his tone simpering in a way that made Michelle want to thump him. "Senator Kensington is just finishing up. She is on the phone with the education secretary."

If that was supposed to impress her, it failed. "And I am a busy woman. Tell Senator Kensington I am here. My time is of equal importance to the senator's."

Far more important, she'd have dearly loved to say, but Bolt was clueless as to who she really was or what power she held. To him, she was probably just one of Phyllis Kensington's many businesswomen allies, donors, or supporters.

His disbelieving expression confirmed Michelle's suspicion that he had no idea his boss was one of The Fixers' biggest clients, or what that meant.

"I'll tell her." He disappeared and then returned immediately, wearing an expression like a smacked kitten. "Senator Kensington is now off the phone. I have to attend to business elsewhere." Bolt glanced at his iPhone. "You have twenty minutes until she has a scheduled meeting."

"Fine." Michelle pushed past him, shooting him a withering look that he shrank from.

The door gave a satisfying heavy clunk behind him as he left.

"Michelle, darling, you really have to stop terrorizing my staff," came a rich, throaty voice, followed by the senator stepping into the room.

Phyllis Kensington was a graceful, stately woman of sixty-two with more gravitas than the rest of the members of Congress put together. The senior senator for Massachusetts was famous for verbally autopsying her colleagues on the other side of the political aisle. And for the wholesome recipes on her website, At Home with Phyllis.

Her Skillet Supper was the most downloaded recipe in the US last year, apparently. Which was hilarious because if Phyllis ever was seen willingly lifting a pan in the kitchen, Michelle would know it was an impersonator. In sum, Phyllis was a shrewd political operator with ambitions that went to the highest office in the land and who collected an interesting array of informants and allies.

"Stop hiring staff so easy to terrorize, and I'll consider it," Michelle said.

Phyllis laughed. "Aaron's one of my biggest donor's sons. I'm stuck with him. For now."

"Welcome to DC," Michelle muttered. "Everything's a deal or an angle."

"Don't sound so disheartened, darling," Phyllis said. "Our scheming keeps you and your dastardly team in business. What's with the husky throat? Did you strain it in your part-time job as a chanteuse?" She waved to a silver tray on a counter lined with glasses and bottles. "Drink?"

"Funny," Michelle drawled but wasn't about to enlighten Phyllis as to how she'd strained her voice. "No on the drink, thanks."

"Update, then? Dare I ask what my appalling husband is up to now?"

Michelle exhaled. "I haven't heard anything new. Not since…" She faded out, not entirely sure how to phrase the latest. The senator's husband had taken to banging his staff on his desk in plain sight of the security cameras. He was definitely doing it deliberately now, upping the ante, trying to force Phyllis to agree to a divorce.

Like hell the wily senator would allow that with an election looming.

"I'm aware he's getting more outlandish." Phyllis sighed. "I heard he's now fucking Troy, the intern. A *man* now? Obviously he's trying to make me blink first. Well, he'll have to do a lot worse than that." Her eyes fixed hard on Michelle's. "I assume you're busy burying this latest potential scandal in some deep, dark abyss? Paying off Troy and any others?"

"That has been our forte for several years." Michelle hesitated. "You should know, though, that The Fixer operative assigned to your case has reported that Troy is resisting our overtures. It's also proving unusually difficult to dig up past employment information on the intern. But we're on it, and we're the best. We're working out our next step."

"So, is this a strategy meeting?" Phyllis frowned. "That's not like you. Usually you handle the planning and tell me about it after it's done." She paused. "*Is* that why you're here?"

"No." Michelle cleared her throat. "No," she repeated and cursed her pale cheeks for flaming.

Phyllis obviously noticed something because she paused in raising a glass of spirits to her lips and lifted her eyebrows with interest instead. "Oh." She smiled. "Well, well."

It had been a few months since Michelle had been agitated enough to call on her favorite client for *this* reason. Each time, she told herself she wouldn't do it again because she knew firsthand it was a terrible idea to mix business and pleasure. Besides, needing relief of this sort wasn't something she liked about herself. But given that she didn't particularly like herself anyway these days, maybe that wasn't the problem.

Maybe it just annoyed her that she needed anything from anyone.

She and Phyllis had a longstanding arrangement: when one of them wanted to blow off steam discreetly, they could ascertain the other's availability.

Michelle wasn't gay. At least, she didn't think so. Well...the jury was out. She'd only ever been in a relationship with one woman—if relationship was the right word. Did a target count as a relationship?

After Catherine, when her need to fuck burned too hotly, she'd opted for a discreet, top-level male escort. Only, she'd not enjoyed the experience. She'd spent some months analyzing why.

And had decided it was something to do with power, or lack of it.

Her ex-husband had reeked of power and danger. Alberto had thrilled her younger self.

Catherine Ayers had held a different kind of power. The journalist had terrified and cowed the elite in DC. At the peak of Catherine's influence, it had been exciting just being near her. To have her complete focus had been an aphrodisiac, one Michelle had found impossible to resist.

Clearly, her body responded to power, and the escorts had been lacking. The men—and, later, one woman—had confidence but not power. It wasn't the same thing.

But Phyllis Kensington? Here was a woman who stirred her in that oddly familiar way. She could crook her pinkie and Washington's power brokers and donors would bend at the knee before her.

So when she'd asked Michelle, as CEO of The Fixers, for someone she could have discreet fun with, where the paper trail would never lead back to her, ever, and lastly but importantly, someone female... *well*.

It had seemed the perfect solution for them both. Neither wanted a relationship nor the risk or expense of exchanging money for sexual favors. They both found the other attractive. Phyllis looked like some high-class TV lawyer, with her expensive suits and effortless command of rooms. She was cold, though, even if she had the world fooled. The senator had a chilled, distant, brittle beauty that she could transform into a down-home warmth for constituents as easily as turning on a tap.

The first time Michelle had suggested her solution, the senator had her half naked and bent over the desk within minutes. Well, until Michelle had pushed Phyllis to her knees and explained how things would be. She would not be dominated. Ever.

And hell, if Phyllis didn't love being bossed around too. Michelle smirked at the memory. The woman was a damned demon in bed despite her sweet, respectable, church-on-Sundays Republican facade.

Michelle removed her earrings and rings, dropping them into her handbag. She slid off her heels, lining them up, then reached under her skirt and pulled her pantyhose and panties down. "I understand from your minion that you have twenty minutes."

"Fifteen now," Phyllis murmured, voice thick. "Do you think you can get me off that fast?"

"Who said I'm here for you?" Michelle retorted. "Maybe I want you on your back while I sit on your face and ruin that four-hundred-dollar hairdo and perfect makeup?"

"Ah." Senator Kensington's expression might be professional and practiced cool, but her eyes sparked with hunger. "Keep the outfit on." She waved a hand up and down at Michelle. "If you're planning to be above me, I'd like to look at you coming apart while you're in that prim excuse for a suit. It's positively sinful. Like fucking a morally upright lady in a church pew." Her eyes darkened to black.

Michelle snorted. Morally upright? No one in this room was that, despite appearances. "Fine," was all she said. She could give Phyllis Kensington her fantasies while she got off. After all, everyone had their secrets.

It didn't take long. Soon, after thrusting and writhing against the senator's naughty mouth, Michelle came with a gasped-out snarl. Her hands tangled into Phyllis's blond hair and raked her nails along her scalp, earning an approving grunt.

She rubbed herself against the senator's mouth a little harder, enjoying the wet sounds and the glint in the woman's eyes. God, it was obscene. All of it. Michelle exhaled. Hair escaping from her bun clung to her slicked face.

Well, that had been… acceptable. She leaned back a little to give them some space.

Phyllis reached up with a hand to smooth the strands away, but Michelle slapped it away. "No. No one touches my hair."

"What?" The word was playful. "Not even that vengeful security agent of yours?" Phyllis asked with interest. "Or should I say your ex-husband…?"

Well, that had soured the mood. And trust Phyllis to be well-informed. "No mentioning exes, either," she snapped.

Phyllis offered her an amused glance but conceded with a nod.

Why had Michelle broken her drought of eight weeks to seek out Phyllis now? She might enjoy the woman's intoxicating power and flexible, yoga-fit body, but her personality—her real one—was brutal.

She eased off Phyllis, shifting herself to sit on the woman's stomach, creating an indecently slippery wet trail across her bare skin. Then, as she'd promised, she leaned over and destroyed Senator Kensington's immaculate bobbed blond hair with more than a little enthusiastic savagery.

Phyllis's eyes fluttered closed and clenched at that, her body arching and spasming under Michelle's center, which was leaving slick scribbles all over Phyllis's twitching stomach.

The senator's hands suddenly shot out and grabbed Michelle's "prim excuse" for a skirt in two tight, white fists. She gasped and whispered, "Oh, *yes*." Slipping a hand under Michelle's wetness to reach between her own thighs, Phyllis then rubbed herself furiously for barely a minute, moaned, and came.

When she stilled, her smile was one of immense satisfaction. Still thinking of her church-lady fantasy, no doubt.

Trust Phyllis to get off on innocence. It was the rarest commodity in DC.

———◦◇◦———

Thanks to Senator Kensington's exceptionally talented tongue, Michelle was a lot more relaxed come eight that evening when the incoming Skype call sounded.

She straightened in her seat and tapped a button to answer.

"Hey, Michelle," Lawless said cheerfully. "How's it going?"

Michelle. The impertinence of calling her by her first name still burned a little, but she was in too good a mood to argue the point when Lawless was never going to budge. "It goes," Michelle said neutrally. "Report."

"It's going well here," Lawless said, then grinned wide and bright. "And, hey, I've come up with a plan! I had to spend the day driving all over Wingapo to work out the how of it, but it's totally doable." She bounced a little in her seat.

"What plan?" Michelle asked, trying to sound unmoved, but Lawless's enthusiasm was infectious. Either that, or Phyllis's adventurous tongue had left behind some endorphins.

"It seems Francine Wilson has developed a bit of an addiction."

"Oh?" Michelle leaned in, interested now. Could it really be this easy? "Gambling? Drugs?"

"No... solar power." Lawless snorted.

"Solar. Power."

"I know, I know, it sounds out there. But she's been going crazy the past three years championing solar plants for Wingapo. There're a few here now, but there are a dozen more on the books she's signing off on after the election."

"Why?" Michelle asked. "And how does that hurt her?"

"Well, see, being Francine, I'd say her love of solar is less to do with jobs or replacing lost farming markets or even clean energy. I'm pretty sure the three main companies behind the plants have been bribing her to push this agenda. And maybe she's bribing the planning boss to authorize it. But I can't prove it."

"Then how does that help?"

"Because the point is it is *excessive*. It's going to swallow up every beautiful bit of green all over Wingapo County. There'll just be rows and rows of solar panels. Everywhere. It'll be unsightly as hell."

"And no one's protesting this?"

Lawless laughed hard. "Oh, hell, that's a good one."

It was?

"Michelle, you don't protest against Francine. Even if you did, these plants aren't approved yet. They're coming after the election. And she's making it sound awesome, as if Wingapo will be the green-friendliest county in the US when she's done—capable of selling power to the world. Which is total BS. It's only fourteen plants."

"But they're fourteen *solar* plants." Michelle got it now. "All right, I agree that would be hard to oppose in the traditional way with environmental activists and so on. So I presume you know a way to get the media on side and prevent her reelection? A way to attack these solar plants?"

"Okay, first, I have to say that never in a million years would I predict I'd wind up doing something to diss solar power. And, I've gotta say, I'm still making my peace with it." Lawless shook her head.

"And I'm assuming your attack of conscience has passed and you will be getting to the point soon?"

"Yeah, yeah." Lawless laughed. "Okay, right. So I'm going to run a massive scavenger hunt."

"You're...what?"

"Didn't you ever do this as a kid? Follow a clue, find another clue, and on it goes until you get to the end? All my clues will lead to something special about Francine that'll sink her. But the buildup, all the questions, will seem so benign. Nonpolitical. Therefore, safe enough that even Wingapo's media will follow it, because nothing much happens around here."

"What makes you so sure anyone will participate in your scavenger hunt?"

"I'll make it go viral. I'll hire the biggest billboard in town to put up the first clue. There will be a website to go with it that'll amp up the excitement and explain how it all works and show clues once the public has found them. I'm working on a media release about it, which will have all the details. Trust me, Wingapo is boring as hell, and this will have the whole town talking. So by the time the hunt's almost over, everyone will be so caught up in it, the media won't be able to not report on the final answer."

"The answer that will sink Francine."

"Exactly."

"How does this relate to the solar plants?"

"The early clues will be placed in innocuous locations. The later clues will all lead to somewhere scenic that's earmarked to be taken over by solar plants—which participants won't know at first.'"

"The mayor might work out early on what the clue sites all have in common even if the public doesn't join the dots."

"I think she might. But what can she do? Tell everyone to stop playing a fun game…for *reasons*? Which she won't specify? No, she'll pretend the scavenger hunt doesn't exist while secretly trying to get to the organizer. But I'll make it exceptionally hard for her to find out it's me."

"I see. How many clues are there?"

"An even dozen. I figure since we've got ten weeks before the election, a clue a week and a few extras at the end just before election day is best. It'll keep people interested, and everyone has a chance to work it out for themselves before I put the next one up." Lawless grinned again. "I've worked my clues out all this afternoon. I feel like I've covered every square inch of Wingapo County!"

"Send me your clues and answers," Michelle instructed her, "and I'll assess whether I believe they're exciting enough to whip a whole county into a fervor."

"Nope. No fun there. I want to see if you figure them out too. Besides, I'm a master at making things go viral. You don't need to check my work on this."

"I am your boss," Michelle said, defensively. "I *can* order you to divulge this information as pertinent to my job."

Lawless's expression dropped. "I guess you could. But then that'd just make you a massive spoilsport."

Michelle stared, staggered, at this…*upstart*. How did Lawless even think this was a normal way to converse with one's CEO? Apparently last night's talk had failed to enact any change whatsoever.

"And frankly, Michelle," Lawless continued, her eyes round and sad, "if you ordered me to give away the game, I'd be *really* disappointed."

Oh. Michelle inhaled. For some reason, she didn't want Eden Lawless disappointed in her. She chose not to analyze why.

This was so unorthodox. All of it. Their interactions. Lawless refusing to obey simple instructions—galloping over the line, not merely crossing it.

And yet...

Michelle had to admit it might be quite interesting to try and guess the answers to each clue whenever Lawless disclosed them. In fact, what might be even more enjoyable would be besting her. Working out the answers quickly.

So sue her, she was competitive.

"All right. You will supply me the clue after you put each one up." Michelle tried to sound stern, given she had just capitulated. "I'll assess them then."

"So I can go ahead with my plan?" Lawless asked, a smile breaking, delight filling her eyes.

Dear God. It was like Michelle had told her unicorns were real.

"You're saying you approve my scavenger hunt?"

"I..." Michelle exhaled. "Fine. Yes."

"Awesome!" Lawless looked relieved and a lot like a puppy that had worked out where its kibble was kept. "That's good because I already booked the billboard and paid the deposit. I promised the billboard's owner a big secrecy bonus at the end of the hunt if no one learns who paid for it. That's in case the media or the mayor's people sniff around. And..." she paused and looked down, tapping something. "Also, my friend's almost finished working on the secure website, so that'd be a waste of time if you'd said no. Here." Another tap and a link appeared in the chat box.

Michelle clicked on it.

A website opened up with the words: *Join Wingapo's Exciting Scavenger Hunt!*

A how-to-participate list appeared, along with a lot of generic, picturesque snaps of trees and streams that Michelle had to admit looked enticing. It was being billed as a new way to explore the beauty of Wingapo and have fun at the same time.

"No prizes?" Michelle asked.

"No. I'd have to state in the terms and conditions who's running the scavenger hunt then. This way it can stay anonymous."

"Well," Michelle said, impressed in spite of herself. "It seems you've thought of everything."

"I hope so." Lawless's expression dimmed. "I talked to the main candidate trying to replace Francine today. He's a retired pediatrician, beloved and kind, but he's going to need all the help he can get. He won't be able to cut it against the mayor if she decides to pull out all the stops. She could destroy him in one debate."

"Then you'd better make sure your scavenger hunt scheme works," Michelle said. "Or do you have a Plan B if it fails?"

"No." And with complete seriousness Lawless added, "It won't fail."

"How can you possibly know that?"

"Because it can't." Another flash of teeth appeared. "But it won't." And with that, Lawless lifted her hand in farewell and ended the video call.

Michelle stared at the now black screen and frowned at the young woman's circular logic. It was no better than "It can't be true because I don't want it to be." Or "I won't fail because I can't fail."

She exhaled and shook herself. "I hope you know what you're doing," she muttered under her breath.

Michelle wasn't sure if the warning was for herself or her newest employee.

Chapter 7
Nor on a Fish

THE SCAVENGER HUNT BILLBOARD WAS up, containing the first clue. It was the biggest sign Eden could rent given Wingapo's lack of available billboards of any size. But even though the thing wasn't enormous, it dominated thanks to its position in the center of town. It was guaranteed to generate interest.

Eden hoped she hadn't been BS-ing Michelle about how her trail of clues would become a viral sensation. Everything in Eden's gut told her she was right. Small towns were usually bored towns. Anything new was noticed, in much the same way any*one* new gets noticed. Wingapo was no exception.

So far, the local media hadn't bitten on her press release. It was also too soon for them to have noticed, let alone reported on, the big clue billboard which barely had the glue drying on it. The one local paper, radio station, and TV news station would likely only bother reporting on the hunt when there was a fuss generated or a really slow news day.

Eden sipped a coffee from a street cafe and watched pedestrians discover the billboard plastered two stories high on Main Street. It contained one line, and below it, the scavenger hunt's website address in much smaller letters.

Neither in the kitchen, nor on a fish. Where in Wingapo am I?

It wasn't the most taxing of puzzles if locals thought about it, and that was intentional. No reason to make people feel stupid and not want to join in if they couldn't work out the first clue.

Several passersby had stopped cold, drawn out their phones, and kept glancing up at the billboard. Typing in the web address, no doubt. There they'd find a cheerful guide explaining how scavenger hunts work and urging all the locals to have fun taking part. And it explained that in a week, a new clue would appear at the site of the answer to the previous clue. That would give people enough time to discuss it with their friends before the next answer went up so they wouldn't be spoiled early.

The website had about 600 hits so far, and the billboard had only been up since dawn.

As the day progressed, wherever Eden went, the hunt was already all anyone was talking about. She hoped they'd retain their interest as the weeks progressed, but for now it looked like she'd created a hit.

By dinner, with 4,750 hits on the site, it looked as if her prediction of a viral sensation was a strong possibility. Eden was daydreaming when Melba cut into her thoughts.

"What do you think it's all about?" she suddenly asked the room. "The billboard? The clue? What do fish and kitchens both have?"

Jimmy furrowed his brow and, being the cook that he was, said softly, "Scales?"

It was the right answer. Eden smiled. She wanted to tell him he'd half solved it, but she couldn't, of course. "Great answer," she said instead.

He smiled shyly.

"Ooh, yes. Yes!" Melba said, waving her fork in the air. A string bean on the end of it detached and succumbed to gravity. It landed on her plate in a splat of gravy. "Scales. So..." She stopped. "Where does that take us next? Who has scales? The produce department in the supermarket has scales."

"There are weighing scales outside the supermarket too," Jimmy said. "Like, to see how much people weigh for a dime."

Eden let them debate Wingapo's surprisingly vast collection of scales—far more than she'd been aware of—as she finished yet another delicious dinner. Then she offered to help with the dishes.

"Goodness no, not on my watch," Melba said askance, dropping her cutlery with a clatter. "You're our guest." She paused. "By the way, what's the right answer? Which scales do they mean?"

She looked so certain Eden would know that for a second, she faltered. But then she realized Melba was simply seeking another opinion.

"I don't know Wingapo well enough to guess at which set of scales is the most iconic," Eden said, trying her best to look perplexed.

"Didn't you say you grew up around here?" Melba frowned.

Oh. Oops. "But this is my first time back in well over a decade, and the clue could relate to something new," she said, rallying. "But I guess we'll find out in a week when the answer appears next to the right scales."

Melba gave a dissatisfied humph. "That's straddling the barbed-wire fence, if you ask me. I thought you might have an actual opinion there for a second." She smiled to show she was teasing.

"Well, I'll let you have one for both of us," Eden teased back with a grin. "But it does occur to me that whatever scales they're referring to would probably be close to the billboard. I mean, why else put it where it is?"

"Or, they simply bought the biggest billboard in town?" Melba said.

"Possibly." Eden shrugged. Her watch buzzed, alerting her to the time. "Sorry, I have to call the office. Thanks for a lovely dinner." She bolted to her feet, calling "Good night!" over her shoulder.

"Night," Melba said distractedly. Behind her, Eden could hear the woman ask her son, "Which scales are closest to the billboard?"

Eden left them debating it as she headed for her room. She was still grinning by the time she connected with Skype.

She half expected it not to be Michelle this time. After all, the CEO had approved her plan now, so there was little reason for her to check in personally. Would she be handing Eden off to someone else to oversee the rest of the assignment?

The disappointment that flooded her at that thought was surprising. It was replaced quickly when she realized Michelle Hastings was now staring back at her.

Her hair was pulled tight as ever, in the tautest bun, low on her neck. Her suit was sky blue, with a white silken blouse under it. And what was that on her neck? Like a scratch? But too thin? It was faint, but Michelle had cut herself somehow? How do you cut your neck like that?

She'd have love to have asked, but Michelle seemed awfully fixated on her professional Line That Shall Not Be Crossed. For some reason, asking about bodily injuries seemed like something that would get her hung up on again.

Besides, Michelle's expression was even more intense tonight.

Eden's breath caught. It was a little unsettling how much her boss's eyes seemed to burn into people. As in, *Oh don't mind me while I drill holes into your brain and work out what you're up to.*

She squirmed in her chair, trying to get more comfortable, as if that would somehow remove the laser-like stare.

"Ms. Lawless. I trust you've had a productive day?"

How could anyone make such cold, professional words sound so... taunting?

"Yeah, I have. Great, actually," Eden said and grinned. "The billboard went up. First clue's on it. And everyone's talking about it."

"And what clue would that be?"

Hadn't she checked the website? Eden had posted the clue to it minutes after it had gone up in town. Well, she supposed CEOs of top-secret organizations had better things to do with their time. Eden cleared her throat. "It's *Neither in the kitchen, nor on a fish. Where in Wingapo am I?*"

"I see. Isn't that a little simple? Too easy to solve?"

"Is it? What's the answer?" Eden asked, curious.

"The courthouse, obviously. Scales of justice." Michelle's eyebrow lifted. "Are you making the clues easy to draw more people in or to make the smart ones not bother?"

Oh, *ouch*. And yes, she was right about the answer. "The clues do get harder—but not too hard. I'm creating a sensation, not a demoralizing exercise. I want people into it."

"I suppose I can see that." Michelle leaned back. "And are they?" she asked dryly. "Into. It?"

That taunting tone was back, and Eden found herself staring at Michelle's mouth, the way it curled slightly down, then up when she was delivering her tart one-liners.

Wait, was this Michelle's version of teasing? It was so hard to tell with her. She was impossible to read.

"Yes, they're into it. It's all anyone's talking about." Eden clicked through a link on her phone and checked the tally. "Sixty-five hundred hits so far and counting. That'll grow as people discuss it with their friends. Tomorrow, I'll be kicking off a hashtag campaign on Twitter and tagging the news outlets again to see if they'll bite. As long as it looks harmless and nonpolitical, they might."

"I hope you're right." Michelle's expression cooled. "Won't people get progressively bored as you drag it out, though? Isn't that a risk?"

"It might be if this was somewhere with lots of other things going on. But people love a mystery. A puzzle to solve. And deep down, everyone wants to play a game. We're all kids at heart, no matter how fancy the suit and the car."

"You might be wrong about that one." Michelle folded her arms.

She meant herself, of course. And she'd intended it lightly, dismissively, almost certainly, as that was her thing. But her tone was all wrong and so was her body language. Her shoulders were hunched and tense. Nothing about her seemed normal, not even Michelle's weirdly uptight version of normal.

There was something wrong. Maybe there'd also been something wrong the time Michelle had been so furious she'd hung up on her. That incident might not have even been about Eden at all. People dealt with stress in different ways.

"Are you okay? What's wrong?" she asked gently, willing Michelle to see she wasn't kidding anymore.

"Nothing," Michelle snapped. Her eyes flared in indignation. "I'm...*absolutely* fine." Her teeth gritted.

Whoa. Eden raised her hands to show she meant no harm. "You're fine. That's great. I just wondered if you'd had a bad day at the office or something. Happens to the best of us. Even me, though I don't even have an office."

Michelle's expression was tight and cold. "Yes. Gloria. The office in a former FedEx van."

"Don't knock her till you've tried her," Eden said with an easy grin. "She even gets TV...after a fashion. And has a really comfy double bed in back. Not to mention high-end bathroom facilities."

"I fail to see how any of this is relevant."

"It's not, I guess. I just wanted you to know that if you wanted to let off steam, I'm told I'm good to talk to."

Michelle stared for a long beat, then rolled her eyes. At least she no longer looked iced up enough to crack. "Remember that line we talked about," she said with a sigh. "The one you seem to blithely ignore? The line I have asked you not to cross as I am your boss?"

"That old thing?" Eden teased. *"Please."* She smiled. "Okay, no chit-chats, got it. No teasing, either. Well, I'm working on that, but that's two-thirds of my personality, so you might not always win on that one. Or, like, *ever* win. But please know I gave it serious thought before discarding it as unworkable."

"Discarding it?" Michelle's eyes went flinty hard.

"Chamomile tea." Eden suddenly snapped her fingers.

"Excuse me?"

"With honey. It's good for whatever malady or malfunction you care to name. Mom swears by it. And it helps you sleep, if that's an issue."

Before Michelle's outraged expression could turn into an out-loud threat, Eden quickly added, "Not that I'm suggesting you're anything less than perfect in bed."

Oh shit. Oh shit, shit, shit. Had she really just said that?

The innuendo sunk between them like a falling anvil.

"Oh goddess." Eden whimpered. "That is *not* what I meant, okay?"

Michelle's face was a cold, granite mask.

"I was referring to *sleeping*." Her voice was now embarrassingly higher, like the squeak of a dog's chew toy. "I'm sure you're perfect at *sleeping*!" Eden rubbed her face. "Look, just kill me now. And do it fast. Like quick-acting poison or something, okay?"

"In my experience, poison rarely acts quickly," Michelle drawled evenly. Amusement filled her eyes. "The movies have a lot to answer for. It's like they do no research whatsoever. Good night, Ms. Lawless. Oh, and sweet dreams," she added, now looking on the verge of an actual fucking smile. That taunting was definitely back.

The screen went blank. Eden slumped in her chair.

Oh fuck! I just suggested my boss is fabulous in bed.

And wait...poison? In my *experience*?

How the hell did Michelle Hastings know about poison? Or was she joking?

It was all too hard. Eden groaned at herself as the conversation replayed on a loop in her brain. Her pained groan turned into a half smile. Well, she'd at least seen what her boss looked like when she was amused.

In a word? *Hot.*

Michelle closed her laptop with a decisive click. She had no idea what had just happened at the end of that Skype call. Then, before she could stop herself, she burst into laughter.

Kill me now, Lawless had informed her so, so mournfully. She was all soulful sad eyes and soft expression. The woman would be dangerous if she could harness that into a weapon.

Was this to be a pattern? Michelle would conduct an entirely appropriate conversation seeking updates from an employee, only for the woman to completely derail it? She was chaotic and problematic. And now she'd announced she would be "discarding as unworkable" Michelle's demand not to tease her. That had been a completely reasonable request, and Lawless had just said the equivalent of "yeah, nah"?

She massaged her pounding temples. Michelle had been skirting a bad headache all day. She'd almost emailed to cancel the call but ultimately decided to just go ahead. Maybe because Lawless could be amusing. For some entirely incomprehensible reason.

Michelle had allowed yet more lines to be crossed. How inappropriate Lawless had been. And then…how contrite.

She smiled again and gave a soft gasp at the pain from her headache. Funny how she hadn't even noticed it during the call.

It was the work. She sighed. Ordinarily, work should never be one's whole, sole focus in life. It wasn't healthy. And she was getting too old for this at forty-seven. Her doctor had warned her that her stress levels were off the chart. But what else could she do? Michelle had a unique skill set. Her power and contacts were what made her important.

Who am I without The Fixers? What am I without my job?

"Bubbeleh?"

Hannah's call forced Michelle to her feet. She groaned as her head protested the movement.

"Are you okay?" Michelle called back tightly as she made her way down the hall.

"Oh fine, fine. Just an old woman with aches and pains. I wouldn't say no to a hot-water bottle, though. And my bad knee is making me regret many things from my youth."

Michelle snorted. "You? With regrets?" She entered her grandmother's bedroom and found her under a blanket on her bed, a discarded book on her stomach. "I heard you were the queen of the party circuit back in the day. You can't tell me now you regret all that attention and all those cha-chas."

"Never," her safta said with a pleased smile. "But I do regret my decision not to take good care of my body after I had your father. I got so caught up in all my little projects, and everything went stiff from lack of use. That's something you should think about too—you're too young to be hunched over a computer from the moment you get home. And I know you have a headache, so don't be stubborn."

"Not this again."

"I say it with love."

"You say it as a meddling old safta." Michelle gave her a fond look as she picked up the old woman's reading glasses from where they'd fallen to the floor. She folded them up and placed them on the bedside table as her grandmother studied her with far too much interest.

"A young woman should be out on the town, finding that special someone who makes her hum," she announced.

"I've never hummed over anyone, so that's a bit silly. Not even my husband."

Hannah's eyes turned knowing. "Oh, you hummed once. It was a little before I moved in with you, just before your divorce. I found it odd you'd divorce a man still making you hum like that."

"You're imagining things," Michelle said lightly, even as an image of Catherine slipped into her mind. "And besides, you hated Alberto. I'd think you'd have wanted us to be divorced even sooner than we were."

Her grandmother had side-eyed Alberto from the moment they'd met. "He is so dangerous, bubbeleh," she'd warned. "Don't you see his eyes? He might be good to you while he likes you, but what if that changes?"

It *had* changed. And those dangerous eyes had not given rise to whatever violence her grandmother had feared for Michelle. But there was more than one way to hurt a person. Alberto had indeed been dangerous. He still was.

She heard whispers from her contacts quite regularly of him trying to punish her by bringing her and The Fixers down. He'd tried before. He'd likely try again. Some dangers never went away. The stress of them just got added to the pile on her plate. "I'm going to get your hot-water bottle."

Hannah didn't reply, just gave a slight nod. It was a relief that she didn't comment further on Alberto or humming. But the eighty-three-year-old's face contained an expression that said she wasn't buying whatever Michelle was selling.

Michelle hurried to the kitchen. She carried the hot-water bottle back five minutes later.

Her grandmother had lost her inquisitive look and smiled at her. "Thank you. Now then, tell me, who was it who had you laughing ten minutes ago?"

"I..." Michelle frowned. *Laughing?* "What?"

"In your office. I heard you."

"Oh. That. Eden Lawless. The troublemaker employee who never met a cause she didn't like."

"I want to meet her," Hannah said serenely. "Anyone who can make you laugh is special."

"Not special; annoying," Michelle shot back. "She has no regard for decorum or professionalism or any other boundaries. And you and her meeting is never going to happen, so don't ask."

With a firm smile that could have been welded on by Rosie the Riveter, Michelle fussed over her grandmother—placing the bottle in the best position and adjusting the blanket—to avoid looking too deeply into the old woman's speculative eyes.

Her grandmother didn't say another word on the topic—which constituted a minor miracle.

Michelle would take it.

Chapter 8

Does Not Bleat

EDEN YAWNED, BARELY ABLE TO keep her eyes open. She'd been much better at doing midnight missions in her younger years.

"Listen to me. Ready to be sent off to pasture at thirty-six," Eden muttered to herself. "I need a nanna nap before noon."

"What was that, hon?"

Eden started, not having realized Melba had come into the sitting room. She'd been slowly munching away on a ham-and-cheese sandwich, lost in her own world. "Sorry," Eden said. "I didn't get much sleep last night. I might have a nap after lunch."

"Oh, that's a shame. I hear chamomile tea does wonders," Melba said.

"With honey?" Eden asked and grinned. "My mom loves it like that."

"Mine did too," Melba said happily, clasping her hands in front of her chest. "Oh! Did you hear we all know the answer to the scales clue now?"

Eden forced her eyes to her sandwich. "Nice. What was it?"

"The courthouse! You know, like scales of justice. Everyone's saying they correctly guessed it, but they're full of it." She chuckled. "You were right, though. That's in spitting distance of the billboard." Melba leaned in. "Anyway, I heard from Mrs. Thornlie at the drugstore that there was a new clue stuck up next to the courthouse sign this morning when she opened at seven."

Eden swallowed her mouthful. "A new clue? What is it?"

"Does not bleat, does not cheat." Melba's gaze shot up to the ceiling as she thought. "I'm thinking *sheep*? Although what cheating and sheep have to do with each other..." She tapped her chin as she trailed off.

"Could be a lamb," Eden suggested. "They bleat. But neither cheats, so..."

"True, true." Melba frowned for a second, then smiled. "I should consult Jimmy. He was right about the scales part. That boosted him right up."

"I'm glad," Eden said.

"All righty." Melba rose. "Let me take your plate, and I'll shoo you off to that nanna nap. I think you must be on a different clock than the rest of us."

"I came here from Ohio, and that's on the same time as Wingapo."

"Well, something's knocking your body clock off. You can barely keep your lids open."

Eden decided she was too tired to think of an answer. "Okay, you're right. I could use a nap."

With that, she trundled back to bed.

Eden was mid-yawn when Michelle answered her Skype call that evening. She sheepishly turned it into a weird hand-mashed-to-mouth rub that probably hid nothing. But a girl could dream.

"Am I keeping you up?" Michelle drawled. Her eyes darted to the bottom of her screen. "At...eight in the evening?"

"Sorry," Eden said. "Pre-dawn mission today—I'm still getting used to them again."

"The youth of today are so weak," Michelle noted.

"Hey, I'm closer to your age than a youth's." Eden pouted. "Or I think I am. How old are you, anyway?"

Michelle's mouth tightened, and she reached for a pen and paper. After a moment, she held up the paper, which had a line drawn on it.

She tapped it. "Does this or does this not ring any bells?" She sighed. "At all?"

Right, right, no crossing the line. "Yeah, yeah," Eden said with a grin. "Okay, so to get down to business—"

"I do wish you would."

"—I put the next clue up." Eden waited for dramatic effect...or until irritation flitted into Michelle's eyes. "*Does not bleat, does not cheat.*"

Michelle looked up and to the right as she thought. Then she said, "Goats bleat. And people cheat in games. Games and goats..." She met Eden's eye and smiled in triumph. "So, does Wingapo have some favorite sporting son or daughter memorialized somewhere? Who's the GOAT?"

Eden stared at her.

"Have I got it wrong?" Michelle said more cautiously, her smile dropping away. "It's a sporting term. Greatest of All Time?"

"No, I know. It's just, you're right." Eden shook her head in amazement. "And you worked that out in, what, two seconds?"

The triumph was back, but Michelle masked it quickly. She huffed. "Your clues are not difficult. But, as you say, purposely so."

"Right. Anyway, so Wingapo loves its baseball. There's a statue of Babe Ruth that sits in the park off the main street. As the local history goes, he played a single game at our humble baseball stadium just before Boston signed him, and we've never forgotten."

"Ah. How exciting for the locals." Michelle's lips twitched.

Eden shrugged but felt oddly defensive on Wingapo's behalf. Why should her old town be mocked for honoring a beloved celebrity's visit? "It *was* exciting. Hell, it's still a huge deal here."

"Right." Michelle cocked her head. "You said *our* humble stadium. Is Wingapo yours once more?"

Eden stopped, startled. She *had* said that. "Oh. No, I don't think so. A slip of the tongue."

Michelle eyed her closely, and those burning eyes were boring into Eden's soul again. "Have you done any reconnecting since you've been there? Visited friends or family or maybe your old haunts?"

"What? No!" Eden snapped. "I mean...I'm here to work."

"I don't imagine furtively slapping up a clue once a week in the middle of the night takes up every waking second of your day. What else have you been doing?" Michelle's expression was indecipherable.

In truth, Eden had been coordinating her other consultancy work remotely when not running the scavenger hunt. There were the nurses in Ohio, for instance. Causes abounded that needed her expertise. She could do more than one thing at once—but it probably wasn't wise to tell her boss that.

Instead, Eden asked in dismay, "You want me to reconnect with people around here?"

"I didn't say that. I was just curious as to whether you had."

"Why?" It came out sharp. Eden knew she was being prickly, but Wingapo's assorted bad memories had always been a sore spot for her. "Do you want me to look up my ex-girlfriend who ditched me because it was too shameful to be seen with me after the mayor began a campaign of lies against me? Or look up my dad who still hates me for ruining his medical career?"

"You really are adept at putting words in my mouth," Michelle said evenly. "I simply imagined you still had friends there. Those who helped you construct your big protest back in the day? I wasn't aware asking after your friends would cause such a reaction."

"I haven't looked any of them up." Eden scowled, furious at the reminder as to why. She was half tempted to draw a line on a page, as Michelle had done, and tap it repeatedly. Eden folded her arms, feeling truly out of sorts now.

After Francine had gotten her expelled, all Eden's supporters except Aggie had gone to ground. The silence had been deafening. Oh, Eden got it: no one else wanted to go down with her. But no one had reached out privately, either. Hell, some pretended they'd never even met when she saw them in the street.

Her heart hadn't taken it well back then. She wasn't sure she was ready even now to face them and their fumbled excuses or history rewrites.

Eden realized Michelle was still waiting for an explanation.

"I'm trying to keep a low profile so Francine won't work out I'm here." Well, that was also true. "If I look up all my former friends, word might get around."

"You're trying to keep a low profile, yet you drive a rainbow-colored van?"

"Well, I'm staying out of town as much as I can. And Gloria's hidden when I'm at the B&B."

"Would it affect any of your plans if the mayor knew you were in Wingapo?"

"Probably not. I'm just avoiding having to face her. She's so… draining. I suppose there's a chance she might guess I'm the hunt's organizer. If that happened, she'd probably order a media blackout on reporting on it because she'll know I'm up to something. I'm not sure if she'd do more, like try and stop it."

"She won't go that far," Michelle said with certainty. "She has an election in two months. She doesn't want to be known as the woman stopping everyone's fun. At least, she won't stop you until you reveal your true intentions. Then she will come out swinging."

Michelle's expression became intense. "You must be ready for that, though. Trust me on this: powerful people with their backs to the wall are exceedingly dangerous."

"Yeah." Eden grimaced. "Seen it all before, remember? Anyway, I'm just putting off having to face Francine for as long as possible. She's such a negative energy. She gets me so worked up. I'm all about being a positive force."

"Then I suppose it must be unsettling for you having an arch enemy," Michelle said with a hint of a smile. "We all have that one antagonistic individual who claims to want to destroy us. Or, in my case, several individuals. But for me, it just comes with the job."

Eden digested that uncharacteristic amount of sharing. "What do you do to acquire *multiple* enemies?" she asked in astonishment. "I mean, I thought you were just righting wrongs for a price."

"Righting wrongs?" Michelle repeated slowly. "Is *that* what you think we do?"

"Well, I'm just guessing based on the available data. That is, my assignment and your company name. The Fixers means you fix injustices, right? But as to all your other cases, I have no clue. So, what *do* you do when not toppling corrupt mayors by proxy?"

"Whatever it takes," Michelle said mysteriously.

"Um, okay, that was suitably vague."

Michelle smiled.

"Oh, come on," Eden groused.

"All I can say is, I have to go up against very important people daily. And some of them think having money or power means they can do anything. It can be quite a shock to them to learn, actually, that that's not always true. And they remember me as the one who caused them problems. I'm sure I'm on a few lists."

"Yeah. Same. I go up against quite a few polluters and bad corporations. They really do hate it when they get attacked by pesky mosquitoes."

"Mosquitoes." Michelle's face went through myriad expressions before settling on incredulous. "Oh, I'm no mosquito to these people."

"I meant me. You're more a cougar, right?" Eden suddenly stopped in panic at how that had come out. "Um, as in face-tearing cats! Like a lion! Or tiger?"

Michelle gave her a long-suffering look. "Forget the metaphors. My point is, if you want to connect with your friends, I'm suggesting it wouldn't be a disaster. It wouldn't matter if the mayor finds out you're there. It will happen sooner or later."

"I'd have thought you wouldn't want your employee distracted."

"I want my employee on an even emotional keel. I'm aware that for some people, especially social types…" she waved at Eden, "it can take a toll when they don't have support networks or friends around them."

Some people.

"Not you?" Eden asked quietly.

This time the pause was interminable. Michelle's jaw worked and worked. It was like the human version of seeing three dots appearing and disappearing while waiting for an instant message.

Something seemed to shut down behind her eyes, and they became cold and empty. "We're not talking about me. I'm just saying I know how people tick. Knowing this is what makes me good at my job. So, long story short, if you need to catch up with half of Wingapo in order to feel at peace, do so. I give you my permission, in case you thought I expected you to be a hermit while on assignment. But if you're not interested in dealing with the past or being sociable, that's entirely up to you too."

She gave Eden such a long-suffering look that Eden wondered if she was regretting the entire conversation. Michelle had been doing that a lot lately. Even though Eden had absolutely nothing to report to her between clue drops, these nightly Skype calls continued. And during the odd little calls, Eden had begun amusing herself by cataloging Michelle's vast array of expressions and other nonverbal responses. There was the frown, the extra grumpy frown, the cool stare, the icicle glare, the lip twist (disdain), and her personal favorite, the lip twitch (suppressed amusement).

Eden hadn't yet worked up the courage to ask why they were even having the calls when Eden didn't have anything new to report. Maybe her boss really was this anal. Someone who needed to know what everyone was up to at all times and clock it with her own eyeballs. Did she do this with everyone else? She must have a night filled with staff calls if so.

No wonder she always seemed so tired and pinched. Oh, the concealer under her eyes hid it, but not perfectly. Eden could sometimes see dark circles.

And occasionally there would be the faintest scratches. Well, more like nicks—on her neck, face, or arms when she was in a sleeveless top. What *did* Michelle get up to when not on video calls with Eden?

She'd add that to her list of things she wished she could ask but never would. After all, as Michelle kept pointing out, occasionally with visual aids, there was a *line*.

"Ms. Lawless?"

"Hmm." Oh, she'd been daydreaming. Friends. Right. She could look them up if she wanted. "Well, thank you. I will take that under advisement." Eden folded her arms.

"You do that," Michelle said. "So, anything else?"

"No. But I can't help but wondering who the client is. I can't see Dr. Ron wanting to cheat his way to mayor by hiring The Fixers. And

Bubba is both offensive and stupid, and the election is just a free publicity stunt for him. He's hardly going to spend money on it."

"What makes you think the rivals are the only ones who'd gain if Francine Wilson loses? Not everything is about the polls. Not everything is obvious, either. Don't be so literal."

Eden turned that over. "Someone hates her for nonpolitical reasons? Well, I mean, I can see that. But don't they have to be rich to hire you? Most people who hate her are tenants, many of whom are poor college kids. And how would they even know about The Fixers?"

"I'm not at liberty to reveal the name of the client. But you love puzzles and clues; work it out for yourself."

"And you'll tell me if I get it right?"

"Of course not." Michelle gave the faintest hint of a smile, leaned forward, and ended the call.

Eden laughed. "Damn." Why did she have to be so… whatever the hell she was? Taunting? Amusing? Even when she was in a bad mood, she was captivating. And those eyes…

Christ, those eyes.

Her phone jangled into life, and warmth filled her at the sight of Aggie's photo ID. How unexpected. Dealing with upset teens on the help line all day made Aggie less enthusiastic about talking on phones in her off hours. She preferred texts nine times out of ten.

"Now, here's a rare treat," Eden announced by way of hello. "I've missed you,"

"There's a coincidence." Aggie laughed. "I was just telling Colin how you must be pining without my awesome self to cheer you up."

"Definitely." Eden shifted to the bed and flopped. "It's so strange being back here. I keep feeling a few degrees off kilter. Nothing's quite normal. Tonight, my boss suggested I could catch up with my old friends if I wanted, and my whole body just went into shock."

"Ah." Aggie's sadness filled the phone. "Yeah, it's a lot, what happened. Was your boss thinking you need closure? With your friends or your dad?"

"She didn't mention him but… I don't know. Dealing with it just feels…" Dangerous? No. Terrifying. "I mean I'm okay with my life now." Eden wondered just who she was trying to convince here. "With me. I'm at peace with my past, as much as I can be. I shouldn't be forced to be raked over coals if I don't want to!" Her voice rose to almost a panic.

"Forced?" Aggie sounded perplexed now. "How can she force you to? And why—"

"No. I mean, she's not forcing anything. It was a suggestion."

"Okay. So why did your boss *suggest* you do any of this in the first place? Isn't that a bit weird?"

"Michelle thinks that someone like me, someone sociable, maybe needs to be around friends for my emotional well-being."

"Ah. Well, she's right."

"I get that. But now I'm confused. One minute she's all 'REPORT!', and the next it's, 'Hey, you checked in with friends yet?'"

"Right. So, Option A, she's picked up on all that unresolved Wingapo tension you carry around and thinks it'd be better if it was gone—either for you or the mission. And, hey, she's not wrong. Or, Option B, maybe she's just…decent?"

"No, she's confusing," Eden corrected. "She was totally off topic, and she is *always* on topic. What the hell does it mean telling me I'm free to visit old faces and places and blah, blah, blah? What if I don't *want* to?"

"Then don't." Aggie sounded even more concerned. "Hon? It sounds like she doesn't care either way and she just tossed it out there. You're the one getting worked up. This is stirring up a hornet's nest for you. Are you okay?"

"Of course!" Eden had merely gone back to the shitty pits of hell that had tormented her in her formative years. Why wouldn't she be fine?

"Eden, hon, you're my best friend in the whole world, and I can tell from here you don't sound okay. And that makes me wonder if maybe your boss has a really good point. If you're not dealing with random emotional stuff that's come up now, you won't be strong enough to face Wilson when everything comes out. You need to get your head ready."

"Michelle did say I need to be ready," Eden mumbled. "Maybe that's why she suggested connecting with friends? She wants me fit, mentally, for what's ahead."

"It's possible. Or…maybe it was just a throwaway line. Edie, you're really overthinking this, and you don't have to. Look, if it's too much being back there, just pull the pin on the whole thing now while they have time to replace you. Come and stay with me. Mom's devastated she missed you last visit."

Pull the pin? The thought filled her with dismay. No more mission? No more Michelle? That didn't bear thinking about. Despite being back home, she was enjoying her little adventure…skulking around, working out where and when to put her clues, listening to everyone's enthusiasm in discussing them, especially Melba and Jimmy. It was just today, and one tossed-out suggestion that had sent her spiraling.

"I'm fine," Eden gritted out and forced herself to remember that she was. She was older and wiser now. Had her own business and everything. Francine couldn't harm her. Well, not like before. "I'll tell you what: Tomorrow I'm going to look at my old house. And then you'll see. I'll be fine. It'll all be fine."

"If you say *fine* one more time, I might start to suspect you're lying to your oldest and most charming friend."

"*Fine*," Eden repeated but then laughed. The tension drained out of her. "I just can't work out my boss. Tonight, she admitted she has multiple enemies. *Multiple*! Said it like it was nothing. I can barely cope with one."

"Seriously?" Aggie sounded enthralled. "So, have you worked out exactly what she does when she's not hiring nice social agitators like you? You don't have to give me specifics, just the vibe."

"All I know is it involves a lot of important, powerful people. And pissing them all off when she tells them no." She laughed.

"So, you and she aren't that different, then. Given how many assholes you've pissed off in your time. Comes with the job, right?"

"True." Eden exhaled. "Well, a mystery for another day." She rolled her shoulders, suddenly feeling knotted. "I need a vacation after this. Somewhere I can disappear off the grid, with only the nicest distractions."

"Cool. I'll fluff the cushions on the pull-out sofa bed."

"I meant somewhere with an actual bed."

"Please, my sofa is phenomenal."

Eden laughed. "Okay, after this, I'll come stay for a few days. And we'll catch up properly. I promise to spend time with your mom too. I miss her as well."

"Sold."

"And while I'm there, I can work out how to get you and Colin to finally go on a date."

"Do not make me rescind my invitation," Aggie said with mock gravity. "I *will* do it."

Grinning, Eden chuckled and said goodbye. She felt better already. Until she remembered she'd rashly decided to visit her family home tomorrow.

Chapter 9

Where the Heart Was

EDEN FELT FAINTLY RIDICULOUS AS she pulled up outside her former home. Why was she even here? To prove that she was unaffected by being back on her old stomping grounds? That was pretty stupid when it was clear to all that she was rattled down to the bones.

She gazed up at the 1952 Cape Cod-style three-bedroom house. It would be called "charming" in a real-estate ad, if you liked vinyl floors and weather-worn sidings.

It seemed so much smaller than she remembered. But that figured, given she'd been a lot smaller when she lived here.

Eden wound down the window. Familiarity flooded her from the smell of a neighbor's freshly mown lawn and the dust from the long dirt driveway.

The mockernut hickory tree had become huge, its great droopy leaves sagging over the dark-gray tiled roof. She used to clamber up its trunk and onto her favorite branch and dream up wonderful stories while she waited for her father to get home from his shift at Wingapo Hospital.

Then she'd swing out of the tree, dropping easily beside him as he headed up the drive, chattering to him about her stories, her day, her world. And he'd smile as he absorbed her enthusiasm, eyes brightening. His improving mood at her tales always reminded her of the way a sponge grows fat with water.

He'd ruffle her tumble of red hair at the door and thank her for the company, before stretching out in his striped, brown armchair with a beer and repeat his sponge-inflation impression with his wife.

River's day usually involved whatever protest, cause, or strike she'd attended or assisted. Her father's eyes would become fond and gentle, his expression indulgent, as River explained in detail all the ways some new special interest needed protecting. Eden would be riveted, watching their unspoken love for each other and for what they held dearest. Her mother—Planet Earth. Her father—River Lawless.

It was only later Eden realized how unusual that difference in priorities was.

The two had met in Haiti when her father had been visiting a colleague who was working for Médecins Sans Frontières—Doctors Without Borders. It had been love at first sight for young medical resident Peter Nelson when a feisty, still-fired-up River had been brought in injured after a protest. He'd volunteered to treat her.

His love for River had never been in question. Peter Nelson let his wife name their daughter whatever she wanted—and didn't mind when she chose Eden's first, last, and middle names. He wanted River to have anything her heart desired because his heart desired only her. And that had been why everything had gone so badly wrong later.

Eden swallowed back the painful reminder. Back when they'd lived here, they'd all been so close. And it hurt seeing that physical manifestation of what no longer was.

She wiped away the moisture from her eyes. She'd screwed up so much in her early life, but she'd never be able to shake her guilt at screwing up her parents' marriage with it. Thank you very much, Francine fucking Wilson.

"Hello?" A rapping sound came from the side of her van.

Eden twisted to find an older man eying her up and down. "Yes?"

What'cha doin' outside my place? Just starin' at it like yer plannin' to rob it!"

Eden wiped her eyes again. "Sorry," she said, hating how thick her voice sounded. "I used to live here as a kid. I was reminiscing." She pointed at the towering mockernut hickory. "Used to climb that every day when it was only a third the size. That lower branch was my favorite perch."

He man squinted at her, then his expression shifted. "You're Pete's kid?"

"Yeah. I'm Eden."

"Oh." He relaxed, shoulders shifting back, brows unknitting. "Welp, I guess I can see the similarities. The red hair mostly. After he sold his place to me, some nights he'd still come 'round here, like he forgot he didn't own it no more."

When your father was drunk off his ass and had lost it, the man didn't say. She'd heard tales of him propped up at one of the three bars around Wingapo. Stories of him being belligerent and aggressive. Those drunk doctor stories became so widespread, they made him unemployable throughout the whole county.

"I'm sorry," she said, wincing. "Does he still do that?"

"Naw." The man rocked back on his heels, then rubbed his white-whiskered jaw. "Got his act together again. Didn'tcha know?"

How could she since he'd cut her off years ago? "I'm glad," Eden said, dodging the question. Her heart was suddenly hammering hard when she asked. "Do you know what he does now?"

He frowned at her.

"We lost touch," she explained.

"Mmm." He sized her up again. "Pete hangs 'round a workshop for fellas going through troubles. It gives 'em a place to go, build some things, talk. Not be alone. It's on Main and Ninth. Called The Shed. Been there once or twice meself, just to check it out. Honestly, the place means well and all, but for me, there's too many sad sacks bangin' on 'bout who they used to be. Those ole boys can get mighty depressin' when they start up comparin' how their lives tanked."

"Oh." She could easily picture her father doing that. He did love to feel sorry for himself.

"But that's just me. I s'pose I gotta give 'em points for tryin'." He shrugged. "Anyways, Pete's pretty much always there. If you're interested."

Am I? "Thank you," was all she said.

"Hey?" he said, snapping his fingers. "Did you want the tour? Fer old time's sake? Don't think my missus would mind. I know what it'd mean to me if I could poke through my ole childhood home."

Eden drew in a breath and stared at the little house in front of her. She'd loved it. All the warmth it had kept inside.

All the warmth had seeped out, though, and that was hard to forget.

"I really appreciate the offer," she said quietly. "Might take you up on it another day. But right now...I'm not there yet."

He shrugged. "Suit yourself." He stepped back, and his tone became dismissive. "Drive safe, now."

"I will." She started Gloria. "Thanks again."

Ten minutes later, she pulled up to the corner of Main and Ninth and turned off the motor, already regretting her impulsive action to come here.

An old, worn-out shopfront with the words *The Shed* on it sat in front of her. A few elderly men sat outside at tables, drinking coffee, smoking, and chewing the fat. Another was up a ladder, sanding back the flaking paint on the sign and calling out some insults to the seated men about slacking off. The men all laughed.

Eden stared at the man up the ladder. She'd know him anywhere, from any side. His graying titian hair was shaggier, like he hadn't seen the barber in a while. Her father had lost weight too, and his blue shirt flapped against his lean, tall frame.

He hadn't seen her yet, and she wasn't ready for him to. She willed him not to turn around. Her stomach clenched.

Suddenly she was furious with herself for coming here—to this workshop, to her old house, to Wingapo in general. Her anger leaked onto Michelle for putting the idea in her head. Why should people have to revisit the very things that broke them? Wasn't that cruel?

How could she face a man who'd blamed her for every bad choice he'd made?

How could she make peace with a man who had been her whole world and then just walked away? Like she didn't matter. Who could do that to someone they loved?

She gazed at the man who'd once been so highly regarded around Wingapo. And now what was his life? Painting old signs and hanging out with other broken souls, bitterly comparing their miseries?

He wouldn't want to see Eden again. She should respect that and leave.

Decision made, she started her van and floored it.

———— ✦ ————

Phelim O'Brian stood before Michelle sheepishly. "Looks worse than it is." He gestured at his black eye.

"I'm not sure how." She tilted her head. "Well, well. I didn't think the senator had it in him."

"To be fair, it was Cavaner's wife," O'Brian said, his grin peeking out. It looked funny on such a grizzled head. He was all pockmarks and battle scars, with a solid pugilist jaw and once-broken nose, covered in pale, pudgy skin that would look unattractive on anyone except her head of security. He always wore his unconventional face as a badge of honor, and the confidence worked for him. She liked that about O'Brian. Anyone who owned who they were without artifice was refreshing.

Her mind drifted to Eden Lawless, but she pushed the thought away.

"The wife?" Michelle leaned back in her office chair. "I dread to ask."

"We were in some fancy games room, and I may have *helped* Cavaner's back land on the snooker table. His missus tried to prevent my fist from making a few...reasonable points...to the senator about bein' a blackmailin' asshole. She started firin' snooker balls at me. I ducked 'em all." He pointed at his eye. "Except one."

"I remember a time you'd have ducked them all, O'Brian." She pursed her lips to hide her smirk.

"None of us is getting any younger, boss." He said it neutrally enough, but his blue eyes twinkled.

Michelle scowled. Informality from her employees was undesirable. "Don't be a smart ass." She tapped her desk to emphasize the point. "Well, what happened next?"

"This is where it got extra interestin'. Turns out Mrs. C and the new baby had been forced to live with her husband's parents when the Cavaners lost credit card access, power, heatin', and the works. Seems she had some strong thoughts on that turn of events."

"Doesn't like the in-laws? Then she should get her husband to stop threatening us, and it'll be amazing how fast she'll be back home in her own bed. We made her husband a *senator*, as he wished. To thank us, he tries to weasel out of paying his bill." Outrage coursed through her, but she schooled it from her voice "Worse, the doughy little rodent threatens to *blackmail* us and out us to the world? As if *he* has any power in this deal."

"I did make that point," O'Brian said dryly. "With fewer fancy words."

"And?"

"And it was the first she'd heard of it. Didn't help her mood that she was sleep deprived from having a cranky little one. She turned on her husband and screamed at him." His tone shifted to a snooty woman's screech: "'We're going through all this over some shitty bill you won't pay? Are you *insane*? Rich-ahrd! I don't need this! Pay them!'"

"Oh dear."

"Right? Then she started hurlin' snooker balls again—at *him*." O'Brian chuckled. "Well, it was more in his general vicinity than deliberately aimin' for him. Except he doesn't have my reflexes. Went down like a sack of spuds. Well, a sack of whimperin' spuds."

Michelle forced down a laugh.

"Anyway, I left them to it. I'll go back when there's no skin 'n' hair flyin' and see how ready he is to settle up. I haven't mentioned the Degas he'll be coughin' up yet. Figured I'd save it for last."

Michelle nodded. "Fine. Just make sure he's crystal clear as to who he's dealing with. Explain in *detail* if you have to," she said meaningfully. "Although, remember we don't like a paper trail." Such as posting bail for her enforcer.

She waited for his nod. For all his comments about fists and pushing Cavaner around, O'Brian did know where the limits were. She'd hired him to be the thinking man's enforcer for a reason. He could be subtle and imply sinister threats to great effect without lifting a finger. Most individuals he terrified folded instantly.

"Good," Michelle continued, voice silky. "Make him understand *who* we are, *how* deep our reach is, and that we can do *far* worse than what he's endured. We will not be blackmailed, especially by some political amoeba."

"Sure," O'Brian said genially. "But I reckon he'll get the message twice as hard from his wife. She looked fit to be tied."

"Do not cross exhausted new mothers."

"Nooo," he agreed. O'Brian lifted his meaty hands in surrender, his eyes wide. "My missus taught me that."

"We're done here. Get Dr. Michelson to look at that." She pointed at his eye.

"Nah, it's nothing."

"Could be a fractured socket. The Fixers have DC's best private hospital and physicians on retainer. Make use of them. Email me Dr. Michelson's report so I know you've seen her."

"Waste of time and resources," he muttered but turned obediently.

"And speaking of resources, I like to keep mine healthy. See the doctor, Mr. O'Brian." She flapped her hand toward the door. "If nothing else, to prove me wrong."

<hr />

Michelle settled into her chair behind the laptop in her home office, anticipation filling her. The computer's clock turned over to eight and she opened Skype, then bit back her surprise as her call connected.

Something was very wrong with Eden Lawless. Her hooded eyes were dark and filled with sadness.

"Report," she barked, partly out of habit, partly to hide her shock. "Please," she added more gently.

Lawless gave a listless shrug. "I'm waiting till tomorrow before I put up clue three. As you know already. Nothing's changed in that regard. Weeks go on, clues go up." Her mouth drooped.

"I see." Michelle fidgeted, suddenly uncertain what to do with her hands. "So, what did you do today?"

"I visited my childhood home. As you suggested." Lawless's eyes became pained. "I don't recommend it. Too many memories."

"Ah." Michelle wondered why she'd even suggested it in the first place. She'd thrown it out as an idea, out of character though it was, because she hated the thought of someone as full of life and sociable as Lawless bunkered down out of sight for ten weeks. And...well, no good deed goes unpunished. She should have kept her nose out of it entirely.

"Found out my dad's no longer a roaring drunk," Lawless muttered.

"Well, that's good news. Isn't it?"

"He's not who he was. Not even close."

"None of that is your fault."

"Oh, it is. Sort of." She paused. "No, definitely."

"No. It's Francine's for pressuring the hospital to fire him. And it's his for not picking himself up, dusting himself off, and moving on to the next job. How is that your doing?"

"You don't know anything about anything," Lawless said crossly. "I don't know why I ever listened to you." The fury in that statement lashed her.

Surprise shot through Michelle. "Ms. Lawless?"

"Sorry," she said, looking shamefaced. "Sorry. It's been a shitty day raking up all the worst of what I went through here. I hate it."

"I recall you being aware of this going in," Michelle said slowly. A chill shot through her. The woman wouldn't quit, would she? That would be a disaster.

"Reality can be worse than my imagination."

Michelle's heart sank at the broken ache in her tone. "Oh," she murmured, unsure what else to say. Should she shut the conversation down now before it veered off into personal matters?

Before she could decide, Lawless barreled on. "Look, back when I first took on Francine, Mom was so proud of my fight against injustice.

And Dad was fine until Francine got him fired. Her huge donations to his hospital spoke louder than his ability. Maryland's an at-will state, so he couldn't appeal it. He asked me to smooth things over with her, to grovel if I had to, to get his job back." She swallowed. "That…was unexpected."

"I'm sure."

"Mom was furious at him for not supporting me. They started fighting. He started drinking. They fought more. He drank more. Mom left him." Lawless rubbed her eyes. "Then Dad came to me and begged me to find a way to get Mom back."

"Did you try?"

"I felt responsible, so yeah. But Mom said he wasn't the man she thought he was. That she didn't want to be with someone who walks away from doing what's right because it's easier, or who asks someone to be less than they are. She said she no longer respected him and felt only pity."

"Your mother sets a high standard," Michelle said carefully. "Is that why you do what you do for a living? You want to make her proud?"

"Doesn't everyone try to live up to their parents' best example? To make them proud?" Lawless asked in surprise.

Michelle's jaw tightened. "Perhaps. So, how did your father take River's verdict?"

"He blamed me. Said my selfishness had broken up our family, that I was just making trouble to impress Mom and didn't care about the consequences. And his big finish was that I'd ruined him, costing him the things he loved—his career and his wife."

No mention of his daughter in the things he loved? Lawless's expression told Michelle that the omission was not lost on her either. "Your father is spineless, lacking accountability for his own failings, and dead wrong."

Lawless's lips pressed together into painful lines. "Yeah. And it hurts because he's still my dad, and I remember when he loved me. But then he committed himself to becoming Wingapo's town drunk. A laughingstock. He always *was* good with a goal." Her sarcasm bit a fat chunk out of the air.

"And what happened with your mother?"

"She disappeared off on a world tour of causes. She's barely ever home anymore." Lawless rolled her eyes as if to say, *that's just River being River.* She bit her lip—a habit she had when nervous, Michelle had noticed. "So, there you have it. One enormous family disaster caused by yours truly."

Michelle opened her mouth to object to that summation, but Lawless got in first.

"Goddess, I'm done talking about him. And now I'm embarrassed I've dumped this all on you."

"Why did you?" Michelle asked curiously.

Lawless stared as a blush reddened her cheeks. "Hell. That was TMI, wasn't it? I'm so sorry."

Of course it was too much information, but that wasn't the question.

Michelle leaned in. "I wasn't asking for an apology. I want to know why you told me any of this. We barely know each other. I'm not your friend. So what prompted it?"

Lawless winced and blew out a breath. "I saw him today. Dad. We didn't talk and he didn't see me, but it stirred up things. Then I got angry. And you'd suggested I kick over some clods from my past, re-connect with people…"

"And you wanted me to know I'd caused that pain." Redirected anger Michelle could understand. Sharing for its own sake? No. That was unfathomable. "I see."

Lawless looked away, embarrassment covering her features.

"Well. I didn't intend you to go through that."

"I know. And I was being ridiculous blaming you even a little. I do get that. I was just…really mad. With everything. Life, Dad, and the universe. And now I feel so…" She threw her hands up. "Pathetic. So," she said, lifting her chin, "I've overshared like crazy and humiliated myself in front of my boss. I don't suppose you'd like to share something back? So I don't feel so exposed?"

Michelle froze. The temerity! She let the silence hang between them, curious to see whether Lawless would walk that impertinent demand back in a sea of apologies.

Instead, the woman held her gaze, steady and direct. "Tell me," she repeated. "Something about your day, maybe? Share a little."

"Surely you understand by now how secretive my organization is," Michelle said. "I simply cannot tell you about any aspect of my day."

"Bull," Lawless said, but there was nothing but sadness behind it. "Not every single thing you said and did today was worthy of being redacted. Tell me one thing. One single thing." She stopped and added, "Please?" Her eyes begged her.

It was the *please* that did it. Michelle was used to clever little mind games to try to get her to open up and reveal some vulnerability. No one ever appealed to her like this, by simply asking her directly. Genuinely.

"Well." Michelle thought over her day, filtering out all the classified content including, regretfully, O'Brian dodging snooker balls. That would raise the question as to why.

"Today I was given a poem," Michelle said instead. "From a potential client who wants me to get it published for him. The thing is, it was awful." She couldn't contain the smile. "I mean, just *awful*."

Lawless eyed her, as if seeking out the lie. "No shit?"

"No shit," Michelle drawled.

"Why didn't he self-publish?"

"No prestige. He wants me to get his piece of drivel, which goes for no less than twenty-seven pages, published by a major publishing house. He wants bragging rights. And he wants The Fixers to accomplish this for him."

Lawless looked at her in astonishment now, the last traces of anger and sadness fading away. "Can you even do that?"

"I thought you understood by now. The power I have at my fingertips?" Michelle leaned in, and her voice took on a faintly husky tone that surprised even her. "I can do anything. However, I decided not to."

"You did?" Lawless seemed fascinated, and suddenly Michelle found herself relishing the tale.

"I decided we don't need the money and the world does not need to be inflicted with a poem that includes the line *Nonna was a goner*."

Lawless burst out laughing. "Oh goddess, that's *terrible*!"

"The worst." Michelle laughed a little too. "I'm still getting over the fact he cannot understand why no one wanted to publish it. And, of course, no one ever will."

"Thanks to you," Lawless chuckled. "See, I told you The Fixers is about righting wrongs. And look at you today, doing the goddess's work. Sparing humanity from drivel."

The goddess's work. Right. Still, she couldn't bring herself to correct Lawless, especially when she looked so much happier. There was a warmth in Michelle's chest she hadn't felt in…years?

Years. Good grief. "You're welcome, Ms. Lawless. I look forward to your next clue. I have no doubt it'll be as easy to crack as the last ones," she added, allowing her lips to quirk up. Just enough to show she was teasing. No reason to be excessive.

"Don't be so sure," Lawless said, her easy manner returned. "This next clue requires local knowledge. I will be very impressed if you get it at all, let alone quickly."

"Don't underestimate me," Michelle said, realizing the challenge excited her.

"Never," Lawless said more seriously. "That's one thing I'd never ever do."

Then she grinned, waved, and ended the call.

Michelle sat back, feeling a little dazed. At least Lawless's calls never bored her. Suddenly she couldn't wait for this new clue that would actually be challenging.

"Bubbeleh?" came a call from down the hall. "Did you know you were laughing again?"

Well. That sounded absurdly habit forming. She always said Eden Lawless was a troublemaker.

Chapter 10

Blue but Not Sad

THE LOCAL NEWSPAPER HAD FINALLY decided to run a story on the scavenger hunt. Over breakfast, Eden read about it with satisfaction on their website, along with the latest clue that had gone up overnight. She felt better now after a good night's sleep. It helped she could still remember the sound of Michelle laughing. It had been light and soft and sweet. Completely unexpected. And Michelle had lit up from inside out as she'd done it.

Eden had been filled with delight and a wash of relief. Her prickly, line-drawing boss had actually shared something. Not much, sure—a silly story about a poem—but she didn't have to share a single thing. And she'd done it because Eden had asked.

"What do you think it means?" Melba asked, reading over her shoulder.

Eden's eyes slid back to the screen at the third clue.

Feeling blue but not sad. Seeing yellow, good fellow.

"Blue and yellow? And fellows?" Melba's brows puckered in thought.

Eden shrugged. "Don't ask me. I haven't lived in Wingapo for sixteen years. I think the longtime locals will have a better shot."

"You think it's a clue for the old-timers?" Melba settled into the seat opposite and began to lather a slice of toast with butter and homemade rhubarb jelly.

Crap. "Wasn't the last one?" Eden tried. "I mean, you had to know who the GOAT was. It wasn't recent history."

Melba chewed thoughtfully, then reached for her coffee cup, adding heaped spoonfuls of sugar to it and stirring with gusto. "Only thing blue around here would be the crabs."

"I hear Maryland is famous for its blue crabs," Eden said casually. "But if you're right, how does the yellow work in? And who's the good fellow?"

Melba's shoulders rose and then sagged. "Has me stumped. Maybe Jimmy'll have some ideas."

"Well, if he doesn't, there's now a community forum board discussing everyone's theories." The newspaper was hosting the forum board. She smirked at that—the most unashamedly pro-mayor newspaper in human history promoting a hunt designed to bring Francine down. They'd choke on their forum board when the final clue's answer was revealed. "Must have a lot of interest if they're doing that."

"I might just sign up and see what people are saying." Melba's gaze became distant. "Put the crabs idea out there." She reached under her headscarf and pulled out a pen, jotting "crabs" onto her palm.

"Great idea. You'll have to let me know what they're debating." Eden was, of course, already a member. Along with 2,700 other Wingapo clue hunters. She finished her scrambled eggs and pushed the plate aside. Delicious. "Jimmy will make me fat if I keep eating his wonderful food. Those were the creamiest eggs I've ever had."

Melba beamed. "I'll tell him you said so. So what are you up to today?"

"This and that. Sorry to be so vague. I'm not really supposed to talk about what I'm doing."

"Say no more," Melba said, miming zipping her lips. "I'm the soul of discretion." She gave a belly laugh. "Ooh, listen to me, will you! Like I'm in a spy movie. Which would make you the spy." She leaned in. "You're not, are you, Eden?"

"Well, if I was, I wouldn't be able to tell you, would I?" Eden said playfully.

"You have me there." Melba slapped her thigh encased in purple leggings. "Okay, okay. You go off and have your spy games. I'm going to brainstorm with Jimmy on the crab theory."

"Have fun."

Judging by the excitement in Melba's eye, she already was. Good. The more fun people were having, the more they would rope friends in to have it with them.

Eden logged into the newspaper's community forum and started anonymously dropping in some random wild ideas as to what the clue might mean. Once everyone was debating her red herrings, she logged off and headed for the shower.

Today, she decided, would be a whole lot better than yesterday. The memory of Michelle's soft laugh made her lips curl once more.

<hr/>

"Okay," Michelle said the moment their video call connected that evening. "Let's hear this clue I apparently won't solve."

"Why, hello there, Michelle, nice to see you too. Nice blouse." Eden grinned. "Is it new?"

Michelle narrowed her eyes. "I didn't take you for someone who gave even a passing thought to fashion."

"On the right woman it can be noticeable. Memorable even. That shade of blue suits you."

Michelle's mouth dropped open. "Please tell me you are not flirting with your boss. That would be a ruinous idea." She glared.

"No, no!" Eden held up her hands. "Sorry. I couldn't resist tweaking you a little since you came on the call all guns blazing. Remember how we agreed two-thirds of my personality is teasing and it's unworkable for me being anything but me?" Eden swallowed.

"*You* agreed to that. I didn't." Michelle was still glaring.

Was she actually upset? It was hard to tell. The thought she might be seriously mad made Eden feel awful, especially after last night's laugh. She thought they'd connected.

"I didn't mean to make you feel uncomfortable. Truly." Regret filled her. "Also, I wasn't flirting." She didn't think so, anyway. Although there might have been some leakage from her not entirely platonic thoughts about the woman. "I'm a firm believer in not hitting on straight women." There. That fixed it.

She expected an eye roll. A snide comment about it being an *obviously pointless exercise.*

Eden did not expect the flash of wariness and vulnerability in Michelle's eyes. The tiny shift in her seat. The way her eyes darted around uncertainly. Her fingers clenching where they had been loosely interlocked in front of her. Her pink tongue, there and gone, darting out to lick her lips.

It was the most emotion she'd ever witnessed from the other woman, and it had lasted point five of a second. Michelle's walls were back up again, sky high and impenetrable.

Eden's mouth fell open. Part of her wanted to scream, "Holy hell, are you not straight?" The air felt a little thin all of a sudden. Oh, that's right. *Breathe.* "Michelle?" Eden croaked. "Are you—"

"Stop. There is a *line.*" Michelle pounded the last word.

"I was just going to ask if you're okay. Why? What did you think I was going to ask?"

A frosty silence fell and then…

"Can we *focus?*" Michelle's scowl was even deeper now. "The *clue?*"

Eden's heart sped up to frantic. *Wow.* It hadn't ever entered her head that her mysterious boss, whom she had the (tiniest amount of) hots for, might be on the same team.

Did Michelle have someone in her life? A lover? For some reason, she seemed too much of a loner to be partnered up with anyone, regardless of sexuality. A sense of isolation and self-sufficiency radiated from her.

"Ms. Lawless?" Michelle said, sounding thoroughly out of sorts now. Gone was her enthusiasm from earlier, and Eden missed it horribly. "The clue?"

"Right. Sure. The clue. Well, first, I'm happy to report it's being hotly debated all over town, including by the newspaper and its new community forum board."

"The *newspaper* has a scavenger hunt board going?" A hint of savage delight edged into Michelle's eyes. "Oh dear," she said with a tsk. "Won't they be miserable in, oh, seven weeks?"

"Yeah." Eden grinned. "So, the clue: feeling blue, but not sad. Seeing yellow, good fellow."

Michelle said nothing and did that 'head tilt, eyes sliding up' thing she did as she processed. Her gaze dropped back to Eden's. "I'm tempted to think this one's musical. Blue...but not sad. As in the blues? Fellow could be a musician's name. Yellow, the name of his or her song? Or a club name? Is there a jazz venue in your shabby little hometown?"

"No. And no to all of the above." Eden offered a sympathetic look. "I didn't expect you to get it. It's for the locals, as I said."

"The locals. How local are we talking? As in Wingapo locals? Or Maryland locals?" Michelle probed.

"Both. Marylanders might get one half of the clue; Wingapo locals should get both."

A triumphant smile appeared. "Then it's about crabs? Maryland's famous blue crabs." Michelle's gaze sharpened. "Yes?"

"Yes." Damn she was good. Give her an inch...

"Yellow, though... Mmm." Michelle tapped on her keyboard for a few moments. "It says here that the 'mustard' of Maryland's famous crabs is what makes them the best. A bright yellow liquid that sweetens the meat—that's your yellow?"

Eden inhaled. "You're...impressive."

Michelle shot her a sharp, questioning look that said the flattery was not appreciated. Or maybe she was suspicious of the praise due to their earlier weirdness.

Eden couldn't quite regret that awkward moment, though, because...holy crap. Her heart sped up yet again at the tantalizing idea that her impossible-to-read, secretive boss might like women.

Michelle tapped again on her keyboard. "Did you know," she said conversationally, "that there's a crab restaurant in Wingapo that's apparently renowned for its blue crabs? It's called Fallowes Crabs. Good fellow? Fallowes? What a coincidence," she deadpanned.

Goddess. Was there no end to how exceptional the woman was? "Only a local was supposed to have gotten that. Right now, over two thousand Wingapo locals have been going at it for a whole day, arguing about the clue. Yet you worked it out in five minutes from DC, having never stepped foot in Wingapo?"

Michelle's expression turned oh-so smug. It was adorable. "I'd like to think my brain is a little above the average intellect of a Wingapo knuckle dragger."

"Hey! Need I remind you *I'm* from Wingapo?"

"And you were smart enough to leave. I rest my case."

Michelle looked far too pleased with herself for Eden to actually be offended. "Fine, fine. Have your superior little victory moment. Because there is no way you'll figure out the next clue, I can promise you that."

"No?" Michelle smiled a maddening, confident smile—the one that was kind of hot. "We'll see."

"Yes. We will." Eden chuckled. "So, Michelle, it turns out you were right when you said you could do anything."

"Not entirely anything. Apparently I can't ever get you to call me Ms. Hastings."

"And I already told you, it flies in the face of my sense of fairness and eradicating classism. When you break it down, are you really better than me because your company pays me?"

Michelle smirked. "I never said I thought I was better than you because *money* was involved."

Eden burst out laughing. "Michelle! That's so…"

"No, do not finish that sentence either." Michelle's eyes contained faint amusement. "As I keep saying, there is a *line*, Ms. Lawless."

And this time, when she said *line*, she wrapped it in honey. Eden gasped at the sensuousness of it. Heat warmed her cheeks, and she was a loss as to how to reply. "Um?"

Oh, very articulate.

Michelle leaned forward, arm reaching to the keyboard. Her lips performed a little dance. It was the suppressed-amusement twitch Eden enjoyed so much. "Good luck with your little hunt, Ms. Lawless."

Before Eden could reply, the screen went blank.

Breathing seemed optional again.

Nope, nope, nope. That did not happen. Michelle's words had been so soft and teasing.

Of course, she was definitely imagining anything more than basic taunting taking place, which was Michelle's default setting when it came to dealing with Eden.

After all, she'd been put soundly in her place for complimenting Michelle on her blouse. And her displeasure was strong over the idea that Eden might have been flirting with her. So, basic deduction, she'd badly misread Michelle's sensual way of saying the word *line*. It meant nothing.

A pity, the small voice in the back of her brain noted.

Shut up, Eden informed the little voice. *I am not romantically interested in my hot boss who maybe likes women too.*

The little voice laughed long and hard.

Chapter 11
Opposites Attract

IT HAD BEEN A WEEK since her last clue went up. Pretty much the whole town had worked out it was Fallowes Crabs before she'd put everyone out of their misery at four a.m. today by sticking a printed sign on the restaurant wall with the next clue.

Opposites attract, writ large

It kind of sucked how this one didn't rhyme.

Eden sat at an outdoor area at a small cafe on Main Street, listening in on the people around her discussing the clue as she sipped her green tea.

Eden was certain there was no way Michelle would ever work this one out. Only a local could figure out it was about a billboard on the outskirts of town.

She'd checked in on the newspaper's community forum board, and debate was raging already. At least one person had figured out a billboard was a possibility based on "writ large." Someone else had begun a list of every billboard or large sign in Wingapo.

Earlier, she'd caught a story online about her nurses securing a win on pay and conditions. Excellent. She'd texted her clients her congratulations and received gushing thanks, which warmed her immensely. And she caught the tail end of a TV story mentioning her scavenger hunt which had "inspired an entire town." It was only a small local affiliate running the piece, but if it got picked up wider, that would be huge.

Maybe she should give that a nudge.

Eden fired off a text to Aggie, asking her to use her extensive social media contacts to flag the hunt story with bigger television networks. Aggie could work Twitter like no one Eden had ever seen.

On it! You want national or just state news?

Eden texted back. *Everywhere. No traceback to me, tho*

Yeah, yeah :)

Eden grinned. She'd pay Aggie for her time in a couple of crates of Bacchus-F and corn chips next time they caught up.

A shadow fell. Then came the scrape of metal as the chair opposite was pulled out.

"Well, well," Mayor Wilson said, sliding into the seat. "I thought I was seeing things. But no, here you are again: Eden Celeste Lawless. Back like mold spores."

"Francine," Eden noted, willing her heart to calm the hell down at the sight of her nemesis. "You haven't changed a bit."

She actually hadn't. Still immaculately dressed, this time in tailored black wool pants, designer ankle boots, also black, and a starched white linen blouse. Her dark brown hair curled perfectly at her popped collar, her olive skin was as flawless as ever, and those rich brown eyes still promised everything and made Wingapo's residents forgive her many sins.

"Oh, I wouldn't say I haven't changed. It's *mayor* now. You might be behind on all the developments around here since you ducked out of town with your tail between your legs."

"*Mayor*," Eden said slowly. "I suppose you paid well for that title."

"Still as disrespectful as ever, I see." Francine's scarlet-lipsticked mouth tightened into a cat-anus pucker. It was her real face. Eden always did manage to bring it out in her.

"Never forget you're the slumlord in this equation," Eden said. "I'm the innocent party who exposed you."

"Innocent. Sure." Francine scoffed and ran her eyes all over Eden, cataloging her every failing in appearance, as she usually did. It was designed to make her feel small. And it was a highly effective tactic.

Eden fought her teenaged self's urge to fold her arms across her flannel-shirted chest.

"I think you'll find your information is woefully out of date." Francine gave the shirt a longer look. "Much like your adolescent lesbian lumberjack look."

Eden rolled her eyes. "What do you mean out of date?"

"I mean every one of those complaints against me you cooked up no longer exists."

"Let me guess: you ran out of bureaucrats to bribe and burned down the complaints department instead."

"The complaints have been resolved to everyone's mutual satisfaction." Francine offered her vote-winning Cheshire cat smile that was all teeth and smugness. "If you'd bothered to stay, you'd have seen me attend to those matters. Personally."

Uncertainty filled her. This was the first she'd heard of it. Had Francine really sorted out her property maintenance issues? Maybe in her second run-up for mayor? Aware it was what was holding her back? Except...

"I'm a student at Wingapo College," Dr. Ron's staffer had said.

"Are you renting terrible accommodation nearby, by any chance?" Eden had asked. "Holes in the plasterwork? Or the floor?"

"Something like that. But I'm not saying that on the record to anyone."

"You're a damned liar." Eden scoffed. "And you've simply found a way to frighten people into shutting up. That does not constitute resolving anything."

Francine gave her a hard, cold stare. "Why are you here? I doubt it's reminiscing about the good old days." She sneered. "Did you even have any?"

"My reasons are personal." She gave Francine a sharp look. "And private."

"Reconnecting with dear old daddy the lush? I hear you can find him stuck in a shed with grumpy old men these days."

Fury rose, and Eden forced herself to strangle it back down. "You saw to that, didn't you? Ruining my dad."

Francine playfully danced a loose strand of hair behind her ear. "Goodness, you do give me a lot of credit. Did I force a bottle into his hand or make his wife leave him? How *is* River these days? Still busy hugging whales off the coast of Japan?"

Eden's eyes thinned to slits. "Mom's fine. Why do you care?"

"Well, I'm just curious as to what brings you here if not for your mother. And I understand there's some…" she lowered her voice and said with faux concern, "*bad blood* between you and your father. It makes me wonder if you're here for some…other…reason." Her expression became intense.

"What other reason?" She gave the mayor her most baffled look.

"You're not seriously about to feign ignorance about my reelection coming up?"

"You don't seriously think I give a flying donkey what *you* do any more, Francine? Is it even conceivable to you that people come and go and live their lives never thinking about you even once? Can you imagine that? That I might have visited my hometown for reasons wholly unrelated to you and your political ambitions?"

Francine regarded her. "Mr. Daly said you visited your old place two days ago. But you declined his invitation to go inside."

Jesus. A chill went through her. Same old Francine. "You're unbelievable. I see your network of spies is still running hot."

"Not *that* hot," she admitted with a small smile. "Where are you staying?"

"None of your business."

"In your van, then? I'm begging you to park that eyesore somewhere illegal so I can have it towed." Francine's smile was evil. "Personally, I'd have that thing crushed, it's such a disaster."

"So are you, but you don't see me advocating your destruction."

"Not this time."

Eden smiled back. "Right. So, why don't you take that as a win, hmm? Let me do my thing and you do yours. We'll stay out of each other's hair."

Francine's lips pursed as she considered it. "I don't trust you. But then again, if you were planning something to unseat me, I doubt you'd be nosing around Daly's place."

"Like I said, not everything's about you."

"Look, friendly reminder: do *not* take me on." Francine's eyes flashed.

"Hey, you forgot the evil cackle." Eden casually gave her a move-it-along gesture. "Really sell it."

Francine's tone was carefree as she said, "If you come after me, this time, I will end you properly." She lowered her lips next to Eden's ear and added, "And if *you* don't have any sense of self preservation, I know where your father lives." She strode off without looking back.

Makes one of us, Eden thought. Because she had no clue where her dad lived. Guilt slithered into her. Maybe she should warn the man that she'd just put him in the mayor's crosshairs yet again.

Damn it. She probably should.

Eden pushed on the glass door to The Shed and entered a dimly lit room filled with the sound of masculine bellows. A pool table in the middle of the space was being used by a trio of men in their late fifties who slunk their gazes suspiciously over her. A few men sat in armchairs in the corner, talking over coffee.

A workshop area toward the back was filled with the noise of a drill, sanding, and country music over the speakers.

Willie Nelson was explaining the rules of poker in a smooth, whiskey-coated voice, but Eden only had eyes for a tall, thin man stretched out in a chair just outside the workshop, reading a book.

"Hey, Dad," Eden said, dropping into a crouch beside him.

His eyes flew from the book and sharpened on her. "Eden?" he said cautiously. He glanced around as if he wasn't sure she was supposed to be here. Hell, maybe she wasn't. Was this an exclusively men's space or something?

"You doing okay?" she asked gingerly. Stupid question. Of course he wasn't.

"You're here," her father repeated slowly. "I thought I was dreaming you."

"Yeah, I'm here." She licked her lips. "Is that okay?"

"Depends." He sat up straighter. "Why are you here? If it's money you need, I haven't got any. Or..." his face brightened. "Are you here for your mom? Has she sent a message?"

"No, Dad," she said, wincing as his face fell again. "Sorry. It's no on both counts."

"Then why? After all this time?" He sounded so confused.

So ended any hopes he might have wanted to reconnect.

"I had some work in the area and figured I'd see how my old town was."

"Really?" Her father studied her. "You hate it here. You ran away."

"Not quite how I remember it, but okay." She stood, suddenly desperate to fidget. Her movement attracted a few curious stares. Eden rammed her hands nervously into her pockets. Why did he have to look so old? It was unsettling seeing more salt in his reddish-brown hair now. His eyes were ancient too, hollowed out—a sign of a man who'd gone through a lot of pain or a lot of booze.

Eden drew in a breath. "Anyway, I came to warn you: I bumped into Francine. She made some threats. She hasn't got any hold over me, so they didn't work. Then she said she knows where you live." She shrugged. "It's probably no big deal, but I thought you should know. In case it's not empty words."

Her father peered up at her and placed his book on the table. *The Grapes of Wrath*. His eyes were oddly sharp but not angry. Not this time. More...resigned. "You've managed to poke at that bear all over again, huh?"

"Don't shoot the messenger, Dad. I promise I didn't do anything to her." *That Francine knows about.* "But you know what she's like. Mean and vindictive."

"I know she retaliates when she feels attacked. Is that what you're doing, Eden? Stirring up trouble like last time? Cornering the bear?

That's dangerous." Again, his expression was oddly empty of anger, as if he were merely curious.

"Pete?" A masculine voice boomed near them. "Got yerself a problem here?"

Eden turned to see a brute of a man in a black leather jacket eyeballing her like she smelled of something foul. *Great. Just great.*

"I was just leaving," she said in frustration, too emotionally wrung out to even be disappointed.

Her father didn't try to stop her from going, but she felt his hooded eyes on her the entire way out of the room.

At the door, she turned, but her father was buried back in his Steinbeck novel. Figured. A story of the disaffected, powerless victims of the Great Depression. Her father probably thought it was all about him. She resisted the urge to slam the door behind her.

The sensation of being watched hadn't left when she stepped outside, though, and she looked up to find the mayor's black jaguar idling on the street, ten feet away. Francine fucking Wilson was studying her from the window wearing a terrifying smile that said she knew exactly what had transpired—that Eden had immediately scampered off to warn her old man.

Eden smiled back and offered her most friendly wave, then trudged away, heart crumbling.

———— ⬥⬦⬥ ————

The first thing Eden saw when she answered the Skype call that evening were enormous green eyes, far too close to the camera, blinking owlishly through thick glasses. The words "you're early" died on her lips.

"Hello?" she asked uncertainly.

The eyes widened in surprise and then leaped back. Well, all of the face did, and it resolved into an old woman with a gentle expression, who had so many of Michelle's features that Eden instantly smiled.

"Hello!" she said warmly. "Are you Michelle's grandma by any chance?"

"Yes, dear!" Excitement infused the old woman's voice. "Goodness, you gave me a start. It's my first time working out these video call things. But I've watched my bubbeleh do it a hundred times. I thought I had the hang of it."

"Bubbeleh?"

"My granddaughter, Michelle. Now I'm hoping I clicked the right button and you're Eden the troublemaker?"

"Yes! That's me." Eden burst into laughter. "So that's how Michelle describes me? That figures."

The older woman settled back into her chair. "Troublemakers are the best kind of people, so I wouldn't worry."

"Oh, I'll wear it with pride. How can I help?"

"Well, I just thought I'd sneak in a call before my granddaughter gets out of the shower." She peered behind her. "I wanted to meet you, but she keeps saying no."

"And now you have." Eden grinned in delight. "May I ask your name?"

"I'm Hannah, or you can call me safta, if you like. That means *grandma* in Hebrew."

"Michelle's Jewish?" Eden's eyebrows lifted. "She never said." She added hurriedly, "Not that it matters, of course. Sorry, I'm just surprised because she doesn't share *anything* about herself, and I'd love all the tidbits I can get and—oh no! Listen to me babbling! I'm a little nervous to meet someone so important to Michelle."

"As am I."

There was a long, long silence. Finally, Eden squeaked out, "You think I'm important to your granddaughter?"

"Yes." The kindly old eyes studied Eden in a way that seemed to miss little. "I do."

"Oh." Eden felt her whole face fall. "I think maybe you're mistaking me for someone else. I'm just one of Michelle's employees. I'm not her friend." She ran her thumbnail along the edge of her laptop, praying her dismay wasn't obvious.

"Yes, yes." Hannah gave a dismissive wave. "She sent you to Wingapo to sort out the mayor. I know who you are. I have exactly the right person."

"She told you all that?" *So much for Ms. Secrecy.* Michelle clearly shared when she wanted to.

"Well... I might have been a little...naggy...until she spilled. But I'm allowed as her safta."

Eden laughed. "Yep. Totally allowed."

"Besides, she didn't tell me much. I worked out most of it myself." She tapped her nose. "She's tight-lipped, my granddaughter. But I'm a crafty old woman with too much time on her hands."

"She really is tight-lipped," Eden agreed. "You know, I'd love to know more about her." She left that hanging in hopeful invitation.

Hannah's eyes sparkled brightly. "Well, I'll tell you a little something you're hankering to know if you answer something I really want to know."

"Sure. Is that why you called me?"

"Well, first I just wanted to look at you. I have to say, you're not anything like the other sneaky people I've caught sight of on her video."

Sneaky people? The Fixers' staff?

"And I really wanted to ask your secret."

"My...secret?"

"Tell me: how is it you make my granddaughter laugh?"

Her expression was so serious that Eden knew she wasn't joking.

"Do I?" she almost said before remembering that there had been at least once when she'd done exactly that. Was this a rare thing even with her grandma, then?

"I...guess I'm just me. She finds me a bit ridiculous at the best of times." Eden grinned. "Although I keep telling Michelle I'm two-thirds teasing whenever she orders me to behave and stop crossing lines."

"Ah." Hannah gave a small smile at that. "So you tease her." Her eyes gleamed. "Good, good. She's far too serious. Too much work, work, work. Never any playing."

Eden tried to imagine that. "Does she never..." She tried to think of how to phrase it. *Date? Party?* Let down her beautiful hair out of that tight bun? "Play?"

"Was that what you really wanted to ask, dear?" Hannah's head tilted in exactly the same way as Michelle's. "If you could ask anything about my granddaughter—and I'm not saying I'll answer—but is *that* your question?"

Eden blushed hotly, from the roots of her hair, as she thought about what she most wanted to know. "Is she seeing someone?" she mumbled, not looking up.

Silence fell. Yeah, the question was *totally* inappropriate. What was she thinking? Talk about invading her boss's privacy. *Hell!* And of course a grandmother would take a dim view of being asked by a woman if her granddaughter was dating.

Not to mention, what if she was homophobic? What if Eden had just made things really awkward between Michelle and her safta? What if the older woman was next going to round on her granddaughter and demand to know if she was into women?

As regret rushed into her, Eden's head snapped up, determined to fix this by spinning the question into something completely vanilla and innocuous and super hetero like gal pals asking gal pally things…

Hannah was watching her with such kindness and understanding. "*That's* your question?" she asked gently.

"Only if it's not out of place," Eden whispered. "If it is, if I've overstepped, I could ask about what she loves? Dancing? Music? Favorite drink? Um…chocolates?"

"You like dancing?" Hannah's whole face lit up. "Which kind?"

"All types, of course," Eden said, beaming. "Mom's a lifelong hippie, and as a kid I was always dancing around someone's hand drums or Tibetan singing bowls. It's really freeing, you know?"

"Oh, I know." Hannah beamed. "I love all the old twenties dances, but especially the Charleston—although before you ask, they're way before my time. I'm not a hundred!" She cackled. "I used to dance on the stage, once upon a time. People paid to watch me; can you believe that? Oh, it was magical." Her face lit up; eyes bright. "But then my knee gave up." She shook her head. "Those were the days. I loved them."

"I'm sorry you can't dance anymore."

"I still dance," Hannah said with a tiny smile. "In here." She tapped her temple. "And here." She patted her heart. "Dreams never die. You can replay them as much as you like. But I don't deny I'd love to dance again the way I used to. Sadly, Michelle never had much interest in dancing or dreaming or anything but work."

Hannah gave a soft sigh. "To answer your questions, she does enjoy, very occasionally, classical music and chocolate so dark it's almost all cocoa. Most of all, she's a champagne lover, but I learned my lesson never to buy her any."

"Why not?" Eden asked, fascinated.

"Because she's a collector. She already has all the bottles and labels she wants and doesn't need some amateur picking the wrong one." Hannah paused. "She's very choosy like that. And on that front, no, she's not seeing anyone. No one since her husband."

"*Husband?*" Michelle was straight? Or...well...maybe bi? But still, *husband?*

"Mmm." Hannah's eyes narrowed. "Nasty piece of work, Alberto was. That's no exaggeration, either. His eyes were dangerous. Gave me chills. That ended nine years ago, and there's been no one serious since. I wish she'd find someone lovely to amuse her. Someone with good vibes. With joy. She's so driven." She stopped as if for effect, eyebrows floating up angelically. "Someone, perhaps, who likes to dance?"

Eden swallowed as a tiny shock skittered up her spine. Surely Michelle's grandmother wasn't saying what it sounded like? No, that was unlikely. And even if she was, Michelle had no interest in Eden beyond finding her repeatedly irritating between rare bouts of amusement.

"Well, I have to go now," Hannah said airily. "The shower's stopped. Let's keep this chat between us for now. I think we'd both be facing some cranky words otherwise." Her eyes twinkled. "It was lovely to meet you, Eden the Troublemaker."

"You too, Safta Hannah," Eden said warmly.

"And, Eden? Don't ever listen when she tells you to behave. She needs those lines crossed." Hannah's eyes were earnest now. "We all do. But her most of all. Bye, dear."

The old woman's face suddenly appeared enormously close again, and then the screen turned black.

Michelle settled into her chair, slicking her hand through her damp hair, and glanced at the clock. On time as always. She flicked Skype on, and an incoming call alert sounded almost immediately.

"Okay," Lawless said before Michelle could open her mouth, "I promise *this* clue you won't get."

"You sound so sure," Michelle murmured, settling into her chair with satisfaction. "Didn't I work out the last one without local knowledge?"

"Yes. But this one you won't."

"Let's hear it," she said with interest. "Test me."

"Opposites attract, writ large."

"Not very catchy, is it?" She hid her smile as Lawless pouted.

"Hey, I'm not a published poet, okay?"

"Oh, I believe it." Michelle considered the clue and thought hard. "Writ large—obviously a large sign or billboard."

"Go on," Lawless said, eyes warm.

"Opposites attract will be the content of the billboard, then?"

"Yes."

"Which I won't know without knowing the billboards in your area."

"Right." Lawless's expression was triumphant now.

"A billboard will only be in a well-traveled area, otherwise, what's the point?" Michelle continued, and she tapped rapidly, keying into Google Maps. Then she switched to Street View, taking in actual images of the various streets at ground level. She swiveled her mouse up. "All I need to do is look at the main street of Wingapo, and then all main roads in and out of Wingapo, yes?"

At the silence, she glanced back up at the video feed to see Lawless's astonished face.

Bingo.

Main Street yielded only one major billboard—probably the one Lawless had booked for the hunt's first clue. That clue wasn't on the billboard in front of her, but then, Google Maps images weren't always recent.

That could be a problem. Even if she found the right billboard, if it didn't have recent content, she wouldn't be able to solve the clue. She had to hope the advertiser was one who had a long-term ad booking.

She widened her search, traveling farther and farther out of town. After a few minutes, she gave up on that route and switched to the other road going toward town.

And then she saw it.

"Got it." Michelle shared her screen. "That Virgin Hotels ad. Right? Virgins; hotel rooms? No sex; synonymous with sex? Opposites attract."

"Wow," Lawless whispered. "That's…" She glanced at her watch. "Three minutes! You did that in three minutes! The Wingapo locals are still debating whether it's a billboard or some skywriting thing planned later."

"Well, as we've already established, I consider myself smarter than the average Wingapo local. No offense to anyone related to one." Michelle smiled.

Lawless's expression fell. Well, more than that, it shattered.

Surprise coursed through Michelle. "What is it?" she demanded. "What's happened?"

Lawless's head snapped up. "How do you do that? Know when something's happened?"

"Your face is an open book. So?"

"I saw Dad today."

"Intentionally?" She'd thought Lawless had no interest in reconnecting.

"Yeah." The other woman fidgeted.

"It didn't go well, I gather?"

"No. I think he got excited for three seconds that I might have been there on a mission from Mom. But when he realized I wasn't, he just withdrew. So, then I told him about the mayor's threat and…"

"Wait. Stop. Back up. What threat?" Some vicious political troglodyte was threatening Eden Lawless? Her eyes narrowed. This would not do at all.

"Oh. Sorry, yeah." Lawless shrunk a little, which was even more worrying. "She sat down next to me at this cafe I was at and started grilling me like a freaking cheese sandwich to find out why I was in Wingapo. I think I've convinced her I'm on a personal mission. She has spies everywhere, but I don't think she knows I visited her rival candidates. She'd definitely have brought it up if she did."

"Her *threats*, Ms. Lawless. What were they?" Michelle asked impatiently. "Please," she gritted out when Lawless shot her a startled look.

"Just the usual vague nonsense. That she knows where my dad lives." Lawless huffed out a breath. "And *I* don't even know where he lives."

Michelle ran a quick threat assessment in her head. "Is she serious, do you think? Do I need to send security to your location?"

"You'd do that?" Lawless asked in astonishment. "For me?"

"Of course. You're an employee. It's my duty of care to protect you—*and* your family."

"Oh. *Duty*. Right, yeah. Of course." She rubbed her head absentmindedly. "I'm sorry. I've got a Francine headache coming on. She used to give me the worst migraines when I was in college. I don't think I should hang around talking for too long tonight. I need to be lying down with the lights off."

"Understood." Michelle knew how bad a migraine could be. Until she'd discovered her own form of stress release, she'd suffered from them quite often. "Rest now. Inform me later if you feel that you or your father do need some protection, and I will have operatives in your locations within two hours."

"That's really nice of you, but I think I'm okay for now. And as I said, I don't know where Dad lives."

"He lives in a small cottage at the rear of the property of one of his former colleagues."

"He...what?"

Michelle shrugged. "Our researcher turned it up." She flipped through a folder in her computer. "63B Treeridge Lane."

"Oh." Lawless looked stunned. "I didn't realize he'd stayed in touch with any of his old friends. It's nice someone's looking out for him. How are you better informed about my family than I am?"

"I wouldn't go that far. I'm sure you have River's address, and I don't."

Okay, that was a straight-up lie, because the background report on Lawless had pinpointed exactly which protest boat in the North Sea her mother was on at this minute. But Eden didn't need to know how far the Fixers' tentacles reached.

"Okay." Lawless gave her a wan smile but seemed to be fading fast as she rubbed her temples. "It's really nice of you to keep an eye out for your employees like this."

"Get some rest. And, Ms. Lawless?"

"Yeah?" Lawless's drooping head lifted again.

"For the record: I *never* do nice." Then she ended the call with a chuckle.

Chapter 12

Fifteen

WHAT A DISASTER. MICHELLE DROPPED the pages of the operative's report to her desk and glanced at Tilly. "Is this for real?"

"I'm afraid so." The PA eyed her for a long moment. "Senator Kensington doesn't know yet."

Well, that had been her next question.

Goddammit.

It turned out that Phyllis's husband had made a grievous error in his quest to force his wife's hand and get that divorce he so badly wanted. The intern that he'd been screwing—Troy Plymouth—had turned out to be underage.

Fifteen.

Fucking fifteen. Michelle's stomach twisted.

"We do *not* cover up crimes for those harming children," she gritted out. "The Fixers have a line. And even if they didn't, I sure as hell do. Remember that pedophile ring last year? Wanting a way to avoid their computer network being hacked or infiltrated? I sent them packing."

"To be more accurate, you sent them to prison," Tilly corrected.

Michelle stared at her in astonishment. *No one* was supposed to know she'd leaked their details to the police.

"The timing was suspect," Tilly explained. "Like how the secret use for MediCache's technology became public knowledge just before the scheme was due to be implemented nationally. Perfect timing to stop it."

Michelle might have let a lot of things sit on her conscience over the years—many more than could possibly be healthy. But actively hiding pedophile nests or a sneaky scheme to track people? She'd never allow that if she could prevent it. Even if the latter had meant raking over old wounds to make sure it never went ahead. "You thought those leaks came from me? You never said."

"Actually, it was a board member who noticed the timing on both. Five thought it was suspicious."

Of course it would be Five; he was the sharpest.

Due to the secrecy of The Fixers, the five board members went by numbers, not names, although years ago Michelle had worked out who all but one of them were. She'd never pinned down Five's identity, as he was based in Hong Kong now.

Tilly's duties included attending all board meetings to take notes, fetch drinks, and set up conferencing for any out-of-state members to virtually attend. She was beyond discreet, never even hinting about anything she'd heard take place. So why had she let this slip to Michelle now?

"And on the Kensington matter?" Michelle returned to the point. "The intern *is* underage. And we don't hide crimes against children."

"No." Tilly said, then paused before adding cautiously, "Ordinarily, we don't. But he's three months shy of his sixteenth birthday, which is the age of consent where the offenses occurred. And, as you know, Senator Kensington is a *top-tier* client."

Top tier. As in hugely powerful or hugely rich.

The fact Phyllis Kensington would probably be president one day meant The Fixers organization was heavily invested in keeping her happy as a client. The board *would* want this matter resolved to Phyllis's complete satisfaction. And now Michelle understood: Tilly was gently reminding her of that unpalatable fact, as well as that she was under board scrutiny—in case she had another attack of conscience.

"Christ," Michelle muttered. "This is such a mess. If this came out, it could ruin Phyllis as well as her husband. And then there's the intern. Monica Lewinsky ring any bells? She's been the butt of jokes for decades and has never been allowed to forget that scandal even though everyone else involved has moved on."

"Did you see the operative's conclusion?" Tilly asked.

Michelle's eyes darted to the final paragraph again. It was just as bad on the third read.

> *The young man doesn't appear to have been leveraging Mr. Kensington for blackmail purposes. He has a strong case of hero worship. Further, he has been led to believe that his affections are mutual. Mr. Plymouth refuses to believe any stories that his boss has done this many times with many employees. Mr. Plymouth is adamant he and Mr. Kensington share "true love" and will be living together, possibly even marrying, once he's of age and Senator Kensington grants her husband a divorce. He would therefore be uninterested in any offer we could make to bury this matter.*

Seriously, how low a person would you have to be to toy with the affections of an impressionable teenager just to screw over your wife?

"How bad will the underage issue be for Mr. Kensington?" Tilly asked.

"I just heard from our lawyers about that. Unfortunately for Kensington, he chose to sleep with his intern in Massachusetts, the state with the worst laws for statutory rape." Michelle flicked to the lawyers' email. "There are even more rigid rules about consent if one partner 'maintains a position of power' such as a teacher or employer. Then there's the additional issue of criminal inducement, which Kensington is absolutely ripe for being charged with. That reads, 'Whoever induces any person under 18 years of age of chaste life to have unlawful sexual intercourse shall be punished.'" Michelle looked up. "He's up for at least a couple of years in jail."

"A *chaste* life?" Tilly repeated distastefully. "How archaic."

"Worse than archaic. While that particular law is rarely used, if it ever did go to court, lawyers would have no choice but to argue Troy slept around, as it's their only defense available. The kid's reputation will be trashed purely because they *have* to try to prove he was unchaste. The law is cruel."

Michelle slammed closed the report. "But it won't go to court. I'll take care of this myself. Order our jet for a flight to Boston this afternoon."

"Covering this up to avoid a scandal for the senator and the intern means Mr. Kensington gets away with it, correct?" Tilly's tone was curious more than disapproving.

"Actually, I plan to fix both." Michelle stood. "And I will. I'll have Mr. Kensington terrified of breathing too loudly by the time I'm done. Book me a hotel in Boston for this evening, somewhere close to Kensington's workplace. I don't know how late it will be by the time I get this mess sorted out."

Tilly made a quick note on her phone. "Yes, Ms. Hastings."

Michelle grimaced at a new thought. "And afterwards, I have to explain to Phyllis that her husband came *this* close to embroiling her in an underage sex scandal. I can't tell you how much I'm looking forward to that."

Tilly offered a sympathetic wince. "Good luck with that. Would you like me to also inform Ms. Lawless you'll be unable to attend your video call with her this evening?"

"Now, why would I cancel that? I'm capable of multitasking, even from a hotel in Boston. All right," she shooed Tilly out. "Thanks. Get on the rest."

"Yes, Ms. Hastings."

<hr />

Troy Plymouth was a sweet young man. He had brilliant blue eyes, wild, curly blond hair, and a natural tan that spoke of his love of surfing. At least he looked older than his fifteen years, certainly old enough to be hired as an intern.

The boy's shy smile drooped into confusion when Michelle leaned over his desk and announced that they'd be having coffee together. *Now.*

"Um, excuse me, ma'am?" Troy said. "I don't know you."

"I'm your boss's wife's problem solver," Michelle said pointedly.

He paled.

"Right," she said, dryly.

Ten minutes later, at a coffee house a block away, Troy eyed her furtively over his nonfat latte.

Michelle carefully stirred her own black coffee as she spoke. "It's like this: Senator Kensington hired me years ago to make sure she looks good. She would like very much to have a clean run at the White House one day. Her husband, who is someone you know intimately, might prevent that." She waited.

Troy didn't deny it. He looked down and his cheeks reddened, making him seem years younger.

Oh, Christ. He was just a baby. Michelle hated dealing with innocents. It just felt so much more *grubby*.

"I know Mr. Kensington has made you promises," Michelle continued. "And said that he doesn't want to be married to Senator Kensington any longer."

The young man raised his gaze to meet hers with an earnest look. "She's fighting to keep him, and that's *not* right. Bill wants a divorce. Bad." He sounded eager at the thought.

"Yes. To get a divorce, he'll do anything." She hesitated before adding, "Or *anyone*."

Troy shot her a dark look. "Some dude was here a few days ago telling me Bill's been fucking half the office. If you're gonna tell me the same to scare me off because his wife doesn't want me around, it won't work. You can't bluff me. 'Sides, I'm loyal. I love Bill. He loves me back." His chin lifted in defiance.

"Let me show you something." Michelle pulled out her tablet and scrolled down the screen. "See all these documents? Each represents a woman who was seduced by Mr. Kensington for the sole purpose of him trying to pressure his wife into a divorce. He threatened to embarrass her with his many indiscretions unless she agreed."

Troy started shaking his head.

"It's true. And I know this because my firm investigated each case thoroughly and then paid the women a sizable sum to keep them quiet—much to Mr. Kensington's frustration." She pulled up a page with an anonymized summary of payments. "No one throws hundreds of thousands of dollars away to hide something that *didn't* happen. Why would we?"

"I don't believe you. That stuff..." Troy waved at her tablet, "...could be about anything." He looked about two minutes away from a panic attack. For someone who didn't believe, his eyes said something else.

Time to remove all doubt.

Michelle cued up on her tablet a recording from Phyllis's answering machine. In it, her husband could be heard ranting that "next time I'll find a scandal even you'll think is worthy of divorcing me over."

Confusion flickered in Troy's eyes as his gaze went to her tablet.

"All right." She adjusted the volume to low enough that only their table would be able to hear, and then hit play.

Two minutes in, Troy's horrified eyes scrunched up. "Stop," he whispered.

Michelle stopped the playback. "That threat was on August 9. Tell me, when did Mr. Kensington initiate his affair with you?"

Troy's entire face crumpled. All questions and doubt were gone, replaced with anguish. "How could someone do that?" he whispered.

Awww, hell, kid. People did worse to each other all the time.

"How can what I gave him mean nothing? How can love mean nothing?" His teary eyes met hers. "I don't understand."

She had to look away from all that stark pain. "People are not always...their best selves."

"Fuck that," he said, voice thick. "This is, like, setting out *on purpose* to hurt someone. Someone w-who'd do anything for them? How could anyone *do* that?"

A stab went through her, and just for something completely different, she hated herself all over again for what she'd done to Ayers so many years ago.

Troy's eyes were so huge and blue and his expression so broken. "I...mean, it's kinda like a pact, isn't it?"

"A pact?"

"Like...when you get to the point you're that close to someone and you share who you are? Y'know...*underneath*? And they share back? It's like agreeing without saying it—that you won't take their private shit and hurt them with it. And they agree not to do the same right back?" His voice cracked. "A pact."

Now Michelle wanted to crush William Kensington into smithereens.

Troy looked at her, confounded. "I trusted him." He wiped his eyes with his sleeve. "Who does that to another person? Like, as a...game? Who takes someone's love and trust and...and *dreams*...and throws them away like it's nothing?" Hurt radiated from him. "Like your feelings are just a pile of shit?"

Michelle sighed, wishing her stomach would stop churning.

Who does that to another person? The list was long. She was on it. So were her parents. Her former boss at the FBI. Three-quarters of the client list of The Fixers. Probably her entire staff.

"So, great," Troy gritted out. Tears ran down his cheeks again, and he scraped them angrily away with his sleeve. "You win: I believe Bill thinks I'm just some stupid idiot to fuck with and throw away. Now what? Why are you here?"

"Obviously, Senator Kensington doesn't want your affair to be public knowledge," Michelle said quietly. "She wishes to be scandal free for the next few years. Your relationship is even more problematic since you're a man. It would lead to speculation about *her* sexuality. Is Mr. Kensington a beard? Was it a fake marriage? That sort of nonsense. How is that fair for her? She's the victim in all this. Well..." she flicked her gaze to Troy. "Another one."

She'd probably go to Hell for that exaggeration alone. Phyllis had never been a victim of anything in her life.

Troy stared at her miserably.

"And of course it gets worse given you're underage."

Surprise lit his features.

"Yes, I'm aware you lied on your employment forms. Why did you?"

"I upped my age coz I really wanted to work for him. He came to our school for some careers talk thing and I thought he was so... perfect." His eyes filled with tears again. "Shit."

"Mr. Kensington doesn't know your real age, does he?"

"No." His head drooped.

Michelle drew in a breath. "Troy, if your affair goes public, Mr. Kensington would be charged with statutory rape."

His head snapped up. "But I wanted it!"

"It doesn't matter. The law doesn't care if you consented. He could go to prison. But before that, your name will get dragged through the mud along with his. You could be portrayed as some rent boy."

Troy looked aghast. "I've never been with anyone else!" he hissed.

"Which makes it even worse what he did to you." She glanced to his wrist where a fancy platinum timepiece flashed. "Troy, he has targeted you in a very calculating way. I understand why you fell for him. Here's your boss—good-looking, powerful, interesting. He's exciting. He knows you like him. He listens to you. And suddenly he's lavishing you with gifts. A new wristwatch, a new car?"

Shock crossed his face.

"That's what he gave the others," Michelle said quietly.

"He didn't force me," Troy said. "He was so nice to me. Kind."

"Charmers always are."

"What if…" he choked out. "What if he really does love me? And it just *started out* that I was a game?"

Michelle gave him a long, steady look. "Okay, say you're right. Maybe it was a scheme at first to hurt his wife but then he fell in love with you. He wants you two to stay together. But at what cost? You can never be open about your relationship, your age, or when you became a couple. The risk of charges will always hang over his head for his past, even when you're an adult. You say you love him. Is that a life you want for him?"

Troy gave her a mournful look.

"But you strike me as a smart man. I think you know the truth, deep down." She watched him closely. "Don't you?"

He looked away and fidgeted.

"You *could* stay with him on the off-chance he isn't still playing you," Michelle went on. "But is *this* what you want for yourself in life? Don't you deserve more?"

Despair crossed his face as he met her eye.

God. The poor kid.

"You deserve to be all someone wants and dreams about. And you owe it to yourself for your love to be returned." Michelle exhaled. "Want to know what I've learned about love over the years? That everything you ever want to know about someone—who they really are—lies not in what they give you or promise you. It's what they *do* to you. How they *treat* you. And after we've finished here, I'm going to march into Mr. Kensington's office and break the news to him that you're a minor. And you'll know fairly soon by his actions how he feels about you."

"You think he'll dump me."

She held his eye. "He *will*. Actually, he'll be terrified of you after this. You have the power to destroy him completely."

Troy swallowed.

"You have to be ready for his reaction to that, okay? He may call you up and say cruel things. So, if he does, ask yourself this." She waited until she had his complete attention. "'Why am I even listening to someone's bad opinion of me when they don't care about me?' Can you remember that?"

Troy gave a grim nod.

Michelle forced from her mind the memory of how her father had done something similar to her. His fury had shocked her and had sliced her heart to ribbons. How he'd talked to her had told her everything she needed to know.

Her beautiful safta had been the one to gather her broken soul in a hug as deep as eternity and give her advice to live by: only take to heart the words from those who care about you.

Troy was wiping away his tears with his sleeve again while trying to look like he wasn't.

Michelle rummaged through her bag to give him some privacy. "I'm sorry," she said as she continued to look down. "Really, I am."

She was. But now that she'd shattered his heart with the truth, she still had business to conclude. Michelle pulled out some paperwork.

"This is our standard nondisclosure agreement. It's the same deal we gave to the women he was involved with. There's no reason the senator has to suffer for the actions of her husband, wouldn't you agree?"

"But I won't talk." Troy sounded so certain.

"It'll give her peace of mind."

"I. Won't. Talk." He glared at her.

"It'll give *him* peace of mind too."

Troy hesitated.

"The agreement comes with a lot of money to make things easier for you."

"I'm not after any money. I love him, I *told* you that!" Troy looked indignant at even the suggestion.

Shrugging slightly, Michelle said, "So don't cash the check. Or use it to get therapy or a college degree or do a world surfing trip, I don't care. But you've earned it—whether you understand that now or not."

Troy glowered but after a moment held out his hand for a pen. He scribbled his name and the date and pushed it back. "I signed only so he sleeps at night knowing I'm not out to hurt him. Maybe he'll even feel a bit guilty about it." His voice broke.

"He won't feel guilty; he never did before." Michelle took the NDA from him and slid it into her bag.

It wasn't worth the paper it was printed on, of course, given the young man was underage. He didn't realize that, and she wasn't about to share. The signing was purely performative. The Fixers could renegotiate with him later when he was of age, if it ever came to that. But right now, as long as Troy believed the contract was legally binding, he'd probably keep his mouth shut.

The money was real, though. And cashing the check would be seen as compliance. The lawyers would then argue everything was all about the money if it got ugly down the road. Well, *uglier*.

So, for the young man's sake, Michelle really hoped he'd put his head down and get on with life far away from the likes of William Kensington.

"Don't go back to work," Michelle instructed as she zipped her bag closed. "I'll have someone forward your effects to you. Now, here, take this." She pushed the check over to him.

He stared at it with wide eyes. Well, it did have a lot of zeroes.

"Shortly, I'm about to explain to Mr. Kensington how his poor decisions have given him a terrifyingly close brush with being charged as a statutory rapist," Michelle said. "However, I have a suggestion." She met his gaze. "Let me tell him you were in it for the money."

"But I wasn't!" Troy's eyes widened.

"I know," she assured him. "Still, let me tell him you were. That way *he's* the sap who got played."

Not you, hung in the air.

Michelle continued, "I know he's not capable of guilt or shame, but he is capable of humiliation. It's the only payback you'll ever be able to inflict on him. It might make you feel better. Or not. It's up to you."

"Payback?" He stared at her in disgust. "Who thinks like that? You're no better than he is."

Michelle took a sip of her coffee. "I'm not a good person," she said casually. "I don't pretend to be. None of us is decent in this scenario, except you. That's just how politics is: it makes everyone awful. We're all cynical, manipulative, and self-serving. And, on that note, you should know something. If it suits us, my organization will have no problem throwing Mr. Kensington under a bus at a later date—revealing your relationship with him. Which would be unfortunate for you."

He stared at her. "But the NDA..."

"The NDA you signed is about giving *us* control of the narrative. *You* may never talk about your affair. But that doesn't mean we can't reveal the information as we see fit, *if* we see fit. That may never happen. And, no, it's not likely, but be aware it is a possibility."

While that was true, Michelle would fight tooth and nail to prevent it ever happening—for the kid's sake. Not that Troy needed to know that—it would undermine her warning.

Troy lurched to his feet, hip crashing against the table, causing the cups and spoons to clatter and clang. "You're so fucked up," he said far too loudly, attracting curious eyes. "And so's Bill. You're *all* fucked up. And no—don't tell him I played him. Because I *didn't*. Because I *loved* him—a concept none of you...*fucking assholes*...seem to get at all." He stormed off.

Michelle watched him go, taking another sip of her coffee. Yes, she was fucked up. And, no, that wasn't news to her. This was all in a day's work.

The familiar sick feeling in the pit of her stomach rose up and swirled, but she was used to it.

She finished her drink at her leisure, focusing her mind on the hours ahead—after she'd blackmailed Kensington into a terrified new reality.

Michelle imagined heading to her hotel, having a soak in the enormous whirlpool tub, forgetting her day, and then...

Then it'd be...eight o'clock.

And for just a moment, as anticipation kicked in, the awful, sick feeling went away.

———✦———

Three hours later, Michelle sat in her bathrobe in her hotel room, thoroughly wrung out. Blackmailing Kensington had been exhausting. Not because of his fury at being defeated or how he'd folded so easily when he realized he might be headed for prison if this got out. No, it was his complete indifference to Troy's broken heart. And the fact he hadn't even blinked at the revelation it had been a *minor* he'd been fucking for the office security cameras. How could that not bother him?

Scum. And today she'd helped keep the slippery bastard out of prison because it served the interests of her organization. Some days the corner office just wasn't worth it.

She felt dirty. The scalding shower hadn't helped.

Pulling out her phone, Michelle finally did what she'd been dreading.

After it rang for a long time, Phyllis answered. "Okay, what's so urgent? You know this isn't a good time for me to—"

"It's about your husband," Michelle cut in. "I've handled the situation. Permanently. He will never put a toe out of line with you again."

"Well, now! That *is* exciting news." Phyllis's tone was upbeat now.

"The intern turned out to be a fifteen-year-old boy. That's statutory rape if it comes out."

There was a shocked gasp. Phyllis, remarkably for her, did not say one word.

"Do yourself a favor and divorce him."

"I thought you said you'd fixed it? So why—"

"Because he's *scum*, Phyllis." Emotion finally spilled into her voice. "He's so empty—no shame or guilt. Only his fear of criminal charges stopped him. He shouldn't *have* to be threatened to not be a sexual predator and not blackmail his wife. He has shattered that young man, and his only response was terror and fury at being caught. Cut him loose."

"Divorced women do not become president," Phyllis snapped.

"And no married women have ever become president either. Make voters want you regardless. If anyone can, it'll be you. Or if that's too hard, just find a different husband. Someone with an ounce of humanity."

"No, thank you. Not when I've finally got this one right where I need him. Terrified and broken? With the fear of being charged at any time hanging over his head?" Phyllis's tone warmed considerably. "It sounds like he'll do anything for me now."

"Probably." Michelle deflated at the senator's ghastly enthusiasm.

"Exactly!" Phyllis was positively gleeful now. "Well, well, haven't you been busy!"

Michelle sighed.

Phyllis's voice turned playful. "Are you in the mood to celebrate, darling? I've decided if you're *very* good, I'll let you tie me up this time. I have some lovely Dior scarves that should do nicely. I'll even…"

Michelle shuddered and drew her fingers over her eyes. A headache was forming. She couldn't think of anything worse than sleeping with a woman so cavalier over learning her husband had destroyed a teenager. Worse, Phyllis thought that was good news because of how she could leverage it. Suddenly, for all the woman's power, elegance, and talented mouth, Phyllis was repugnant to her.

The sick feeling making her stomach lurch warred with her headache. "I can't. I'm still in Boston."

"Rain check then," Phyllis said airily. "Talk later. And *very* good work today. I'll send you a completion bonus." She hung up.

Michelle closed her eyes, sank back on the bed, and threw her forearm over her eyes. She'd known all along who Phyllis was: powerful and morally compromised—but then, so was everyone else in DC's political circles. Michelle *knew* that going in. So why was she so disappointed in Phyllis now?

What had she expected the senator to say? "Why, yes, of course I'll absolutely dump my lecherous husband now that I know how low he was prepared to go?"

She'd at least wanted to hear her acknowledge Troy in all this. The pain her husband had caused to an innocent teenage boy.

Phyllis hadn't even cared, though. Just like her husband.

"You're all fucked up." Troy's outrage and pain danced through her exhausted mind.

Yes, kid. We really are.

━━◆◇◆━━

It felt like only a few minutes later, but the skies were dark when Michelle woke. A mechanical-sounding noise chimed a few bars, then repeated. It took a moment to rub her face and shake her brain before she realized it was an incoming Skype call.

Her fingers hit *Accept* before she could stop herself.

"Whoa," Lawless exclaimed with surprise. "I thought *I* had a crap day. You look terrible, Michelle! Are you okay?"

She glowered. "Is that any way to talk to your boss?" She ran a hand self-consciously through her hair. "*Of course* I'm okay."

Lawless's cheeks reddened, and she made a vague wave toward the camera. "Um...I think you...should adjust your..."

Michelle looked down. *Oh, lovely.* Her bathrobe was gaping open, and she didn't have a stitch on underneath. And she'd obviously given Lawless an eyeful of cleavage. *Christ.* She jerked the robe closed and wrenched the tie at her waist tight.

"I can call back if you'd like to get dressed?" Lawless suggested, eyes now gazing heavenwards. Michelle doubted the light fixture was that exciting. "Or skip to tomorrow if you need to go back to sleep?"

Michelle should agree. Except she suddenly just wanted to...talk. About things that had nothing whatsoever to do with empty, soulless powerbrokers.

"No. Report: what's happening at your end?"

THE FIXER

Lawless grinned and wriggled in her seat like an excited puppy. "A few people have guessed the clue correctly now. I'll put up the next one at the base of the Virgin Hotels billboard later tonight."

"And the next clue is?" Michelle asked slyly.

"Nuh-uh-uh, nope. You'll have to wait till it's up like everyone else."

"Well, whatever it is, I'm sure it can't be hard," Michelle taunted. "You have yet to challenge me."

"Oh, I've noticed. But you're not as smart as you think you are. In fact, no one's noticed what's right under their nose."

"How mysterious." Michelle had no idea what that meant and decided to mull over it when she was less wrung out. "Well, then. Has anything else happened?"

"Not a lot." Lawless pouted and somehow managed to look both petulant and cute. "I spent a lot of the day feeling sorry for myself and thinking of all the witty comebacks I should have said to Francine when she confronted me. Especially when she said I had a lesbian lumberjack look."

Michelle laughed at her aggrieved expression. "I take it that wasn't the case?"

"Well, maybe I did. And I am. But that's not the point."

"Am what?" Michelle asked, puzzled.

"*Am* a lesbian. *Did* wear flannels. And, yes, they were of a certain lumberjack-esque variety, but in my defense, they're warm." Lawless folded her arms with a huff.

Am a lesbian. There it was again. Not that it mattered. *At all.*

"But it was rude!" Lawless was barreling on. "She does it all the time—runs her gaze over me like I'm the worst eyesore in existence. Like she's so perfect, with her perfect hair and perfect outfit and perfect boobs. Ugh! You know, she might be beautiful on the surface, but she has one of the ugliest personalities I've ever met. I can't stand people like that—ones with ugly souls."

Suddenly Michelle felt dirty all over again. Her traitorous head throbbed in agreement. Apparently the universe had decided everyone and everything needed to remind her today of all the ways in which she was a shitty human.

"Duly noted." Her tone came out chillier than ice.

Lawless blinked. "Uhm… you know I wasn't talking about you, right? I don't think you have an ugly soul. How could you? *You're* the entire reason I'm here removing a corrupt person from power!"

"I didn't take it personally," Michelle lied—and was rather impressed at her acting skills.

"Oh right, yeah, good," Lawless said sheepishly. "Damn, always sticking my foot in things with you. So okay, let's just move on. Tell me about your day?"

"Why?" Michelle's head was aching now. "What relevance is it to your job? And just because I told you one minor detail about my day *once* doesn't mean I owe you anything more. It will not be repeated!"

Lawless gaped at her in obvious surprise. "Okay, what *on earth* is wrong?"

"Nothing!" she said with a growl.

"Riiight." Lawless reeled back as if from a physical hit. "You know, Michelle, I was just being friendly. I don't think I'm owed anything from you. I'm always happy when you share, though."

She sounded vaguely hurt, which made Michelle feel like a total heel. She couldn't find enough energy left to care. Her headache was thudding like a concert speaker. Didn't that just cap off a perfect day? And it was what she deserved for helping Mr. Predatory Scum get away with crushing some poor kid's heart.

"Be friendly with your *friends*, not me," Michelle snapped. "I'm not your friend. I'm *no one's* friend."

Lawless's eyes widened.

Hell. There it was. The truth had just fallen out there like a fish flopping around on a boat deck.

"You have *no* friends, Michelle?" Lawless asked quietly. "None?"

Michelle glared at her, but it was too late. Her walls were in ruins. Lawless was looking at her as if she could see right through her. The sympathy radiating off her was deplorable.

"But how can you decompress after a long day in the office?" Lawless asked in dismay. "Who do you share bad Netflix shows with? Or eat ice cream with because you've had another shitty date?"

"I'm not fourteen." Michelle stared at her, at a loss. Who did all those things, anyway?

"I know. But it's really hard to live life without someone else to talk to. And I'm sorry for overstepping, and I know I am, and I *know* we're not friends, because you've made that super clear, don't worry, but okay, I'm just throwing this out there: If you need to talk, I'm told I'm a good listener. I've even got a playlist I can send you for whatever occasion ails you. Like, broken heart? Or new promotion? Just had your ex kidnap your goldfish on the way out? Whatever. You say the mood, and I've got the tunes sorted."

Michelle grimaced. "Well, I doubt you have a playlist for telling a teenager his much older lover is really a manipulative creep who's been using him to hurt his wife. Because breaking a poor boy's heart is just *so much fun.*"

Silence fell. Michelle wished she could cut out her own tongue. Why had she revealed any of that? Even without any identifying names, she'd said far too much.

Lawless's eyes softened. "Oh, Michelle. That must have been awful."

"Imagine how the young man felt." Her heart squeezed at the reminder. Tears, stupid, stupid tears, pricked at her eyes. It was just the stress. And the kid. And his aching, innocent eyes. Michelle had seen the love and trust and hope fade from them. She blinked hard.

"Yeah. That poor kid. I'm so sorry for him."

Finally someone got it. Troy's pain should be—

"*And* you."

—acknowledged.

"Don't do that," Michelle said, voice thick.

"Don't do what?"

"That sad thing with the eyes. I'm a *professional.* And *this* is my job. I find and fix problems. Some are easy. Some are..." she inhaled, "less so." Michelle scowled. "I have no idea why I even told you that. I will not be requiring any advice from you on this matter."

"I understand. No advice. But I'm glad you told me. It helps me understand the pressures you're under. Puts your moods into context."

My...moods? Could her employee *be* any more impertinent?

"No one would be good after a day like that," Lawless continued. "If you want to vent, I'm available to listen." She gave a grin. "Given my day job, it's kind of my specialty hearing people shouting about what's wrong with their world."

"I don't doubt it."

"So, you'll be okay, then?" Lawless asked kindly. Too kindly.

"It's my job, as I said. And I'm fine." Michelle put steel into her voice. "I can certainly deal with scheming assholes and put the fear of God into them in case they plan on repeating their transgressions. I can make them cry in fear. Hell, I did." Yes, William the Lech had actually sobbed. But not once because he'd been thinking of Troy.

"Good," Lawless said with a satisfied nod, surprising her.

"You approve of me making him cry?"

"Hell, yeah. Bad guys suffering? I'm down with that. Did you think I'd want to hug it out?"

"You are a touchy-feely, social justice type." Michelle's eyebrows lifted.

"And I hate people who inflict pain. I hate people being hurt. Look, on that score, I know you're all self-contained and professional and have your shit a hundred percent together and all that, but just so you know, that's still a lot. What you faced today? Even for people as together as you are, it's a lot. So, it's cool to *not* feel okay right now."

"I'm so very glad I have your permission to...not feel okay," Michelle said sarcastically.

Instead of being offended, Lawless laughed. "Hey, I'm not going to bite at that. You've earned one free punch at the universe today. If you're in the mood to take the universe up on it, of course."

"Or maybe that's just me on a regular day? Punching at every-thing?" A smile almost threatened to tug her lips at the absurdity of all of this. "Ever think of that?"

"Yeah? Well, you go, Michelle. Rule the world! In the meantime..." Lawless leaned forward and clicked some buttons on her keyboard. "I've just sent you the *perfect* playlist for coping with your shitty universe-punching day." She grinned and gave a double thumbs up. *Like an idiot.*

"I find that hard to believe."

"*Believe.*" Lawless's grin widened.

A cute idiot.

Michelle's computer pinged with an incoming email. She had no intention of touching it.

"Well, I'll leave you to it. I can see you need space to decompress or punch the bejesus out of something. Remember, ice cream helps. And I'm always available for venting purposes if needed. Later!"

Her screen went blank.

Michelle slid her eyes to the email and did a double take at the name on the attachment.

Snoopy Playlist.

Okay, what? She clicked on it—purely to satisfy her curiosity.

Dear God. Every single song had a dog name. How utterly absurd.

Michelle determined she absolutely would not play it.

Ever.

Her fingers tingled.

No, really.

Two hours later, she found herself, to her complete stupefaction, on her hotel bed, eyes shut, as the strains of Johnny Cash's "Dirty Old Egg Sucking Dog" crooned from her laptop speakers.

And weirdest of all, her headache was gone.

Chapter 13

Bowing to the Inevitable

MICHELLE ARRIVED HOME FROM BOSTON early the next morning and immediately called in sick at work. That would raise eyebrows, she had no doubt. In all her years at The Fixers, she hadn't taken a single day off outside of scheduled vacation time.

The moment she set her overnight bag down in her bedroom, she made a call. "I need a Room Four Special. One hour."

Michelle was pushing it, she knew, asking this early. But the establishment's manager knew he'd be exorbitantly well tipped if he pulled this off.

"It'll be ready, Ms. Hastings," came the deep voice down the phone.

It was nine-fifteen by the time Michelle returned home, pain coursing through her neck, back, and shoulders. Self-inflicted pain, so she could hardly bitch about it.

She shed her clothes and studied herself. Scratches and cuts covered her body, tiny red flecks of dried blood the only outward sign of what she'd done.

It was called a rage room. Somewhere people could go to let off steam in privacy.

Michelle was addicted to it as a pain reliever. Sometimes it alleviated stress, sometimes something deeper.

Rooms ordinarily contained computer equipment, old TVs, microwaves, or DVD players—the usual annoyances people liked to thrash with a mallet, baseball bat, or hammer to let out their frustrations. Michelle, however, had no interest in such mundane sources of anger. Her tastes were specialized.

She rolled her aching shoulders. May as well indulge in a long, decadent shower since she was having the whole day off.

Under the blasting water, too hot to be anything but a form of torture for most people, she let memories wash over her from an hour ago...and nine years ago.

Room four. She'd paid for an hour and had been given the usual paper coveralls and plastic safety goggles and directed to the room.

"Special request is ready and waiting," TJ said, nodding his bald, dark-skinned head. He was an exceptional and discreet manager of such arrangements. He always kept a stock of what she needed. His eyes betrayed no emotion, no judgment as he left her in the sound-proof room. Michelle locked it behind him.

She ignored the coveralls and eyewear, pulling out her own custom-made, high-end protective goggles. Michelle had no desire to be blinded. She also wanted an unobstructed view while she did this.

She stripped down to the undergarments she'd worn just for the occasion—boy shorts and a sports bra. The tight, black material contrasted against her paper-white skin, another sign she rarely left the office anymore.

In the middle of the room was an enormous mirror. Gilt-edged, old, probably hauled out of some estate sale. Other smaller mirrors surrounded it, most cheap and nasty, chipped and secondhand, although one or two had probably once been quite lovely.

She could see angles and corners of herself in every direction. A glimpse of mouth—lips pressed together in disdain. A slice of hard hazel eyes. Her biceps, small but tight thanks to a strict free weights regimen at the office gym, wielded a long-handled, metal-headed mallet. It was painfully heavy, but that made it perfect. She wanted to embrace the ache of destruction and carry it with her for the rest of her week like a bruise.

She swung.

The smallest mirrors were first, giving way majestically in showering arcs of glass that exploded across the room. Shards nibbled at her legs, arms, chest. The pain was a minor, instant inconvenience.

Michelle swung again. Mirrors, medium and small, went flying. One was almost whole, and she could see her slightly slack-jawed mouth in its arcing reflection before it slammed into the far wall and ruptured.

Her feet, in her designer black Givenchy mules, crunched carefully over the glass, then stood before the main mirror. TJ had outdone himself. She'd tip him extra for this beauty. Michelle tilted her head back as she soaked it in. This was like something from a mansion in a fairytale. *Beauty and the Beast*? Or *Snow White*? She imagined a captive princess would glimpse herself in it. Or maybe an evil queen.

Yes. Villain fit better. Much better.

Michelle hefted the mallet one last time and, with a furious howl, whooshed it up and outward. The tool's sinister metal head rammed into her mirrored stomach, smashing into a thousand shards.

Her own flesh-and-blood stomach caught the flying shrapnel of indignant little arrows.

It wasn't that she liked the sensation of pain—at least, not the way some people coveted it. Rather, Michelle saw allowing the tiny cuts as accepting the consequences of her actions. She'd chosen her path, for all its ills; now she was living with it.

Michelle dumped the mallet with a thud, dropped to her knees, and howled until her throat ached. It was so freeing. There were no words for the experience. Everyone expected her to be so poised, cold, perfect, aloof. She wasn't expected to feel anything. How could she? Hadn't she destroyed a woman—a target—to advance herself? A woman she'd cynically fucked to get her to trust her?

That was the consensus around the office. Well, the original consensus had been the story Alberto had told them all. That while Michelle had been assigned to stop Catherine Ayers from writing some stories a client didn't like, she'd gone soft on her target. Oh, Alberto hadn't been *entirely* sure his wife had fallen in love with Ayers, but he'd picked up that there was something there.

There was no greater sin at The Fixers than to be seen as weak. Soft. Emotional.

So she'd shown them. Michelle had blown up Catherine Ayers's career by feeding her a fake story, then walked away without a word, as if the target been nothing to her. Someone to throw away as worthless.

After that, no one ever dared suggest Michelle was weak or—Alberto's term, "cunt-struck"—for good reason: there had been no need to ruin Ayers so completely.

Michelle had been supposed to make one phone call to alert Ayers's editor that the story she'd slowly fed Ayers for months was a pack of lies—just before it was due to go to press. The huge scoop would have been pulled at great expense and embarrassment in-house. Ayers would have been castigated, demoted, and shamed *in private*. Few would have known outside of her newspaper.

Michelle hadn't made the call, so the false story became a national scandal.

Why hadn't she chosen the less public, less brutal option?

Obviously because Michelle, being a vicious, cold-hearted monster, preferred cruelty and maximum devastation. Her reputation had been so cemented afterward that she'd been promoted to CEO.

"Psychopaths always prosper," her father often used to warn her. He'd know, of course, given how high up he worked in the government's security agencies.

She almost wished she was a psychopath, someone who felt nothing about hurting others. Someone incapable of empathy or love. Someone heartless. But her own heart persisted, pumping away to spite her. Her traitorous mind constantly reminded her of what she'd done.

Because, of course, the truth was infinitely more depressing than the perception. Alberto had been right all along. Michelle had become addicted to Catherine Ayers. Her body sung whenever she was near. She'd craved the reporter like a drug. The attraction was instant and overwhelming. Nothing had been just business for her.

The moment Michelle was meant to call the story off, she'd been at her lowest. Vulnerable. Afraid. So weak. She'd sat there, literally frozen by her own insecurities, trying to force her hand to reach for the phone. It had been a terrible mistake. A monstrous lapse of judgment fueled by fear.

Later, when she'd heard whispers about how she'd thrown Ayers away, she wanted to round on those acid-tongued gossips. Seize them by their collars and shake them furiously.

I didn't throw her away.

I threw distance between us because I panicked.

I threw myself away. And Catherine suffered for my cowardice.

If regret could right wrongs, Michelle had often thought her self-hatred would have fixed the world ten times over. Not that she could ever admit that to a soul. No, Michelle Hastings, CEO and ice bitch, had a certain reputation now. It had been useful at times. Besides, who would even believe her if she told them?

Knowing she was *capable* of the deed was the hard part. Even though her callousness had been impulsive, born of fear, it didn't matter. She'd done it. That was the wound that would not heal. And why should it? It was entirely self-inflicted.

Memories filled her of a warm smile and witty mouth at her ear, joking about a column that would shake up DC. "Won't it be incredible," Catherine's low, throaty voice whispered. "We'll watch them all burn together."

Except she'd been the one to light the match while Catherine Ayers had burned.

And so had Michelle. She'd immolated right along with her—not that anyone had noticed.

Catherine's hair was the richest auburn, thick to the touch and so incredibly soft. It was a sensory delight running fingers through it, having permission to do so. The memory reminded her of Catherine's fingertips curling hair around her ear and leaning in. "Darling, I've missed you."

That voice. That beautiful, rich Bostonian voice had always undone her. That voice had made her cross lines she'd never realized she wanted to cross before. "Let me show you how much."

Michelle's body trembled in frustration and fury. She wanted to howl.

Enough. Enough. Enough.

Her mantra returned. *Hold tight.* Michelle was cool, controlled, and in charge. *Hold tight.* She could do this.

No one would ever suspect Michelle had days where she was hanging on by a thread. She'd been so careful to never let anyone see. Another benefit of keeping the world at arm's length.

Not even her safta knew how precarious her mind could be, how close to the edge her dark thoughts slid her, although she was aware Hannah worried about her. For years after the incident, Michelle forced herself to get out of bed and get dressed each day. Forced herself to prepare food—for her grandmother's sake, if nothing else. Forced herself to push away the painful reminders of her shame and weakness.

She'd be okay, she promised herself, as long as she held it in. Held tight. Michelle just had to make sure that the knot she'd tied around her heart, compressing all her emotions into a closed-off fist, held tight.

The rage room memories faded, and Michelle lifted her head under the shower's water and held it there. Her pale skin was crimson.

She resolved to try harder to push away reminders of Ayers and to steel herself against anyone who wanted to get close. Michelle was *not* safe to be around.

Eden Lawless's face drifted into view, and she sagged into the tiles in frustration. The absurd panda. Speaking of people who wanted to get closer.

If only Eden knew the truth about who she was professionally involved with. Michelle pictured that guileless, sweet, frustratingly teasing woman recoiling from her the second she found out about the moral cesspool they worked in.

Maybe Michelle should tell her now: she was not a good person. And The Fixers, catering to the prurient whims of humanity's most entitled assholes, were even worse.

Tears pricked her eyes and she straightened sharply. That was the sign. It was always time to pack it in when she veered from anger into self-pity. She was not a victim. Whatever had happened, whatever she'd done, she would live with the consequences.

Oh, and memo to self? The woman's name is Lawless, not Eden. She is not now and never will be your friend.

Michelle blinked at the droplets on her face and realized they were burning. She turned the heat down a little. Then a little more. Some of her wounds—minor as they were—had opened up, and diluted red was swirling down the drain. She watched it go, eyes empty, for the longest time.

Her safta banged on the door. "Bubbeleh? It's been forty-five minutes. You'll wash your whole life away if you stay in there much longer!"

Like that'd be a bad thing? Michelle ignored her.

"If you don't come out, I'll start drinking your fancy Champagne collection, which is bold of me since it's not even ten in the morning."

There was a pause.

She wouldn't dare. Also, this was blackmail!

"I wonder what the one with the black label from Montagne de Reims tastes like? It looks to be...oh my...*twenty-two* years old. I think I'll have it with my challah and eggs."

Michelle frowned. She'd paid almost three thousand for that bottle at a rare-wine auction. She'd been saving it for a special occasion—which had never materialized.

"You know not to bluff me, child."

Michelle heaved a sigh and turned off the water.

Michelle crawled back into bed after a quiet breakfast with Hannah. She tried not to feel guilty about having a day off, but it did feel both decadent and wrong somehow, going against her grain.

Even amidst the Ayers saga, she had refused to call in sick. Michelle had had little choice back then if she wanted to prove to her office that she was unaffected by everything that had transpired. That there was nothing to Alberto's taunting rumors.

But now, she needed the break badly. Earlier in Boston, she'd woken at four in the morning with the worst stress headache and her stomach churning. She shouldn't be surprised, since she'd endured hours of nightmares involving her worst FBI assignment interspersed with the haunting, tear-filled eyes of Troy.

It was sorely tempting to send O'Brian to visit William Kensington and put a whole other level of fear into him—maybe risk the paper trail and break a few nonessential bones. Except Phyllis seemed to want her husband looking presentable to play the doting role of future First Man.

Her teeth ground. She hated both Kensingtons with an unreasonable fury. Or *was* it unreasonable? Did she even have any accurate barometer left after so many years in this work to gauge morality as normal people did?

Michelle hugged her blankets close and wondered if she could sleep through the day to avoid any further self-analysis. She'd thought the rage room might at least take the edge off. But for the first time, it had done nothing.

"Bubbeleh?" The voice came simultaneous with the knock.

"Come in," Michelle said tiredly. "Do you need something? Are you okay? I can—"

"No, no." Hannah came to sit on the edge of her bed. "I'm here to see that you are all right. Have you ever taken even one day off work since I've lived here?" She shook her head. "No, I don't think that you have. Are you ill?" Her hand floated to Michelle's forehead. "You don't have a fever, but you're still warm. I should make you my chicken soup."

"No, Safta. No soup." The woman loved to cook it for absolutely anything that ailed anyone, from hangovers to headaches. "And before you suggest it, no to the raw onion and honey too."

Hannah had that traditional surefire cure as a particularly noxious backup.

"I'm just tired," Michelle said. "Too much work, probably. The nagging headache's back and it hurts to read anything, so it's pointless to go into the office. My trip to Boston took it out of me for some reason."

Her grandmother frowned. "Did something happen?"

"No." Michelle answered too quickly. "Well, nothing I can't handle."

"Hmm." Rising, Hannah went over to the windows and pulled open the curtains enough to create a stabbing shaft of light. "It's too dark in here, and that's affecting your mood."

Michelle winced and turned away from the bright light with a soft moan. "It's not a psychosomatic headache, Safta!"

Her grandmother huffed but twitched the curtains half closed again. "You've always been such a determined young woman. I have never thought you'd ever face something you couldn't handle. Not even when you were with the FBI."

"Please don't go there." Michelle's plea sounded pitiful to her own ears. "Not today."

"Maybe it's time we finally talked about it. What happened. It can't be good, you keeping it all bottled up."

"What good is it now? It's done. Yes, while I was working at the FBI, I had a relationship with a domestic terrorist." She threw up her hands in annoyance. "My parents think I'm shameful and disgusting, yada, yada, yada. I've accepted they'll never get over it."

"Will *you*?" Her safta leaned into the glass and said quietly, "I know that relationship wasn't your choice, by the way. It was you working undercover. Your father always leaves that bit out in his vitriol. But *I* know."

Shock ricocheted through her. No one outside of the FBI should know that.

"You truly expected me to believe that of all the people in this world, my picky, proud, entirely sensible Jewish granddaughter wanted to date a violent neo-Nazi?"

Michelle stared at her with wide eyes. "I don't know what you *think* you know, but—"

"Oh, please." Her grandmother snorted. "One, I know you. Two, you made no effort to explain yourself when it came out. And three, I couldn't help but notice that while your mother was working her way through the entire thesaurus for words that mean *filthy*, your father called you 'too ambitious.'"

Michelle swallowed.

"Too *ambitious*," Hannah repeated. "Imagine that. I did not know that your ambitions lay in working your way up a domestic terrorism cell." Her eyes narrowed. "I knew what it had to mean. Your father's security clearance is high enough to have given him access to your files. All along, he knew you were ordered to do that for the FBI, didn't he? It's the only thing that makes sense."

Michelle murmured, "You're such a meddler."

"It's appalling what they put you through."

Hannah didn't know the half of it. Michelle's stomach clenched at the reminder. She'd resisted the assignment at first. But her manipulative boss had all but begged, explaining how close the target was to finishing a bomb. They just needed access. Still, she argued that he should choose someone else.

Then he told her to be a professional, to be pragmatic, to think of herself as merely a tool. "It's just a body. An effective means to an end." He'd told her that over and over.

She'd believed him.

Michelle had hated the man she had to seduce. She'd compartmentalized the ordeal by convincing herself she might save thousands of lives.

What a cruel joke. She'd discovered later that there had been no bomb. She'd felt used and dirty. And she'd endured *that* for nothing.

The part that really burned came afterward. People acted as if she'd enjoyed it: Her boss made occasional sly jokes. Her mother called her shameful and a whore. Her father wouldn't even meet her eye.

Only Alberto, as a private undercover security agent, had understood the work was just that; it had been a mission, nothing else. He never judged her. He'd been her rock and her salvation. He'd also found her an escape: an interview at his workplace for a job for which she was highly qualified.

That had been the day she'd learned about The Fixers.

"I'm glad you left that organization," her grandmother said with a disapproving cluck. "I have no idea why the FBI chose you for that awful assignment."

"I'm done talking about this." Michelle's headache sliced through her temples like razor blades.

"I worry about you."

"I know. You don't need to."

"Do you think I'm blind?" Hannah asked kindly. "And a fool?"

"No."

"Sometimes I wonder if you do." She ran an absent-minded fingertip along the sill. "I must dust this," her grandmother murmured to herself.

"Don't you mean my cleaner must?" Michelle asked disagreeably. "That's what I pay her for."

"Yes, well, on that note, I suppose I should tell you that whenever Bethany comes around, she does the shower and vacuuming and all the bending work, but after that, we sit and talk and talk, and when she's gone, I clean the rest."

"I will fire her. I'm so sorry..."

"No, you will do no such thing." Her safta pinned her with a firm look. "I appreciate the company, and I've told her you've hired her to keep an old woman happy with conversation."

Michelle slumped. "Now I feel like a failure as a granddaughter too. I didn't even know you needed company so badly you'd hijacked the cleaner."

Hannah shifted to sit beside her on the bed again and took Michelle's pale hand in her wizened one. "I would tell you if I need something from you. But right now, you need to tell me what's happened. What do you mean by failure as a granddaughter *too*? What else have you failed at?"

"It's nothing."

"It's clearly not nothing."

Silence fell for the longest moments as Michelle fought her secretive nature. Finally, she decided.

"Yesterday, I had to tell a young man some bad news about the person he was in love with. That he'd been used and had his emotions toyed with by someone in power. He was upset."

"Did he lash out at you?" Hannah tilted her head. "Darling, you never care what others say about you. I remember even as a child you had such a sense of your own self-worth. It was astonishing. You were so brave. Fearless."

"That's not me anymore. I don't even recognize her now. She died," Michelle said flippantly.

Silence fell.

Okay, that had come out a lot darker than she'd intended.

"When did she die?" Hannah's tone was so kind. "Recently? Or was it back with the FBI business?"

"I'm not...sure." Michelle tried to remember the last time she'd felt herself. When she'd had some innocence about her. "But don't we all become someone else as the years go by? Most of the time, we're not sure where we're going or conscious of who we're becoming. Then one day, we look in the mirror and find out."

"What do you see in the mirror?" Hannah asked.

"Hair, eyes, mouth. The usual."

"*Michelle*." She gave a soft tut.

Her safta's use of her first name was powerful. She so rarely used it, preferring her many nicknames.

"I see the truth." Michelle admitted. "That I'm no longer...that I'm not a good person."

"I beg to differ. And I know you better than anyone." She felt Michelle's forehead. "Your head is so hot. Hotter than before. I should make you that chicken soup. It's called Jewish Penicillin for a reason." She made to rise.

"Wait." Michelle hated the querulous tone in her voice. "Stay? Can we keep talking?"

The surprise on her grandmother's face was brief but clear. "What do you want to talk about?"

"I hate..." Michelle inhaled. Her stomach twisted. "I hate what my parents think of me—that I...enjoyed it. I *hated* that assignment. For months and months afterward, I dreamed of killing him. I hear in my head what my parents say about me. It's not true, but it hurts."

"Oh, bubbeleh." Hannah stroked her hair. "This has tormented you for so long, hasn't it?"

"I'm fine," Michelle said sternly, as if to convince herself. "I will be. I can compartmentalize."

"Yes, you can. You always have. It's alarming how well. Until yesterday. Why was that so different, I wonder? Was he awful to you, the young man?"

"No. He wasn't at all. He was so...he was innocent. But that was taken from him. I watched his innocence die in his eyes. His trust."

"The way the FBI took it away from you?"

Michelle's stomach twisted. "It's not the same at all. The young man was only fifteen. Far more innocent than me. He fell in love and was broken. I wasn't young, and I certainly wasn't in love."

"Betrayal is not a contest. I remember how you were back then. You were idealistic too. And then one day you weren't." Hannah's expression became sad. "Someone you believed in took that from you. Did the young man remind you of your younger self?"

Michelle shoved that thought away, hating the taste of it. She was probably right. It was partly that one FBI assignment that had stolen any innocence she'd had left. And it was the Ayers business again. The reminder that she'd thrown away the one person she'd ever wanted to hold tight.

Her fractured husk of a heart had been hurting so much lately. The walls she'd built so high to protect herself seemed to be made of paper.

"All I know for sure is for some reason, yesterday hurt more than it should. I lost control." Michelle had let down her guard with Lawless. Told her things the other woman had no business knowing. That was so far beyond normal for Michelle that she could barely believe she'd done it. "And the stress headaches are getting worse."

Her grandmother touched her forehead again. "I have been worried about you for so long. I worry when I see you come home late. Bleeding. And you won't say why or how. I worry when you work all hours. And I worry when you hate yourself. And you think I don't notice any of these things? Well, I do."

Michelle sank back deeper into her pillow. "I'm making such a mess of life."

"Is that how you see it? A mess?"

"I might be a workaholic, but even I'm self-aware enough to notice I have no one, aside from you." Michelle gave a self-deprecating smile. "I know I have no friends. Zero life outside the office. I'm just... existing. And some days, when I do something particularly clever at work, it's enough. I'm proud. Satisfied. But other days, like yesterday, it just...hurts. My head and my stomach ache for hours."

"Oh, bubbeleh, how awful. But I wouldn't say that you have *no* friends." There was a glint in her eye. "Did I or did I not hear a medley of dog songs this morning?"

Oh God. "Which answer would give me the most deniability?" Michelle hadn't wanted to listen to it again, but her head had been throbbing and, for some reason, it had helped last night, and...

Hannah chuckled.

After a pained sigh, Michelle confessed, "Fine. Yes."

"And where did these come from? Because, darling, I know for a fact you'd never have chosen them yourself. I did not hear a single classical strain in any one of them."

Michelle mumbled.

"I'm sorry, I didn't catch that."

"Eden," Michelle repeated with more volume. "Lawless. She's decided I need universe-punching music, whatever the hell that is. And, bafflingly, that's what she sent me. *Dogs.*"

"I see." She did not seem remotely surprised by any part of that sentence.

"You do?"

"Oh, yes. And to think you believe you have no friends."

"She's an *employee.*"

"An employee who sends you dog songs."

"Because she's certifiable."

"Or she likes you and is trying to be your friend. Why don't you let her? And before you tell me she's your employee yet again, isn't it for only five more weeks? And then what?"

"And then what, *what*?"

"Well, aren't you free to be friends then? Outside of work?"

Michelle stared at her in bemusement. "Why would I do that?"

"Because you just admitted you need one. I think she's clearly volunteering."

"I don't need a friend, though." Michelle glared at the thought. "Just because I don't have what everyone else has doesn't mean I have to run off and befriend people to fix it. I never said I *wanted* to do that. Besides, even if my life's a mess, I'm getting by, aren't I?" Well, she had been until the headaches had gotten so much worse.

"Says the woman stuck in bed with no one but a meddlesome old safta to talk to."

"And what's wrong with that?" Michelle teased. "You're excellent company."

"Thank you, dear. I agree. But I won't be here forever, will I?" She frowned. "And, to circle back to where we came in, I'm really worried about you. Some days, I worry so much, I check in on you when you're asleep, just to make sure you're still with us."

She...what?

Michelle drew in a breath. "My health isn't so bad that my heart will stop in my sleep. I have pills for the hypertension and stress. Pills for the migraines."

"It's the pills I worry about. Too many, and..." She faded out and eyed Michelle pensively.

"Just how many do you think I'm taking?" Michelle asked in surprise.

"It's not that." Hannah tugged her into a hug. "Darling child, you are so fierce and unstoppable at work. But you are so unyielding to yourself at home. So...*hateful*, almost. I'm afraid you are your own worst enemy. Listen to me closely: You *are* worthy. You *are* good. And I just want you to have people in your life who think that about you as well. People like your Eden."

"But—"

"No. Just think about how she makes you laugh—"

"Except she's irritating half the time. She crosses every line. She—"

"How she makes you play the silly dog songs—"

"She didn't *make* me. I was mildly curious and—"

"And how she knew you needed some 'universe-punching' music. Even if you hated her songs, she knew you needed something. And you knew that too, or you wouldn't have played every track."

"I don't know anything," Michelle mumbled, giving up on this entire conversation as a bad joke. Her safta had lost the plot.

"I think she'd be a good friend for you. Solid and steadfast. She might actually make you remember there's more to life than work. And I get the sense she likes you just as you are."

Michelle eyed her grandmother grimly. "Highly doubtful."

Neither Lawless nor her grandmother truly knew Michelle or the moral abyss she inhabited. They'd be unlikely to want to know her if they did.

"Anyway, whatever she is to you, I'm so glad she's around. I just want you *happy*." Hannah's eyes pricked with tears.

And now Michelle felt guilty for making her grandmother emotional. "I'd like to sleep now," she said diplomatically instead of pointing out she was never earning happiness from the universe. Some things were not possible when you didn't deserve them.

"All right." She smiled. "I know I'm a pesky old woman who gets annoying."

"It's nice you care." It was. Of course, she only cared because she didn't know the truth.

Michelle turned over, pulling her blanket over her into a cocoon. As if it could cocoon her mind.

———◆◇◆———

It shouldn't have surprised Eden how Michelle answered her Skype call that evening. She was immaculately dressed, not a hair out of place, as if to underline how much of an aberration the previous call had been. And her professional mask was welded on.

Eden grinned immediately—her current Pavlov's dog reaction to her boss's resting ice face. Okay, sure, her reaction was partly that Michelle was incredibly good to look at. And partly the desire to see more and know more and make her not look so haunted. The end result, though, was she turned into a grinning fool around her boss.

"Hey—" Eden began.

"Ms. Lawless, for the record, I did not listen to thirty-two dog-themed songs while eating ice cream. Before you infer otherwise."

Eden laughed. "No? But hey the fact you know it was thirty-two means at least you looked at it. Did any of the songs cheer you up?" She leaned in and said, "What about 'Dirty Old Egg Sucking Dog'?"

"That was especially vile." Michelle bared her lips. "Cash spent most of the song threatening to shoot the dog!"

"Well, it *was* getting into the henhouse." Eden laughed even harder. "Come on, you had to like one of the songs? What about Dolly Parton's 'Crackerjack'?"

"Ugh, sentimental claptrap." Michelle rolled her eyes. "The dog was starved and pathetic. Like that playlist."

"Tough crowd." Eden chuckled. "What about..."

"No." Michelle held up her hand. "No to all of them to save you the time of listing every song. All that list did was make me glad I don't own a dog."

Eden digested that for a moment, and it set her off again. She laughed and laughed. She laughed so long that Michelle's lips twitched and a tiny escape of laughter edged out.

"Damn, that's hilarious!" Eden shook her head. "All right, all right. Sorry it wasn't the tonic I hoped."

"I didn't ask for any tonic. What I *am* now begging for is for you to do your job and report."

"Right, right. Okay, so my local knowledge clue has gone up. You ready?"

Michelle made a get-to-the-point signal with her finger.

"Bo...Bowing at nonsense. That's the clue." Eden eyed her. "Seriously, though, local knowledge is required."

"You said bowing in a weird way." Michelle eyed her suspiciously.

"I did not!" Eden protested. But, crap, she so had.

"You did. Like you started to say bow—as in bow string—and remembered it should be bow as in leaning forward."

Eden's lips clamped down hard, willing herself not to give away anything.

"I'm right, aren't I?" Michelle smiled. "Bow as in bowstring? As in stringed instruments?"

Eden didn't so much as twitch.

"Or...as in...archery?"

Are you fucking kidding me? Eden's eyes widened. *How!*

"Don't play poker. I mean it. *Don't.*" Michelle tapped away at her keyboard. "You know, I'm betting Wingapo has an archery club."

Eden shook her head slowly as incredulity rocked her.

Michelle smirked at her expression. "*Three* archery clubs? That seems excessive for a population of forty thousand." She slid her gaze back to her keyboard as she read the list.

"Yes and no," Eden said. "They're all run by the same family. A father and two sons. They're kind of competitive, so they each set up their own club."

"I see." Michelle looked up. "Bullseye Archery."

Eden sighed inwardly. *For heaven's sake, this is ridiculous.* "How do you figure?" she asked neutrally.

"Bull's eye. As in bull. As in BS. Which means nonsense." She drew her explanation out for effect. "Ergo: bowing at nonsense." She shot Eden a triumphant look.

"New record," Eden muttered and tapped her watch. "Genius."

"Hardly. I'm just good at using my brain laterally." Michelle did look more smug, less dark and cold than she had when the call connected. "And I know how to use Google effectively."

Eden shot her a dubious look. "Maybe. But I'm going with you're part wizard."

"Witch."

"What?"

"A female wizard is a witch. I'm clearly part witch."

"Well, I'm glad you find this funny."

"No, I just don't like misgendering people from magicking backgrounds."

Her amusement was contagious, and Eden forgot how miffed she was at how easy Michelle made her scavenger hunt look.

"Nick Drake," Michelle suddenly said.

"Huh?"

"I've decided to throw you a bone—no pun intended. So: 'Black Eyed Dog.' Number 14. *That* song was acceptable. It didn't make me want to commit a murder or throw up over the sentimentality. I liked it."

"It's a song about depression." Did Michelle not realize that? Or maybe she did, by the way she suddenly pursed her lips as if warning Eden not to ruin everything by prodding her about it.

As if she would. Despite what her boss thought, Eden truly did understand that some lines were too personal to cross with someone who wasn't a friend.

"I like it too," was all she said. "It's soulful."

Michelle's shoulders relaxed a little. Her gaze drifted as if seeking a safer topic. "So, any new run-ins with the mayor?"

"No, but I keep expecting the worst. She has tentacles everywhere." Eden scowled.

"I can believe it," Michelle said, after a moment. "Mr. Clemmons said in his report that Wilson is obsessed with you. In the sense she hates that you bested her even once. It hangs over her. That makes her dangerous."

"I think the most fun she ever had was plotting my downfall. I can't blame her since I'm doing the same. The downfall plotting, I mean. I'm not obsessed. More...filled with a fury that can't ever be quenched." She shot Michelle a half smile.

"Same thing, isn't it? Fury and obsession?"

"No, it's not. I can forget I'm mad with her for long stretches and live my life. The obsessed focus only on the object of their obsession."

"Mmm. I suppose that's true."

That reminded her. "By the way, I have a friend trying to get other TV networks and media to pick up the scavenger hunt. If it goes national, it'll maximize the embarrassment for Francine when the end-game is revealed."

"Yes," Michelle said. "I meant to tell you: I saw a small bit on it here in DC. I'll get someone to send you the link if you want it."

"DC?" Eden beamed with delight. "That's fantastic."

Michelle eyed her. "I really hope this plays out the way you hope. It might be easy to anger people. If they feel like they're playing a fun game and get to the end and there's a political message. They may feel duped and dismayed."

"I know." Eden inhaled. "I've thought about that."

"And?"

"And it's a risk. But the biggest problem we have in Wingapo is getting the news out about what the mayor's like. The mainstream media are in her back pocket, and the cops are...intimidating. So even if someone had a rant about her online, which she can't control, the police somehow seem to work out who did it and have a little 'chat' with them about defaming public figures."

Michelle's expression narrowed. "That's censorship. And the local police have nothing better to do than investigate people's online posts?"

"Not a lot else is happening in Wingapo. Even the cops are bored. And Francine gets grateful...financially speaking...when they do her favors."

Michelle sighed. "Politics never changes, does it? No matter who or where. The grubbiness is so pervasive."

Eden studied her. "Still thinking about the underage case?"

"I'm enraged about it," she said, biting out the word. "But I'm not here to discuss that."

"What would you like to discuss?" Eden asked gently. "I can distract you, if you'd like. I've got a great repertoire of distractions. I can even talk about my life-affirming hobbies."

"I'd have bet my life's savings you have a few of those."

"A ton," Eden confirmed happily. "Up to and including knitting, writing spec poetry which I then set to music, and composing protest songs."

"How very on brand." Michelle paused. "Knitting, though?"

"It helps me think." Eden smiled. "About my poetry and protest songs."

Michelle shook her head. "I think I should go if you're threatening to sing or recite something."

"Smart move." Eden chuckled. "Because I never said my knitting, poems, or songs were any good."

"And yet, I somehow suspect they wouldn't be all bad. Probably just dripping with heart." Her smile was taunting.

As her head tilted to one side, Eden got a good view of the dark smudges under her eyes.

She was itching to ask if she was okay. Again. But she'd decided to try very hard to give Michelle her space. It's all she'd asked for: Eden staying on her side of the line.

"Okay, what is it?" Michelle said with a hearty sigh.

"What's what?"

"You have a pained look and have been squirming like a five-year-old. Are you trying to avoid telling me I have something between my teeth?" The faintest uptick of her lips followed, and Eden was transfixed.

"Nooo." She huffed out a breath. "I'm trying…with some difficulty, mind you, because I'm a naturally curious and helpful creature…*not* to ask if you're okay, feeling better, doing better, less moody, seizing the day, and so on."

"Ah, yes. Look at you keeping all that inside," Michelle drawled. "I think you just erupted like Vesuvius."

"Impulse control isn't my greatest-ever thing. But neither is saying nothing when someone I like is suffering in silence." Shit. *Someone I like?* In a panic, Eden rushed in: "And by like, I don't mean, uh, like-like, as in *let's go out*, which would be totally inappropriate because, hello, you're my boss, and for all I know you're married with six kids!" She inhaled even more sharply. *Kill me now.* Good goddess, her babbling was getting worse.

Michelle leaned back, and a curling cat smirk spread across her face. "Six. Kids?" She said the words as though Eden had suggested she might be part lizard. *"Six?"*

"Well…" Eden gave a nervous smile, "Three?"

Michelle snorted. "Try none." She tapped her desk. "I do not do maternal. I have no children, no pets, no life-affirming hobbies for Instagram."

Noticeably, she made no reference to her marital status, which Eden could fully understand, given evil Alberto. Mostly she was just amazed Michelle had shared this much.

Or wait…did it count as sharing if she'd just listed a bunch of things she didn't do or that didn't apply to her?

"You're enjoying this, aren't you?" Eden said with a grin.

At Michelle's startled look, she realized how that might sound flirty all over again.

"The hunt," she said quickly. "It's giving you a kick."

"Hardly."

"Please. I think this is the most fun you've had in ages!"

Michelle's lips pursed. "You mustn't have a high opinion of my life."

"You said it yourself: no kids, no pets, no life-affirming hobbies. What am I supposed to think?"

"You're not supposed to think of me at all."

"Yeah, that's not going to happen." Eden chuckled. "You're a little hard to ignore." *Shit, brain!* "As my boss and all. Whom I check in with every night."

"I suppose." Michelle looked disconcerted.

"And whom I supply cutting-edge music to. Which you also like."

"Now you're stretching it. And why do you care what I like in the first place?"

"I find you interesting," Eden admitted. "And I'm also worried about you. So, I'm killing two birds with one stone. Music soothes the..." She stopped as she realized the saying ended with *savage beast.* "Soul," she substituted.

"Please mark my words carefully: my personal situation is none of your business," Michelle said with the heftiest of long-suffering sighs. "I am your boss. I don't need your constant inquiries as to my well-being, or any eccentric playlists."

At least this time Michelle looked more resigned than annoyed at her temerity.

Eden grinned. "Noted. Well, my offer still stands. For a chat, if needed. And if you don't want any more of my playlists, maybe don't look like you need them so much?" She winked before Michelle could verbally throttle her.

Then, to derail the woman's doubtlessly impending diatribe, she added, "Here's a song for when you're feeling blue." She leaned over and tapped a key, emailing it to her boss. "This always perks me right up."

"I won't listen to it, so don't bother." Michelle set her jaw.

But her eyes? They were interested.

Eden really liked her eyes. They spoke far more than Michelle ever did.

"Just humor a touchy-feely social-justice type, hey? This song has dug me out of some deep, dark holes, let me tell you. I know you prefer classical, but maybe give Israel Kamakawiwo'ole a chance."

"Excuse me?"

"I mean, yes, of course, upbeat ukulele from a Hawaiian dude with the richest voice isn't exactly Wagner, and a song called 'Somewhere Over the Rainbow' might sound uncool, but—"

"What makes you think I like classical?" Michelle looked puzzled now.

Oh.

Oh crap. "Um."

Her face went from relaxed to sheer granite. "I repeat, Ms. Lawless, what makes you think I like classical?"

"Maybe your safta mentioned it?" Eden's voice rose to an uncomfortably high pitch. "There may have been a Skype call involved?"

Michelle's face was even harder. Those emotional eyes flashed with vulnerability, then fear, and then...rage. "A. Skype. Call."

"Yes?" Eden licked her lips. "It was short," she said quickly, as if that made it better. "Sort of a hi there, hello, introductory call with Hannah?" Why did everything she said end up as a question? "Really, it was nothing."

"And in this *short introductory call*, you found time to discuss my love of classical music? Pray tell, what else did you discuss?"

Yep, there was a full-on hurricane brewing in her eyes now.

Eden couldn't lie. That'd make it worse. Besides which, Hannah would likely tell her anyway.

"How you like your chocolate. That you collect champagne. Why I..." she swallowed, "make you laugh."

Michelle's lips pressed into a cold, hard line at that. "Go on," she said, voice low and dangerous. "Don't leave *anything* out."

A ferocious heat infused Eden's cheeks, and she briefly hung her head. "Whether you're seeing anyone."

Now Michelle's jaw clenched hard. Twice.

"And how your ex-husband, Alberto, was dangerous and bad for you."

"That's everything?"

Eden nodded.

"Not my underwear size? The medication I'm on? Religion?"

"Oh. Yeah. That too. The, um...Jewish...part." Eden sagged. Her cheeks could pass as bonfires now.

"I see." Michelle studied her for a long time. "So, when my back was turned, you crossed every line, did not care about my wishes or consent, contacted my grandmother..."

"Actually, I didn't..."

"Or she contacted you. What matters is you knew my rules. I asked only for you to respect my privacy." Her voice was so low now, Eden had to strain to hear her. But body language said plenty. The tightness of her shoulders, the gritting of her teeth. "This was a betrayal of trust, Ms. Lawless."

Eden vigorously shook her head. "No...I..."

"Even now you seek to minimize it. You think it was harmless, as though *your* views on my feelings are relevant. *I'm* the one you gossiped about. *I'm* the one whose dirty laundry has been hung out for display for you to discuss, dissect, and mock." Michelle looked sick. "I've been here before, and I will not go through it again. From now on, our nightly calls will cease. I've been too busy for them anyway."

"But the clues..."

"You will text me the clues as they appear. I may or may not respond. If you have an office matter, go through Tilly. If you have a security matter, text me and I'll send someone to deal with it. Now, is that everything?"

Eden tried to think of something...anything...to make it right.

"Is. That. Everything?"

"Yes," she whispered.

"Good." A finger reached toward Michelle's keyboard, and viciously came down. The screen went black.

Oh, hell.

Guilt and regret flooded her. How had Michelle taken something so harmless and made it seem so sordid?

No, Michelle was right. Eden had done the one thing she'd been asked not to. She'd violated Michelle's boundaries. And clearly something had happened in the past—*I've been here before*—that made her extra twitchy about people knowing her personal information.

When Hannah had called, Eden could have avoided asking anything personal that she knew Michelle wouldn't have divulged herself.

Discussing the ex-husband? Yeah…that was bad.

Shame flooded her when she remembered asking Hannah if Michelle was seeing anyone. That was so wrong, so far over the line. Eden wanted to dive under a pillow in embarrassment.

She really had screwed up everything.

Chapter 14

Down to Earth

"IF YOU DON'T MIND ME saying," Melba said, inching over Eden to reach for the butter, "you've been a bit down for a few days. Actually, it's been about a week."

Eden froze in mid-buttering of her toast and glanced up in surprise. "Oh." She shrugged. "Work stuff." She paused. "Or friend stuff."

She wasn't quite sure where Michelle fell on the work/acquaintance/friend spectrum. All she knew was she missed her. It was ridiculous, given how little time they'd known each other. But those nightly calls had been a highlight of her day.

She'd texted and emailed a groveling apology.

Silence.

The thing was, once she'd picked it all apart, Eden could see two separate things happening between them: on the one hand, she'd crossed a line by talking to Hannah about personal things. That was bad. The worst.

But on the other hand, the bigger hand, she'd seen Michelle's pain and had been trying to lessen it. That wasn't a bad thing, was it? Not to mention Michelle had been the one to share about the young man who'd been hurt. Eden hadn't pried that out of her. She'd volunteered. So there was something there between them. A connection. It wasn't all one-sided.

So, that being the case, she truly couldn't get her head around why Michelle was so adamant about keeping Eden on her side of the line. Their back-and-forth sharing had started when Eden could see Michelle was clearly struggling with something. And it was in Eden's nature to fix things. Why shouldn't she offer to help? How was that so bad?

"Work or friend stuff?" Melba said with a smile. "Not sure which?"

"I'm between definitions right now," Eden said. "I like this person and want to help her, but she's sort of 'No, you stay over there, annoying minion.'" She crunched her toast thoughtfully. "But her eyes say something else, you know?"

Melba nodded. "I have been trying to explain these kinds of situations to Jimmy. He's not the best at picking up body language and nonverbal cues and the like. My baby boy has no sarcasm detector at all. So I tell him, if you want to know if they're your friend, look at how you feel after you've spent time with 'em."

"That's great advice." Guilt washed over Eden. Okay, while *she'd* felt good after their Skype calls, Michelle had clearly just been putting up with her—when Eden wasn't out and out infuriating her. She'd failed the basic friendship test. No wonder Michelle was giving her radio silence.

"What is it?" Melba studied her face.

"I may have been a bad friend...or, well, a bad not-friend. I was sticking my nose in where I wasn't wanted. But my boss really does need a friend right now. Or *someone* to talk to."

"Your boss?" Melba's eyes widened. "Oh, honey, that's a pile more to unpack."

"It is? Why?"

"You sound like you've never had a boss before." Melba laughed.

Crap. Was it *that* obvious?

Melba stopped laughing and regarded her seriously. "Oh, she really is your first boss?"

Eden sighed and stared at her toast.

"I see," she said kindly. "Look, it's like this: most bosses, the professional ones, don't like to be vulnerable. It's a self-preservation instinct, not wanting to show any weaknesses others might use against them. They like to project a strong image."

Eden reached for her coffee. "That's ridiculous. Everyone's a person underneath. We're all equal. I truly wanted to be her friend. Help. Make her laugh. I could see her struggling sometimes."

"And your boss doesn't want you helping." Melba smiled gently. "Honey, that's her choice. You let her be now. Don't push."

"Right." Eden sighed. *Don't push. Also don't breathe. Don't eat.* "That's hard."

"Oh, I'm with you on that one."

"I'm not expected to notice all the ways she's looking like hell? I'm supposed to say *nothing*? Well, to be honest, sometimes I did kind of point out when she looked terrible."

"Oh lord." Melba looked at her askance. "You didn't! A person has their pride, you know."

Eden hadn't thought about it from that angle. "But I was always brought up to believe a burden shared is a burden halved."

"And some people are lone wolves." Melba patted her wrist. "Not you, though, huh? I can see that. You're a woman who just loves to be fixing everyone's messes for them. Can't help it, I bet."

"That makes me sound like a busybody."

"Well, if you are, I'm the same. Or I was. A hard lesson to learn is that some people prefer to figure their stuff out for themselves, crawl out of their own holes, and do their own thing. Number of times I've had to sit on my hands when I was itching to help them out and knew fifty different ways to make it easier for them. That's the hardest."

"It's not weak to need help." The protest movement had taught her that. Strength in numbers.

"It's human, though, not to want to be seen as less-than in the eyes of someone you want to look impressive to."

Eden turned that over. Did Michelle want to look impressive to her? Why?

In the scheme of things, Eden was nothing. A bug she could flick off her windshield and forget about. It seemed unlikely Michelle thought much of her at all. And yet, how interesting that she'd shared, twice now, about her working day—things that amused or troubled her. It felt like Michelle didn't do that often.

So...maybe she was less a bug on Michelle's windscreen. More the windscreen wiper—a little harder to dismiss, and always in her face. She rather liked that analogy.

Eden grinned.

Melba's eyebrows lifted in question.

"Nothing, nothing." She brushed crumbs off herself. "Thanks for another lovely breakfast. I should get on with my day."

"Oh, did you hear, another clue's gone up?" Melba said, leaning in. Excitement lit her eye. "It was pinned to the gate of the Bullseye Archery Club. It's: down to earth, harder still, a dream unburied."

"That's weird. Buried and earth and stuff...sounds like a graveyard?"

"What about *harder still*, though?" Melba asked. "That has to mean something? And if it's *unburied*, it's not about graves, I'm thinking."

Eden shrugged. "I guess you and Jimmy will have to figure this one out without me."

"Mmm." Melba smiled. "The ladies at my yoga group are having the time of their lives with this scavenger hunt. I wonder how long it'll go for? I hope it doesn't end too soon."

"It's a mystery. Like everything else about it."

"Very true." Melba rose and started gathering up the plates. "I'll go brainstorm with Jimmy. Now, you have a fine day."

Eden smiled and left her to it.

———— ⊱⊰ ————

Eden sent Michelle a one-line text after breakfast.

Down to earth, harder still, a dream unburied

Ten minutes later she received a text back that contained only a link. Eden read the opening paragraph on the site.

Rammed Earth Pilot House
During the Great Depression, USDA Chief Plant Pathologist Harry Humphrey built a pilot model of North America's first rammed earth house

in Maryland to test whether it would be a sustainable method of home construction. As dirt was abundant, he hoped it would help poor farmers in the prairies. Humphrey's dream was that rammed-earth homes would be adopted all across the US as a cheap form of building.

There was no other comment.
It was the right answer.
Of course.

Chapter 15
Mortal Enemies

THE MAYOR WAS SITTING IN the garden at the B&B when Eden glanced out her window at eight the next morning. She was sipping on a tea, legs crossed and stretched out as if she owned the place.

Eden stared down at her from the second-floor window with a mix of astonishment, annoyance, and trepidation. With a scowl, she thundered down the stairs and out into the garden.

"What the hell are you doing *here*?" she demanded.

"Drinking Ms. Lotus's delightful green tea," Francine said. "You should try some."

"I have," Eden snapped. "And I repeat, why are you here?"

"Can't I just be visiting an old friend?"

"Who, me? Surely you mean *mortal enemy* instead!"

"Why does everything have to be about you, Eden?" Francine ran a hand through her glossy brunette forelock, pushing it out of her eyes. "I meant, of course, *Ms. Lotus*. She is the owner of one of Wingapo's most respected accommodation establishments, after all. I'm overdue a visit."

Eden swung her gaze around the garden courtyard area. No sign of Melba anywhere. "You and Melba are friends?" she asked skeptically.

"She gave me tea, did she not?" Francine waved at the tall glass of golden liquid. "Seated me in her nicest spot. Went off to find other refreshments."

"In other words, acted like a polite host." Eden drew her lips into a grim line. "How'd you find me, anyway?"

"Your vehicle is somewhat distinctive. It was spotted in the vicinity of this B&B, and so I decided to play a hunch." Francine's smile was cool. "Maybe don't drive such a noticeable hippie van if you're on the down-low."

"I'm not on the down-low." Eden folded her arms. That seemed too defensive, so she unfolded them. Now she felt ridiculous. "I'm taking care of some personal business."

"Personal business? Your only connection remaining in Wingapo is your father," Francine said, sounding almost bored now. "You've spoken to him exactly once, and by my count, that lasted five minutes. So...I have to wonder: What are you really doing in town?"

"How is that any of your business?" Eden folded her arms again and this time, she kept them tightly against her chest.

"It's my business, Ms. Lawless, because the last time you were here, you attempted to play wrecking ball with my career. I'd hate for that to happen again, especially this close to my re-election. And given you're a professional rabble-rouser these days, it's not such a leap to wonder if you're really here in a professional capacity."

"So, wait, I can only possibly be here for you?"

"I repeat, your meeting with your father lasted five minutes. You haven't been back to see him. Conclusion: you're not here for personal reasons."

"It only lasted five minutes because he's still upset that you took his job away from him," Eden said, irritation rising. "For no reason! He loved being a doctor at Wingapo Hospital."

Francine slowly ran a finger across her bottom lip, as if adjusting her lipstick. The action looked more like a threat for some odd reason. "I didn't like the people he associated with."

"Me." There'd been no denial Francine had been behind her father's firing. That was new.

"Yes." The mayor gave a faux sorrowful look. "Of course, how was I to know he'd spiral into despair, take to the bottle, lose his wife, and became a bitter old man who shakes his fist at the clouds? Most people would simply go find another job elsewhere. So, don't put his failings on me. He's a useless waste of space, a sad little man, as I'm sure you've discovered from your brief visit."

Anger flooded Eden at the characterization. Equally she hated how Francine wasn't entirely wrong about her father's choices. He had given up on life the moment River left him. "I think it's time you finished your tea and hit the road, Francine." Eden's voice contained a soft, warning growl. "I mean it."

"Truth hurts." Instead of leaving, the mayor settled back deeper into her chair. "We've gotten off track. I also came to see you today to find out what the point is of your ridiculous scavenger hunt. And before you deny you're running it and look all shocked and innocent, who else? It has exactly your brand of creativity. It began just after you arrived. And it fits in a way nothing else does." She met Eden's eye. "I *know* this is you."

"You don't know anything. Why would I play silly games?"

"Why, indeed?" Francine looked genuinely puzzled. "What *is* your end goal?"

Eden cocked an eyebrow. "Who says this scavenger hunt's mastermind has any end goal at all?"

"Oh, she does." Francine pursed her lips. "Look, can we just skip the part where you pretend it's not you, I press you, you lie, underestimate me, and I crush you once more? Can we just get to the part where you explain what you're up to?"

"It's really killing you, isn't it?" Eden smiled, satisfaction warming her. "There's something's happening in your boring, ordered, censored little town that you're not in charge of. Something you can't control. It's burning you up inside."

Francine lost her placid expression. "I know it's you. It *smells* of you."

"Really. Why? Because someone's doing something original around here that you didn't approve first?"

"Because it's sneaky and borderline clever, and that's you." Francine's eyes flashed.

"*Borderline* clever?" Eden snorted. "Nice."

"Well, the clues aren't exactly challenging. And now your latest? I'm sure the plebeians will work out that one out soon. It's Maryland's famous rammed earth house."

Sometimes Eden forgot how sharp Francine's mind was. She drew in a breath.

"So," Francine leaned in. "Here's what I don't understand; maybe you can explain it to me: Every other clue relates to something *in* Wingapo. The rammed earth house is miles away from town. Half an hour's drive. Why the change?"

Eden probably shouldn't be surprised the mayor had noticed that detail too. It would make sense by the end, but she wasn't about to admit anything now. "I have no idea. And I'm really not sure why you think this is my doing besides the fact you think I'm sneaky and clever."

"Borderline clever," Francine corrected. "So, we're just going to pretend all roads don't lead back to Melba Lotus's charming little B&B?"

Just then, their host arrived, bearing a tray of assorted cookies and cake, looking uncharacteristically flustered. "I'm sorry for the delay, Mayor," Melba said. "I couldn't decide what you'd like, so I brought some of everything." She glanced at Eden. "Oh, hello there, hon, are you joining us too?"

"No," Eden said firmly. "Definitely not. I'll leave you two to socialize."

"A pity," Francine said with a nasty smirk. "We had *so* much to catch up on."

Melba tossed Eden a surprised look. "Wait, you two know each other well?"

"Very well," Francine purred. She lowered her voice conspiratorially and said sotto voce to Melba, "We're mortal enemies." She laughed then, long and mocking.

The grating noise made Eden want to take up a life of violence.

Melba chuckled, confusion clear in her eyes as her gaze darted between them. "Well, now doesn't *that* sound like something interestin' to discuss."

"No, not really." Eden rose. "I'll be in my room."

She left them to it, a Francine-sized headache coming on.

Every damned time.

———◦◇◦———

Half an hour later, there was a gentle knock on her door.

With a groan, Eden flung aside the wet washcloth on her forehead and called, "Come in."

"Just checking you're all right, hon," Melba said. "You looked a bit worked up when you left us."

"Did you enjoy your get-together with Francine?" Eden asked with way too much grouchiness.

"You mean your *mortal enemy*?" Melba lifted her eyebrows. "You sure left some things out. I learned quite a lot this mornin' about you."

"I'll bet," Eden grumbled, then returned the washcloth to her head with a wet slap.

"Well, I had no idea you were the one behind the papering of the mayor's property company. I'd heard stories about that from a long time back, but they were all pretty vague."

"I'm betting no one told you the paper was actually printouts of complaints against Francine for being a slumlord?"

"Is that what they were? Folks seemed to have forgotten to mention that bit. So did Mayor Wilson just now."

Eden snorted. "Sounds about right. I didn't realize you were friends."

"We're not. Her stopping by to see how my establishment was going and whether we needed anything from the mayor's office was a complete surprise. She talked me into a tour. Then she saw your van, and her eyes got a real funny look about them. She asked if she might stay for morning tea. It was such an unexpected request that I obliged. I didn't realize till later it was all about you."

"Everything's always about me," Eden muttered. "She holds grudges forever."

"And do you do that too?"

She turned that over. "I remember injustices. Is that the same thing?"

"Oh, hon, good question." Melba's gaze tracked to the sodden washcloth on her head. "I can see you're having a time of it. Need something for the headache? I have some jalapeños."

"I don't follow."

"My momma swore by 'em. Hot peppers numb the brain's trigeminal nerve and stops it sending pain waves around your brain. And if it's a sinus headache, eating hot peppers will unclog sinuses."

"I'm not really one for the hot stuff," Eden said. "I guess I could try it, though."

"Well, it's not for everyone."

"I'm sure I'll be fine soon. It'll pass." *When Francine's visit is out of my head.*

"Why didn't you tell me about your history with Wingapo? With the mayor?"

"I don't like to relive it. And my boss doesn't want me to talk about much of anything."

"Ah." Melba tapped her nose. "All right, then." She paused. "The mayor did try to find out if I knew whether you were behind the scavenger hunt, by the way."

Eden froze.

"I said that was crazy." Melba gave her a long, considering look. "It's not, though, is it? Didn't think of it till she said, but she's right, isn't she? You're always worn out on the mornings a new clue's been put up overnight. And your van's always in a slightly different spot on those mornings."

Eden sighed. "Please don't ask. Because I really like you." *Too much to lie to you outright.*

A small smile tugged at Melba's lips as she got the hint. "Okay, okay. Goodness me. Dark horse, aren't you?" She chuckled. "Never would have suspected. Don't suppose you want to put me and Jimmy out of our misery on the unburied earth clue?"

Eden grinned faintly. "Afraid not."

"It was worth a try. But don't worry, your secret's safe with me."

"Melba, do you mind if I rest some more? I really do want to see off this headache."

"I understand. I'll bring you some jalapeños, just in case."

"Okay. Thanks."

And with that Melba left, closing the door softly behind her.

Eden exhaled in frustration. Well, she'd known Francine would likely figure out her secret eventually. This was just a little sooner than she thought. That could make things complicated. It also meant the mayor would be watching her comings and goings in town like a hawk from now on. She'd have to be more careful than ever.

⸻ ⬥ ⸻

An hour later, post-Melba's surprisingly effective jalapeño headache cure, Eden texted Michelle. Just as a precaution.

The mayor knows I'm behind it. Well, greatly suspects—enough to pay me a visit.

Thirty seconds later came the reply.

Do you require security?

Good question. Francine didn't have proof Eden was behind the hunt and also hadn't worked out how or whether the hunt would hurt her election prospects. As long as that stayed true, Eden was safe. For now.

No. But thanks.

Her phone pinged an hour later.

Thanks are not required. It is my job.

Right. *Well, that sure told me. And fuck my life, all over again.*

Eden wondered if screaming into her pillow would be effective.

Chapter 16

A Snake on Land

A WEEK CRAWLED BY. STILL no communication from Michelle. Apparently, she was a total pro at holding a grudge.

Eden consoled herself by pretending she did not in any way miss her boss's acerbic commentary and by catching up on Aggie's extensive Instagram posts. Kevin the guinea pig had quite a following now. He was like a Fabio of the rodent world despite only having one eye. She dropped a few supportive comments, telling Kevin he was "looking fine." Boosting his self-esteem suddenly seemed an important life goal, given her own goals had diminished to one thing: hoping Michelle would talk to her again.

Satisfied that Kevin knew his worth and Aggie had at least two hearts and one thumbs-up for her latest hair color (auburn), Eden geared up for her midnight mission.

After an hour, and with a clue left on the fence outside the rammed earth house, she scuttled back to the B&B. She was pulling off her mission-ops black beanie when Melba startled her at the door.

"The new clue's up, then?"

Eden stared back in surprise, offering an entirely too clever "um."

"Could you save me from having to go and look it up or asking my friends?" Melba teased.

Eden gave her a tiny grin. "Wish I could help, but I'm worn out by my scenic drive tonight. Straight to bed for me."

"Scenic drive at midnight?" Melba's thick eyebrows rose.

"Yup. Lots to see. Sorry. I need more rest."

"Go on, then." Melba chuckled. "I hope you feel better tomorrow."

"Me too."

It was so tempting to skip texting Michelle because Eden knew it would only hurt all over again getting a curt reply. Or no reply.

Still, she did it.

A snake on land that loves the water and seeks the light every twenty years.

The reply was almost instant. A demand for more information.

Why twenty? Not forty or thirty?

Huh. Someone was up late. And didn't that reply actually count as engagement? If you squinted?

Eden's heart leaped with excitement. She texted back: *Good question.*

Half an hour went by, then forty-five minutes. Eden was dozing when her phone pinged. With bleary eyes, she opened a text message to discover a link to an old newspaper story from twenty years ago.

The headline read: *Wingapo's water pipe ruptures*

A second text from Michelle followed straight after.

That pipeline of yours has ruptured many times over the years in many places. Why did you choose an event so long ago? One requiring research to find?

Eden replied.

1, I'm mixing it up. I don't want every clue to be solved by locals running around like crazy testing hunches. I want people who love to research to feel involved too.

2, It's the perfect rupture event because it comes with that news story you linked to, which I knew was online. Why? That news story actually says *exactly* where the pipe rupture happened. Ppl need to know where along 90 long miles of pipe to find the next clue. Lastly, that particular rupture happened in a place that's convenient. For reasons.

There was no reply. Eden eventually drifted off to sleep.

In the morning, she found a text waiting for her. She half expected: *Understood*. Or, even worse, a checkmark emoticon or something.

Instead, it read: *smart*.

Eden grinned. So sue her, that felt really damned good.

Chapter 17

The Iron Archer

"Long time no hear," Aggie announced solemnly the moment she answered Eden's call. "I thought I was going to have to advertise for a new best friend. And that's such a pain, recruiting potentials and getting them up to speed to understand nachos should be nuked not grilled and that Bacchus-F is the nectar of the gods."

Eden wiggled to get more comfortable in her bedroom window seat and grinned at Aggie's dramatics. Okay, so it had been two whole months since they'd last clapped eyes on each other. But it was only a week since she'd admired Kevin's Fabio-ness on Instagram, received an eye-roll emoji and comment back from Aggie that her guinea pig's ego was "puffed up enough, thank you very much," and been called "smart" by Michelle. All three events counted as highlights, which probably said a lot about how tragic her week had been.

Christ, it was so boring here. Especially not having nightly Skype calls from a certain prickly but fascinating boss to look forward to. There was no challenge in anything else these days.

"I'm flattered you missed me so much," she teased Aggie.

"Pfft. Missed, schmissed. I'm just making you feel bad because it's my birthday next week and I want to score some major suck-up gifts."

"Aggie, your birthday's not till next *month*. Go con someone else."

"Damn. You're no fun." She cackled. "I was just seeing if you remembered."

"Of course I remembered!" Eden had planned for this momentous occasion weeks ago. Aggie would soon be the proud owner of a new set of lounging pajamas with Kevin's adorable little face printed all over them. Something to replace the puppy PJs she usually wore. Eden anticipated opera singer-level squeals.

She glanced down over the little courtyard, forcing herself not to remember her shock at seeing Francine there two weeks ago, ruining her feeling of sanctuary. "As if I could forget the greatest day in living history."

"Ex-*actly*." Aggie laughed. "Just for that, I'm going to send you my latest intel, no invoice."

"Aggie, I didn't intend for you to work for nothing. At the very least, there was going to be major junk food quid pro quo on offer."

"Eh, no charge coz it was fun." A clattering noise sounded. "Okay, check your inbox. Your little scavenger hunt has now made it on the TV news in fourteen states."

Fourteen? Aggie truly was god-tier level at getting bites on social media. "Amazing! You're so good at this!"

"Wish I could claim all the credit. But a lot of them have been using the hunt as a convenient hook to segue into the mayoral election in Wingapo. Or the other way around. Election, then hunt."

"What? Why do any newsrooms outside of Maryland care about Francine or her piddling local election? She's a nobody nationally."

"It's not about Francine so much as that used-car guy. Bubba's got these atrocious ads everywhere, and the jingle has this annoying earworm catchiness." She burst into song about Bubba being the guy to handle "Cars—Used, New—Trucks."

Eden screwed up her face. "That's terrible. Why the hell is that catching on?"

"The acronym for Cars, Used, New, Trucks. He's telling everyone to vote for the guy who is good at dealing with *cunts*."

"Oh, sweet Jesus." Eden groaned. "So the local race is only getting attention because some jerk has a misogynistic jingle against a female mayor?"

"Yep."

"I really hate Bubba for making me take Francine's side on this. She deserves the respect of being torn down because of her policies, not for being a strong woman." Eden scowled. "That's so gross. The man has no imagination."

"Right? So, as far as I can tell, TV news directors everywhere have been *loving* putting it to air and feigning outrage at the 'maverick candidate in a small town going viral for a crude campaign ad…,' etcetera, etcetera."

"I'll bet. Christ, has Francine seen them? She'll go ballistic."

"She has, and she's going with dignified silence. She's been putting out a bunch of 'no comments,' saying responding is beneath her dignity."

"Wise." Eden hated the admission. "So, basically, because Bubba's an asshole and the people running newsrooms are generally sniggering little man-children, this is getting wide coverage. And in turn, they're also covering my scavenger hunt as 'Meanwhile, in more quirkiness from Wingapo'?"

"Yup. That's pretty much it."

Well. She might have wanted maximum attention on Francine come the hunt's final clue, but she didn't want it *this* way. "Bubba must have a death wish," Eden muttered. "Is he suicidal?"

"I wondered about that too. It's kind of stupid that a small operator like him wants to make a full-on enemy of Francine, given how much power she wields around there. Why would he do that, especially given he knows he's never going to win?"

"It *is* odd."

"Mmm." Aggie paused. "Want me to get Colin to look into it? He'll charge discount rates if it's for us."

"If it's for *you*, you mean," Eden teased. She wondered if it was possible for two people to combust from unresolved sexual tension. "Yes, please ask Colin. Tell him I'll pay double his usual rates if he can do it ASAP. But add that I *insisted* he must convey his findings to you over a candlelit dinner."

"Eden Celeste Lawless," Aggie said sternly, "I'm sure he has better things to do."

"Then he's a fool. But, bottom line, if Bubba's up to something deeper than a butter dish, I really want to know. Or it could just be he's an ass showing his true stripes and thinking being a sexist jerk is hilarious."

"Both are possible. And, yes, despite his sexist idiocy, he *has* managed to raise the profile of Wingapo, Francine Wilson, the election, and the scavenger hunt through the roof. So that's a win for you and your schemes, at least."

"I'll try not to choke on my delight. Thanks for the update. I have to fly. Catch up later?"

"Sure thing."

The call ended.

Eden shook her head. How had a quiet local election suddenly gone from zero interest to a national discussion?

A knock sounded.

"Come in," she called.

Melba stuck her head in. "Hon, I was wondering if you can save me and my yoga friends from having to do a trip out to Mulligan's?"

"Excuse me?"

Melba bustled in and sat on the edge of the bed, looking like a kid on Christmas morning. "The new clue appeared overnight at the water pipe: aiming down, aiming up, the iron archer misses but once."

"Oh, is that up already?" Eden asked innocently.

"You know it is." Melba chuckled. "I thought about it long and hard. See, there's an old apple farm near where the pipeline burst. Mulligan's? It's got this beautiful arrowhead fence. The little arrows go up and go down in a design the whole way along. I noticed it last time I was getting a batch of apples for my homemade preserves."

"Okayyy?" *Damn, score one for Melba. That was fast.*

"So, if I were to drive all the way out there to look at it, I'd find an arrowhead missing, wouldn't I? It's gotten broken off or something, somewhere along the fence?"

"I wouldn't waste my effort driving out there," Eden said neutrally.

"Oh." Melba's expression fell. "It just seemed to fit."

"Well, yes, it does, doesn't it? But, I mean, surely it's too soon for the next clue to be up given this one's just appeared."

"Oh!" Melba's eyes brightened. "Of course! I got all carried away and didn't think of that." She beamed. "Great."

"Hypothetically speaking," Eden added, because it seemed the thing to do.

"Yes, of course. I'm silent as the grave." Melba paused. "When *do* you think a new clue might go up? Exactly?"

Eden shrugged. "Most clues seem to be up exactly a week after the previous one, don't they? So, it'd be…Tuesday night? Maybe?" She wouldn't want Melba driving all the way out to Mulligan's Farm only to find nothing—yet.

Melba nodded, plucked a pen from under her head scarf and scribbled *Tuesday* and *clue* on her palm. "Thanks. I'll tell my friends to cool their jets for a bit." She exited with a wide grin and jaunty stride.

Eden smiled at the delight radiating from her. How easy it was to give people simple pleasures. Eden hoped they'd remember the fun they were having and be forgiving of her when the hunt's true purpose was revealed.

Seven hours later, Aggie called again, sounding a little sloshed and a lot happier.

"Had a great dinner with Colin," she said cheerfully. "Grrrreat."

"I'm pleased to hear it." Eden chuckled. "Soooo… is the night still young?" she asked hopefully.

"Oh no, no. I sent him home. I'm not sure we're ready for more yet."

"Because far be it for you to rush into a relationship after such a short time knowing each other. What is it now? Fifteen years? Sixteen? You'll be retirees by the time you dip a toe in."

"What if we're better as friends?"

"Aggie, do you want to kiss me?"

"What?!" There was an unflattering barfing noise in the background. "Eww. No."

"Exactly. And we're great friends. Yet you don't want to kiss me the way you do Colin. Consider it a sign."

Silence fell.

"I notice," Eden continued, "you don't deny the Colin-kissing urge."

"I hate you."

"No you don't, you love me. And you love Colin. Just not in the same way. Now, tell me what he found so you can go back to thinking about kissing your man and not making your move."

"I'm going to ignore that on account of the fact that I still hate you. And in answer to your question, Bubba has a PAC."

Eden blinked. "You. Are. Joking."

"Nope. And it's a PAC, not a SuperPAC, so Colin can't find out who's contributing to getting Bubba elected. They call themselves the Bubba Bros."

"They sound like idiotic frat boys."

"The name's deceiving. There's nothing juvenile about the support they're giving their candidate. You know PACs aren't supposed to coordinate with the candidate in any way. It's sort of like having a few friends informally going around, putting up bunting and signs and telling everyone that you're really great and should be the mayor, but without running it past you first that that's what they're going to do."

"So, what are the Bubba Bros doing for their candidate?"

"Well, they took that sexist ad Bubba posted to YouTube about being good with...*cunts*..." Aggie hissed the word, clearly displeased she was forced to say it. "...and they made their own version based on it. They turned it into a slick, well-packaged, crazy piece of pop-culture shtick that would play well on social media and news services. *That's* the version that's been playing everywhere. They're the reason the ad got widely distributed and landed on news desks across America. No way Bubba had the means or the brains to do that himself."

"And *that's* why all the networks picked it up," Eden concluded. "Sounds like the Bubba Bros PAC has connections?"

"They definitely have media or PR training. They're a really sharp outfit."

"Why would they want to help *Bubba*?"

"Maybe they hate Francine?" Aggie suggested.

"Then they should back the doc. At least Ron's not sexist."

"He's boring, though. Bubba is capturing attention. He's exciting and funny. Face it: the media and the masses enjoy being entertained." Aggie tutted. "Anyway, that's all Colin could dig up for us: Bubba's backers are pros. And, for no reason discernible, they've chosen a used-car jerk to get behind who has no hope of winning."

"I don't like this. It's giving me 'something's off' vibes."

"Imagine how Francine's feeling. She was sitting pretty and had her re-election all nicely stitched up. Now the whole of America is watching her being mocked and called a cunt in a catchy jingle."

Eden gritted her teeth. "Shit. I *really* hate feeling sorry for her."

"Me too. Still, look on the bright side: now the mayor has someone else in her evil laser sights, not just you."

"I suppose. I'll take it."

"Good," Aggie said. "Not much else we *can* take from this."

Eden had an awful thought. "Aggie? You don't think Bubba could win, do you? I know he's an idiot and an oaf, but unfortunately that doesn't automatically make him unelectable in this country. He'd be like voting in a wrecking ball."

"A better question is which would be worse? I mean as awful as Francine is, she's at least competent at running the city."

"She's corrupt! Aggie, she *censors* people! She bribes the police! She got Dad fired!" Eden's outrage spiked. "How can you defend her?"

"I'm not. *Edie*, I promise I'm not." Aggie's voice was soothing. "But I'm asking a serious question. Who would be worse: the sexist pig who thinks calling women the c-word is funny and has no policies at all? Or, the corrupt, cunning mayor, who terrifies everyone into getting into line…*including* all the services and departments running Wingapo County? She oversees an efficient ship, even though she's the pits in every other way and cuts corners on maintaining her own properties."

Eden fell silent, outrage filling her every pore. "Well, I choose option C, the sweet, retired doctor. He might be kind of checked out, but at least he'd do no harm. Which is kind of fitting since he's a doctor."

"Option C it is. I'm glad I don't have to choose between A and B because those are terrible choices."

"Yeah." Eden sighed. "Let's just hope Dr. Ron is exactly the brand of steady and boring the voters want. Especially once I've roasted their queen."

"Well, maybe take some heart in the fact that no one loves a used-car salesman. I think we're good."

"From your lips to the universe's ears."

Please be right, Agatha Teo.

Aiming down, aiming up, the iron archer misses but once.

Michelle mulled over the new clue that had just landed on her phone. Another archery-themed clue?

It wouldn't be about targets or bullseyes because Lawless had done that already. Not bows, either, for the same reason. Which only left arrows. Iron ones.

Arrows go down, arrows go up. It almost sounded like a pattern. A... repeating pattern?

Hold on. She'd seen wrought-iron fences with arrowhead designs.

Michelle grabbed her phone and searched for the pattern, confirming she was right. The head of the arrows went up and down and crossed on the shafts. She saved off a photo of it, then sent Lawless a text.

Obviously I don't know who in Wingapo has an arrowhead fence but someone clearly does. I'm guessing there's a gap in one somewhere? Where the archer misses but once.

A minute later, Lawless texted back.

Remind me never to bet against you.

"That is not a sound course of events, no," Michelle said to herself. Her phone pinged with a new incoming text.

The fence is outside Mulligan's Farm, which can be seen from where the last clue was at the water pipe. The farm's old fence is well known enough that locals should figure it out sooner or later. Melba already has.

Michelle debated whether to reply. It wouldn't do to encourage Lawless—she'd already seen where that led. But on the other hand, the woman had been behaving herself lately.

And it's not like I miss her or anything.

Michelle scowled at her inner voice. That unfortunate *missing Lawless* business had been a surprising side effect of terminating their Skype calls. Lawless might cross lines more frequently than a subway map, but she'd also been entertaining.

She sent back a reply in spite of every part of her brain sounding off warning klaxons.

Good for Melba. Anything else to report?

Perhaps Lawless *could* manage to stay on topic for once. Okay, that felt a little churlish. But Michelle was allowed to be furious. Lawless had invaded her privacy and blurred the professional with the personal—along with her grandmother, who had apologized at length when confronted with her collusion.

"I meant no harm, bubbeleh. I'm sorry I love to meddle," Hannah had said, looking crestfallen. The old woman had even tried to argue *she'd* been the one to bring up all those invasive topics.

The topic of Alberto, Michelle could well believe was her grandmother's doing but not whether Michelle was dating anyone.

No, there had definitely been *two* traitors tangoing that night. Her lips thinned at the reminder. It had been a nightmare when Alberto had aired her private business in her work sphere, and she was in no mood for a repeat performance.

She was still having trouble entirely forgiving her grandmother. That counted double for Lawless.

Her phone pinged again.

There is something else. I should switch to email to fill you in. It's too long for text.

That sounded tedious. With a sigh, Michelle opened Skype and initiated a call. After the longest of moments, Lawless answered.

"Um, hi?" The woman appeared to have a bird's nest for hair. And she looked... paler? Had something happened?

"What's wrong?" Michelle demanded, concern flooding her before she could stop herself. Had the mayor been threatening her again? What else had been transpiring in Michelle's absence?

"Wrong?" Lawless blinked. "Oh, well, it's not wrong so much as weird." She looked uncertain, her eyes darting to Michelle's and then away. As if she half expected to be scolded. "Just that Bubba Nevada, that used-car salesman in the mayoral race, has a PAC now, and they're promoting a sexist ad of his all over the place. It's being picked up by the media."

Michelle scowled. *Oh that.* "Yes."

Lawless sounded surprised. "You knew?"

"Of course. It's a bit hard to avoid that awful jingle. Every misogynist in DC seems to think it's funny to hum it under their breath whenever a powerful woman is around." A fact to which she could personally attest—and she had fired the man on the spot. "Do you know who is behind the PAC?"

"No. PACs don't have to disclose donors."

Michelle rolled her eyes. "Obviously. But I meant have you decided to find out?"

"Is that relevant?" Lawless asked cautiously. *Too* cautiously. "I mean, do...did you want me to find out?"

Her newfound timidness was grating. "I didn't say that," Michelle said in irritation. "I was just curious as to whether that was a thread you're pulling or not."

A confused expression creased Lawless's brow. "Um... Should I *want* to pull it?"

"How would I know? *You're* there; I'm not." Frustration mounted. "This is *your* assignment, not mine. Am I expected to think for you too?"

Lawless reared back, hurt searing across her gentle face. "I was asking what you wanted from me. I'm checking with my *boss*," she emphasized, "in case this was important to you, because my assignment is actually about the mayor. Personally, I don't think it matters. Bubba feels like a red herring. A man hunting his fifteen minutes of fame. But if you want me to dive down that rabbit hole, I will, and I'll be extremely thorough, but I need to know if that's what you want me to put my time into." Her wide eyes turned stormy.

Michelle quashed the urge to apologize although suddenly she felt like a panda torturer. No. She'd done nothing wrong. Lawless wasn't thinking for herself. And why was she acting so unsettled and nervous? She wasn't usually like this. She was side-eying Michelle as if half-afraid to say the wrong thing.

She's acting like your other employees. Don't forget, this *was what you claimed you wanted from her.*

Michelle's lips curled into a sneer at that appalling thought. "What I *want* is for you to use your initiative and not ask me for permission on every little thing."

Lawless leaned back in her chair, and finally a flash of old fire entered her eyes. "Riiight. Well, *using my initiative*, I'm going to end this call because you're taking your weird, bad mood out on your *employee*. And, as said employee, I'm not putting up with it. So good night. I hope you're feeling better tomorrow."

She ended the call with a stab of a finger and a glower on her beautiful face.

Michelle exhaled. Well, that had been…unsettling.

The very end of the call had been a relief: The woman had some gumption left, at least. If Lawless had turned fawning or apologetic, it would have annoyed her even more. Was seeing the upfront, blunt woman who had passed her truth test on day one too much to hope for?

"Darling?" Her grandmother stuck her head in.

Michelle swiveled sharply in her chair, wondering how much she'd heard.

"Would you like a kichel and tea?" The old woman smiled encouragingly. "I made a batch today. My cookies are always good for what ails you."

"What makes you think something ails me?" Michelle asked irritably.

"Well, you finished your call early with your friend, so—"

"She is *not* my friend," Michelle snapped. How many times did she have to point this out? Then she choked on something—God only knew what—and her vision became weirdly blurry.

Her grandmother's face turned remorseful. "I'm so sorry, bubbeleh. My meddling has finally ended in tears."

"I'm not in tears!" Michelle gasped at that preposterous statement, trying to get in some breaths. She lifted her fingers to her eyes and was staggered when they came away wet. *Am I finally having a breakdown? Is that it?*

"She's an employee!" Michelle pushed the words out in a rush. "An infuriating, rule-breaking one at that. Yet she suddenly needs hand-holding, asking all these meek questions and seeking guidance instead of taking her own initiative. She wasn't like this before!"

"Mmm," Hanna said. "Fancy asking your boss questions. Scandalous." She smiled gently, but it came off as concerned. "So... kichlach?"

Michelle slumped and ran up the white flag, too weary to be argumentative. "Fine."

"Such enthusiasm. Do you know I slaved over a hot stove for hours today?"

"Hours?" Michelle snorted. "Is that a fact?"

"Oh well...at least," her grandmother huffed out a breath and made a *whatever* motion, "two, three hours."

Having helped her safta make the cute, twisted, bow-tie cookies many times over the years, Michelle was well aware exactly how long kichlach took. The complete prep and bake time under Hannah's expert eye was a slick fifty minutes. "Well, I'd better make the most of your Homer's *Odyssey* in the kitchen."

"Indeed you must," her safta said sagely. "And then you can explain to me properly why you're so angry that an employee bothers you just by asking questions."

Michelle's expression fell. "Must we?"

"No, but if I could make one small observation: I'm thinking Eden's suddenly all business because you told her off for being too interested in your life. And could it be…you miss her other questions? Maybe you don't mean to be angry with her about work at all? You're just sorry that the woman you liked challenging you and being interested in other things has gone?"

"No." Michelle said nothing more, clamping her jaw hard enough for pain to shoot upwards, and strode into the kitchen.

Later, feeling grumpy the entire time, she endured an admittedly delicious kichel and two sickly-sweet cups of tea to which her grandmother insisted on adding too much sugar.

The urge grew to send Lawless a text apologizing for being unreasonable.

Fortunately, she resisted.

Chapter 18

Hooked on Going Low

MICHELLE'S WORK WAS GOING FROM bad to infuriating. Two deals they'd lined up fell through for unrelated reasons. Each had been several months in the making. One had collapsed due to an employee's unforgivable error. Michelle had fired the woman immediately.

The other... She wasn't sure what had gone wrong, but heads would roll. Time was valuable. The Fixers couldn't afford to waste it on dead-end assignments.

"Tilly," she called with a weary sigh. "Why are the Ankara files I asked for not on my desk?"

Her PA entered her office, clearly so surprised that she'd actually forgotten to hide it. "Because I gave them to you and then you gave them to Peterson three hours ago."

Michelle cursed herself, appalled at her error. Forgetfulness was not one of her traits. She prided herself on being razor-sharp at all times. "I'm...not impressed," she muttered.

"By?"

Me. "Everything." She glared around her office as though it held the answers. "Why did Maddington screw up so badly? He's never given us any issues before."

Tilly didn't answer.

"Well?"

"Oh, I thought it was rhetorical."

That almost counted as snippy for the consummate professional Tilly.

Michelle narrowed her eyes in warning. What was going *on* around here? Why was everyone suddenly screwing up and challenging her?

"You're taking your weird, bad mood out on your employee," Lawless had said last night.

Michelle did not appreciate being told she was in a *weird, bad mood* to start with. Though perhaps, given Tilly's reaction, Lawless had been close to the mark.

Goddamn it.

"Why did Maddington screw up?" Michelle repeated evenly.

"I assume it was because the deadline was too tight," Tilly said cautiously. "He cut corners to meet it. Therefore, he hadn't finished backgrounding by the time he was supposed to present his report and begin the mission. And…I'm speculating here…Maddington hoped he was right when he theorized that the billionaire would still be lying low at the time we started our operation."

"So it's my fault for setting such a tight deadline?" Michelle frowned. "I cannot control when elusive businessmen stick their heads out of the woodwork. Maddington should have *adapted*. Figured out a plan B in case the man suddenly reappeared on a whim." She glowered. "Now we've lost our one shot *and* our client. Christ, Maddington's a disappointment. Why must I think for my staff too? Again!"

"Again?" Tilly tilted her head in curiosity. "What else has happened?"

Michelle stilled her features. "Nothing. It's nothing. Lawless is…" She faded out.

"Lawless is what?"

"Badgering me for specifics on her assignment when she should work it out for herself."

Tilly considered that. "If she bothers you so much, why not cease Skyping with her?"

Michelle couldn't admit she'd already stopped Skyping with her because Tilly would only ask why. "Because she's too green not to require supervision."

"So when she seeks advice because she's green, you regard that as an error? Even though you've just said she requires supervision?"

"Yes! She should just know!" Michelle glared at her PA even though she could hear how ridiculous she sounded.

Tilly looked just plain confused.

Michelle couldn't blame her. She was acting way out of character. So much for being the cool, controlled, levelheaded boss at all times. A headache threatened to sink its claws in, and Michelle wanted to scream in frustration. *Not now!*

"Why does it bother you she asked for direction?" Tilly finally asked.

Because she didn't used to treat me like her boss and now she does, and I hate it.

"I believe you were correct the first time." Michelle sidestepped that neatly. "I should sever the Skype calls. Treat her like everyone else. If she fails, she fails." Her lips pinched.

"Do you think she will?" Tilly asked curiously. "Fail?"

"I'm not sure. She has a sound approach, but the mayor in Wingapo is cunning, powerful, and corrupt."

"Like half of DC," Tilly noted.

"And the rest," Michelle muttered to herself. She waved Tilly out of her office, then tried to focus on her work.

Ten minutes later, her phone pinged with a text.

Why is Tilly suddenly telling me our Skype calls will cease because you've become too busy?

Oh, great. Her PA had decided to take the initiative. And Michelle couldn't complain about it since she'd just been grumbling about staff not doing that. What a perfect day.

Suddenly the thought of Lawless revealing to Tilly they'd already stopped Skyping seemed a distinct possibility. She did not want that can of worms opened.

Michelle sent a hurried reply.

Do not contact my assistant. She has actual work to do.

Um, she texted me?

And that was a one-off. Michelle harumphed as she hit send. Actually harumphed. *Ms. Zimmermann was taking the initiative.*

Unexpectedly, by the sound of it, Lawless shot back. *Okay, what's going on over there?*

Just focus on your work. Continue to send the clues each week for quality control purposes.

Quality control? Who was she kidding? She'd been thoroughly enjoying solving the puzzles.

Quality control. Uh-huh, came the text back as though Eden had just read her mind. *I'll do that, but it's less fun solving them alone. Don't deny it; we both know it. ;)*

Michelle stared. Lawless had actually sent her a winky-face emoticon. As if Michelle wasn't one of the most powerful forces in DC, someone who could crush anyone like a bug, up to and including a sitting president.

And Eden Lawless had just sent her a *winky face.*

Michelle should probably think up something suitably acidic to say about that...except she couldn't help but notice the heady wash of relief that Lawless wasn't being overly cautious around her anymore.

With enormous satisfaction at that, Michelle returned to her work. And this time, for some odd reason, her headache unclenched its claws and she found her focus.

Some days, Michelle absolutely loathed knowing everyone's secrets. It made it hard to respect people.

People such as Phyllis Kensington, for instance. The woman had been all over her like a hot rash at their business meeting this evening, hands wandering under Michelle's skirt every time the senator's minion's back was turned. They were seated side by side at a conference table that afforded the senator far too many opportunities to be indiscreet.

"It's been too long," Kensington whispered hot against Michelle's ear. "And I need to get off soon or I'll explode."

"You have a husband for that," Michelle reminded her churlishly. "Divorce him, and other opportunities might present themselves. I'm somewhat busy at the moment covering up his statutory rape of an underage teen."

"I don't need other opportunities when you're here," Kensington purred, completely skating past the barb. "I could make it worth your while, make you forget your work. I'll slide my tongue deep inside—"

"Ma'am?" Kensington's staffer, Aaron Bolt, interrupted.

The man saved Michelle from having to find a way to say she never wanted Kensington's tongue anywhere near her ever again since the woman didn't seem to find her husband's sexually predatory behavior to be a deal breaker.

"Your car's ready," Bolt finished.

"Oh, such a shame," Kensington said airily. "I thought Ms. Hastings and I had a little more time to…*catch up*."

The innuendo might only have been obvious to Michelle, but she hated it anyway. The presumption. As if she were some cut-price street walker who would say yes to any demand because of who was asking. She darted Kensington a warning look as the staffer exited the room.

"We should extend our private discussion," Kensington told her, eyes hungrier now that Bolt was gone. Without warning, she suddenly slid over and straddled Michelle's lap and rubbed against her.

The heat from between her thighs was searing. *Jesus*.

"We'll go to the back of my car," Kensington decided. "And I'll get the driver to circle the block for half an hour. Or maybe an hour. I haven't taken you in my car before. We'll have to be *so* quiet." Her lips slid to Michelle's earlobe. "Can you do that for me?"

Michelle's phone pinged in her pocket. *Thank you, universe*. "I'm very sorry," she said with immense gravity, "I really must attend to this urgent matter."

"But you didn't even look at your phone," Kensington said with a pout. She pressed herself hard against Michelle and slid a hand under her skirt to cup her center. "How do you know it's urgent?"

Michelle hated her body's automatic reaction to the touch, the lurch in response. She eased out from under the senator, murmuring rapid excuses before Kensington could argue further.

Once alone in the elevator, she pulled out her phone.

Hooked on going low

Finally. All day, Michelle had been aware it was clue day. She'd been looking forward to this for hours, although she would rather not admit that to herself.

Hooked on going low. She repeated it a few times as the floor numbers ticked down.

Her mind was a complete blank as she stepped out of the elevator and headed for her town car. Maybe Kensington's raging arousal had short-circuited her brain. It was hard to think with that many pheromones in the air. Her body was still thrumming a little, having not yet gotten the memo that Kensington's touch was a no-go zone.

"Evening, ma'am," her driver said, opening her door.

She nodded at him and slid inside the luxurious leather interior, mind still on the clue.

Hooked on going low.

Total blank. Nothing. Nothing at all. That wasn't like her to be completely tapped out.

It occurred to her how much she'd been picking up nonverbal cues from Lawless to solve these things. Not every time, of course, but often. The other woman sometimes punched words or lifted her eyebrows when she spoke, giving hints as to what was important.

"Mr. Ward," she spoke to her driver, "what would come to mind if I said: Hooked on going low?"

The man glanced at her in the rearview mirror. "Is this like a game?"

"A puzzle."

"Ahh," he said thoughtfully, "Hooked? Like a fishing thing? Maybe?"

How on earth hadn't she even considered that? It was the simplest of guesses.

"Got no clue on the going-low part," he added. "Sorry."

She thanked him and settled back into her seat.

Lawless had given away a hint last time about how her hunt was structured: all the newest clues, the ones outside the town itself, were in proximity to each other. So the rammed earth house was near the water pipe, which was in sight of the arrowhead fence. The answer to this clue therefore had to be in sight of the previous one.

What had Lawless said was the name of the farm was with the arrow fence? Mulligan's?

Michelle called it up on her mapping app, then zoomed out. Several water bodies appeared. Water…fishing… She scanned their names.

One caught her eye instantly.

Bass Pond. She clicked the description.

Bass Pond is famous for its beautiful bass (largemouth and smallmouth). The largest bass ever recorded at Bass Pond weighed…

Bass. As in fish. As in *hooked*.

Bass. As in music. *Going low*.

She took a screen shot of the map, the pond in the center, and texted it to Eden without comment.

Her phone dinged with a text a few minutes later.

You're freaking me out right now. Tell me the truth: Did you sell your soul to the devil for all the hunt's answers? Let me know if I should send around an exorcist to peel that demon soul right out of you. I know a guy. No charge.

Michelle could not hold back the laugh that burbled up. It was shocking enough that her driver's wide-eyed gaze shot to hers in the rearview mirror.

Eyes front, she wanted to say. *This is private.*

Wait, *private?*

"Can't we go any faster?" she snapped. Her tone was part warning, lest he get any ideas of sharing around work that he'd seen the CEO laughing it up in the back of his car. All she had left was her lethal reputation, and that needed to be preserved.

"Yes, ma'am," he said, nodding sharply. And stepped on it.

Smart boy.

Chapter 19

Separate the Pair

"My boss is mad at me," Eden confessed to Aggie over the phone between bites of lentil burger from her now favorite café. She was at an outside table that gave her the best street view of Wingapo at lunchtime.

"Well, who wouldn't be," Aggie informed her. "I mean, you *are* super annoying, and I only put up with you because you're my best friend. And because I'm expecting a good birthday present."

"Hilarious," Eden said dryly. "Anyway, she's stopped Skyping me, and we're down to a text or two a week."

"Isn't that a good thing? She trusts you more and doesn't have to supervise you? I don't know why you thought it was a good thing in the first place having your boss demand a progress report every night. That's pretty insulting."

"It wasn't insulting. I mean, at first, yeah, I thought she was checking up on me, micromanaging. But then I realized she wasn't. I was a diversion from her high-powered job, I guess. When I realized that, it became sort of a thing, trying to make her react." *And she needed it. She's way too stressed.*

"So maybe she's too busy to be diverted right now? And need I remind you that you're always telling me that people can be going through their own drama, so if they give you static over nothing, it might not be about you at all."

"I suppose. It's just..." Eden screwed up her face as she tried to find the right word. "I don't know. She's hella prickly and cagey and always telling me off about crossing lines, but she was also smart and challenging. It was fun. For me anyway."

"Well, if you were having fun then she probably was too."

Eden hoped so. "But now it's over."

"And the job will be over soon too, so it doesn't matter, right? Isn't the election happening in a little over a week? Whatever you're doing there will be done, and that'll be that with your mysterious boss?"

Eden's chest tightened a little at the reminder. "Yes. Of course." The spread of election posters all over town had been making her feel oddly deflated for weeks now. The closer it came to the day, the more depressed she felt.

"It's not like you're friends or anything," Aggie said. "Right?"

Of course, never that. Michelle would sooner die. "Right," she ground out. And hell if that didn't hurt.

Soon, too soon, Michelle would be gone. Might as well get her brain prepared now. Stop trying to be friendly with someone who didn't want to know her and had repeatedly made that clear. Eden would start with the next text, being all *just the facts, ma'am*, and leave it at that.

"How's the mood in town?" Aggie asked. "Election-wise? And the polls?"

"Expectations are that Francine will romp it in. That stupid sexist jingle is everywhere. Bubba's hired people to drive his trucks around with it blasting from speakers."

"Ew."

"Yeah, it's really annoying."

"Francine must be furious."

"Yep. Not that she can do anything. The words *cars, used, new*, and *trucks* aren't obscene in their own right. But I'm sure she'd love to single-handedly smash every truck Bubba owns. God, I wish I knew who the Bubba Bros were. It seemed like Michelle wanted me to find out, but she didn't outright say, and that's why we argued and stopped talking."

"That is the dumbest reason I've ever heard of in my life."

"It *is* pretty stupid."

"She sounds like hard work. She's your boss, right?" Aggie huffed out a breath. "So if she wants you to do something, she should ask! Clearly!"

"Right?" Eden said, loving how her friend always *got* her. "I mean, why is it weird that I asked what she wanted me to do? Why does she think I should psychically divine her wishes and take the initiative?"

"Is that what she said?"

"Something like it."

"Mmph." Aggie sounded aggrieved. "High-maintenance women, my friend. *Avoid.* That's advice for the personal and professional."

"I know." Lord, how she knew.

"So, what are you up to today?"

"A new clue's up."

"How many are left?"

"This is number ten of twelve. I'll drop in the final pair a few days apart throughout this week. Last one will go up the day before the election. And I'm stoking a bit of mischief in the newspaper's forum group, keeping some wild theories going. Not that I need to do much. There are twelve thousand people now in that group. The paper itself has stopped even pretending to not care. Every new clue is now a little story on page one entitled: *For those in the hunt.*"

"Cool. So they'll be forced to cover the end result, then."

"That's the plan. They can't talk about everything up to the last clue, then ignore it because it's politically uncomfortable for their preferred candidate."

A shadow fell over the table, and she looked up. Eden swallowed. "Aggie? I gotta go," she squeezed out.

"Hon? You sound weird. You okay?"

"Yeah…it's just…it's Dad. Dad's here."

"Whoa! Okay, call me later. Bye!"

The phone went dead, and Eden stared up into her old man's lined face.

"May I join you?" he asked, waving at the chair opposite.

"Yeah," Eden said, then worried that sounded too indifferent. "Please."

Peter Nelson lowered himself into the chair and leaned on his forearms. He seemed craggier than his sixty-five years. White stubble edged his jaw, and he was less rounded, more angular than she remembered. The cloud of annoyance from their last meeting was absent.

"Hi." He looked at her. "I was passing by and saw you. Was deciding whether to make myself known or not. I heard you on the phone. That was Aggie, right?" His eyebrows went up.

So shaggy and familiar. A wash of nostalgia flooded her.

"How is she?" her dad asked.

"Same old Aggie." Eden offered a cautious smile.

"Still in love with that Colin fellow?"

"Like I said, same old Aggie."

He smiled. "I always liked her. So much gumption."

"Since when do you like gumption?" she asked, genuinely surprised.

"You *have* met River Lawless, right?" His eyes crinkled. "The woman I *married*?"

"So it's just me you have an issue with. *My* protest work."

"Maybe we shouldn't go there. I come in peace." He lifted his wide hands, and she saw immediately they were rough now, as if used to doing manual labor.

When she'd been a girl, she'd loved how smooth his doctor hands were, soft and gentle. "What are you doing with yourself these days?" Eden asked, diverting the topic to safer waters.

"I'm teaching woodshop and leatherworking," he said. "I picked it up as a hobby when I got myself sorted out. The kids at the local high school seem to get a kick out of my classes. And I run the workshop at The Shed."

"You run it?" She studied him in surprise. "I thought you were a participant?"

"Well, I was once. That's where I learned my new skills. Then I took over the program. Not just the woodworking stuff, all of it. The Shed is now my operation. It's good to give something back."

"Oh." Her eyebrows lifted. "Wow, that's something."

"You thought I was a hopeless case, didn't you?" Another smile tugged at his mouth. "I know, I know. I didn't exactly disabuse of you the notion because you caught me flatfooted and I was more than a little shocked. My moods aren't always great. I just wasn't in a good place the day we saw each other."

"And you are now?"

"I think so." He glanced around. "Sun is shining. Birds are singing. And my girl's back in town. So tell me, what have you been up to?"

His eyes fixed on her with an intensity she wasn't accustomed to seeing. It had been a long time since he'd seemed so focused. In fact, she hadn't seen this expression since she was in her teens.

"A bit of this and that," she said. "I wanted to see some old haunts. I checked out the old house. Weird seeing the little tree you planted much bigger."

He nodded. "But what brought you back here? I thought you hated Wingapo."

"I hated who drove me out of town more," Eden said. "You sound like it's shocking I'd come back home and see what's changed."

"It *is* shocking. When you left, you vowed never to come back while Wilson lived here. Well, she doesn't just live here, she runs the place. So I have to wonder, Eden, why you're here? And please tell me you're not behind that disgusting ad Bubba's blasting everywhere." Disapproval crossed his face.

"Why don't you think it's Bubba himself?"

He inhaled. "Man's about as sharp as a rusty lawn mower. It can't be him behind it."

"I agree. Even if Francine deserves to go down, *that's* not the way."

He studied her for a long while. "Not the way?" The question was loaded. "Are you saying *you* have another way?"

Her heart sank. Then sank some more. Eden gathered up her things. Put some money into the leather folder on the table with a generous tip. Shoved her sunglasses on her nose and made to rise.

"What?" he asked.

"Francine sent you." It was too much to ask the universe that he'd been here just for her. "Of all the lowdown, underhanded, shitty things to do."

She truly wasn't sure which was worse: the mayor using her father or her father going along with it.

"Excuse me?" Both shaggy eyebrows shot up.

"What did she promise you?" Eden asked sharply. "What's your betrayal earned you?"

"*My* betrayal?" he asked, his lips tugging down. "That's an interesting choice of word. I'm here, preparing to forgive you, and you accuse me—"

"Forgive *me*?" Eden cut him off. "For what? Doing the right thing by trying to tell everyone Francine was a common slumlord? I'm *sorry* you lost your job, and I'm *sorry* Wilson's a vindictive bitch who did that to you. But blame her, not me. You've fixed so much of your life, and that's great. I'm happy for you. But why can't you fix this?" She tapped her temple. "The part of you that blames me for your own mess."

He stared at her. "I don't blame you for what Francine did to me."

"You don't?" Shock rippled through her.

"No." He stared longer. "A part of me blames you for your mother leaving me. If you had never pulled that stunt, River never would have been forced to take sides. And she always loved you more." He sagged. "I was never *quite* enough, but you...you were almost enough."

"Almost enough for what?" Eden whispered.

"Almost enough to love more than her causes. And knowing that stung; I guess it still does a little." He shook his head. "And I know it's not rational. But because I can't bring myself to hate the woman I love for not loving me enough to want to keep me, I channeled my frustration to you. I know that's not fair, honey, but it's what happened."

"I'm glad you agree it's not fair." Eden regarded him. "I'm just surprised you admit it. You didn't used to be this self-aware."

"Been a few years now. Time makes you take stock. Quitting the bottle does that too. Maybe one day I'll be able to look at you and not see River in your eyes. Not see her fire. Not see all the ways you're just like her: captivating and astonishing and charismatic. And just like River, you were everything that impresses me and makes me want to be a better man while I also feel unworthy. The thing is, Eden—everyone is flawed."

"I know that."

"Do you? I made *one* mistake."

"It was a pretty huge mistake. You asked me to back down on a moral issue. To grovel before Francine the slumlord in the hopes you'd get your job back. Mom would never endorse that. She could never forgive…" Eden trailed off.

"Exactly. Now do you see?" He glanced up Main Street then met her eye. "Your mother could never forgive. One strike. Once you're out of favor, you're out. I made a mistake. River held me—hell, holds everyone—to an impossible standard."

"It's not an impossible standard to expect you to do the right thing morally."

"That's not the standard I meant: it was her expecting I could never make a mistake. And when I did, she no longer wanted me. After I understood that, I fell."

"But, Dad, you didn't make *one* mistake. You kept doubling down. How many bars did you hit? How many fights were you involved in? You were unemployable as a doctor. That's a lot of falling."

"I'm only human." His eyes met hers. "And so are you. Bear that in mind. Holding people to impossible standards isn't fair, certainly not any more than deciding that those who fail some rightness purity test can never be forgiven."

She supposed he made a good argument. It was complicated. Humans always were. Eden conceded his point with a small nod. "So, tell me the truth: Did Francine send you here?"

"Yes."

Damn him. Anger coursed through her.

He regarded her. "The mayor offered me Health Adviser to Wingapo Council in return."

"Lucky you," Eden snapped. "Back in the medical game at last."

He shrugged. "I'll be turning her down. She might have sent me here—in fact she has someone watching us as we speak to make sure I'm doing it." He again squinted down the street. "But once she'd put the idea in my head, I thought, why not? Is it too late to mend bridges with my girl?"

Eden stared at him in astonishment. "I don't know how you can even talk to her after what she's done."

"That's the thing about being at rock bottom, honey. You learn there's very little in life you can no longer consider beneath you. I've done some of the worst things imaginable when I was too drunk to care. I found that pride is the biggest lie we tell ourselves. Pride is *nothing*. If you can put ego aside, you can do anything. It's freeing not to care about how things look. How you look. What others are thinking. I would talk to anyone now about anything and feel no shame for it. You can learn a whole lot, if you listen."

"She's evil, Dad! You know she tore our family apart!"

"She's a woman with a whole lot of fears. More than she lets most people see. She's really worked up about that Bubba Nevada ad. She wants to know who's been smearing her, and she's so busy being mad as hell that it's all she can see. And most people who look at her see only her power and her perfect politician mask or her fury. I see someone hurt and alone."

"Oh, Christ." Eden's stomach lurched in dismay. "Don't you dare go soft on her."

He chuckled softly. "That's never happening. I've not forgotten what she did. What she's doing. But I take people how I find them these days. The parts of them that *are* understandable I try to understand. It really simplifies life. The world really isn't good and evil, black and white, despite the way you and your mother see it. It's a patchwork quilt of many things. A bit of this and that makes up a person. And Mayor Wilson is someone going through a heap of pain who is terrified of losing her power. And I know exactly how that feels."

"You are *nothing* like Francine Wilson!"

"Aren't I? Some days I think I have more in common with her than I ever had with your mother."

"Don't say that!" Horror swept through her. She still loved her dad, warts and all. She loathed Francine, who did *the* worst things just because she could. What an unfair comparison.

"The mayor understands we're all weak. Your mother doesn't."

"Dad, stop talking like this. Please?"

"Why?" Her father met her eye earnestly. "Does the truth make you uncomfortable?"

"It's not the truth!"

"Which part? That I'm not weak? Because I assure you I am. Everyone in Wingapo knows I am. Or is it that your mother doesn't forgive weakness? Despite me pleading for a second chance? It's pretty obvious that she doesn't."

The blood roared in Eden's ears. Her mom was her hero. A role model! She stood up for what was *right*. So did Eden. How could that ever be a bad thing?

Suddenly, Michelle's throwaway line slid into her brain. "Your mother sets a high standard. Is that why you do what you for a living? You want to make her proud?"

Your mother sets a high standard.

Was it an *impossibly* high standard? Had that been what she meant?

Was her father right, that he'd never been allowed to be human and flawed? His first mistake was unforgivable? *No, that's crazy.* He'd made multiple mistakes, the drinking being one of many.

But before that, a voice whispered in her head, *before he spiraled, didn't Mom reject him as unworthy?*

River *did* set a high standard. Her gaze hardened on her father. "She means well."

"She does." There was no acrimony in his tone. "She believes it. And if she didn't practice what she preached I'd be angry. But she does believe it. She lives by her standards. And I've come to the point of thinking there's no one else like her. No one will ever live up to her. Not even you, no matter how hard you try."

"What?" Eden frowned in confusion.

"Don't destroy yourself trying to be perfect, Eden. I can tell you, it's not what it's cracked up to be."

"You hurt *yourself*, though. It wasn't Mom's doing."

"Yes. I really made a mess of things. Like I said, I'm only human. You are too. No one can be River. No one ever will. Deep down, do you fear you'll be tossed away like I was if you make a mistake? If you do, relax. Cut yourself some slack. It's okay not to be perfect, not to be too rigid about defining what's allowed and right and ethical. It's okay to live in the shades of gray. It's especially okay to accept that people are a bit good and a bit bad and not all evil."

"Except the mayor," Eden shot back, her pulse racing at her father's comment. *Do I fear failing in the eyes of my mom? Am I trying too hard to be her? Am I being…rigid?* "She's all villain."

"The mayor has a lot of bad in her, no denying that." His eyes crinkled. "It's a spectacularly bad thing sending me in to pump you for information. Even I was a little shocked at her audacity." He shrugged. "But like I say, understanding people without judgment helps me get my head around the worst parts of them."

"Don't you dare forgive her," Eden said.

"Bit late for that. Sorry, honey."

"You forgave Francine?" Eden gasped. "How could you?"

"I had to let it go. All of it. Otherwise, the toxicity eating away inside me would kill me. Forgiving her served me well. Look at me, running The Shed and teaching shop to kids. At this rate, I might even be creeping up on contentment." He tilted his head. "Only thing that'd make me happy right now is if you were too. So, are you? Happy?"

Eden blinked at him. She couldn't get her head around any of this. Her father doing Francine's bidding. Developing a self-awareness streak. Claiming River had a rigidly unfair high standard that could be warping Eden's thinking. Forgiving Francine.

Forgiving. Francine.

"I'm happy enough." She winced. That sort of felt like a lie. Which was odd. It wouldn't have been ten weeks ago. Before she came to Wingapo, she'd felt settled in her life. Now everything was shifting about like sands.

"Well, it's a start," he said. "Can you just tell me one thing: are you really not behind the Bubba ad?"

"Why? So you can race off and tell Francine?"

"Yes." He met her eye. "I will put her mind at rest that it's not you. She can take her energies elsewhere, if that's what pleases her."

Eden sighed. It'd be something, wouldn't it, driving Francine mad with rage if she thought Eden was the ad's mastermind. Part of her would love to make the woman burst a blood vessel. But it wasn't true. "I'm not behind the ad. Because as much as I loathe her and every-thing she stands for, no woman in power deserves to be treated with contempt just for being a woman."

Her father nodded, looking pleased. "I did tell her it wouldn't be you. But she told me to find out anyway."

"Ugh." Eden scowled at him. "Stop reminding me you're in cahoots with her."

"I'm not. I just decided to follow my heart after she *strongly suggested* you and I talk."

"Your heart?"

"Yes, honey. And here we are. I'm hoping one day I won't see your mother when I look at you because even though that's not your fault, that really hurts."

"Until then?"

"Until then, I'll keep working on the fact I'm a flawed, simple man. One who's only human." He rose with a small smile.

"Don't take too long working your stuff out," Eden murmured. "I've missed you."

"And I've missed you." He leaned over and kissed her cheek. "Whatever else happens, can you remember you're *my* daughter too?"

She gave him a questioning look.

"That means you have my permission to make mistakes and I'll never judge you for them."

"Dad…" Her tone was warning. She didn't like that dig at her mom one little bit.

"I mean that without any edge or agenda. But also remember that no one is purely evil."

"Except Francine." Eden grinned.

"Not even her," he shot back. "Bye, honey."

Oh, Francine was. But Eden laughed anyway.

Michelle's phone beeped, but she forced herself to ignore it despite knowing it would be the next clue.

She was stacking the dishwasher with her grandmother, who was telling her, with much excitement as she passed Michelle plates, about how her friend in Florida had discovered bucket lists and was working on one for when Hannah next stayed there. That was a lot of anticipation for something that wouldn't be happening for at least three months. She slapped the dishwasher closed.

Speaking of anticipation, Michelle finally made her excuses and headed to find her phone. She opened the text.

Separate the pair at dawn

Michelle studied the message. *Dawn.* It was obviously a clue based on somewhere you could see the dawn from. Or...the sun rising, specifically. That gave her a direction. The pair...a landmark of some sort? Hills or a mountain? Side by side? Separated somehow... or separated *at dawn* when the sun peeked through them!

A few minutes later, she found a pair of mountains in Wingapo called the Gemini Peaks. She scowled.

That was the least challenging clue yet. It took me barely a minute, she texted back peevishly, along with a screenshot of the map.

No reply was forthcoming.

Michelle stared at her phone.

And stared some more.

She knew she was right but turned it over again. Gemini—twins. A pair. And she'd found a photo online of them at dawn; the sun quite clearly bisected them. More than that, they were visible from the farm with the arrowhead fence. So...it fit.

It did.

Maybe Lawless's phone was out of range? Or she was busy?

Not too busy to send the text in the first place.

Suddenly reality crashed into her, and she saw herself as someone else might. She was actually fretting about whether a subordinate had received her text message. She'd come to expect, and enjoy even, Lawless's awe at her working things out so quickly. Not receiving the dopamine rush of exuberance had disappointed her.

How utterly, utterly ridiculous she was. Michelle tossed the phone aside, jumped to her feet, and stalked out of the room, determined not to care if or when a text ever landed acknowledging her reply.

And that was as it should be.

Chapter 20

A King Never Alone

AGGIE HAD BEEN RIGHT. EDEN's time with Michelle would be over soon.

It had been hard, though, not responding to her gloating text last night. She could imagine the triumphant look on her face as she sent it. The way her intense eyes glowed with pleasure at solving it, and quickly. But Eden had to prep herself for the inevitable—when her time with her boss was over.

Michelle was quite correct; it wasn't a difficult clue. But it perfectly fit the hunt's larger purpose, and that mattered more right now. She wondered if anyone had noticed what else the clues were pointing to. No one on the forum boards had.

Of everyone, her money was on Michelle...or maybe Francine... figuring it out. They both had intelligence to burn.

Michelle was probably who Francine might have been if she hadn't chosen to side with corruption and greed. The Fixers' CEO seemed genuinely decent, even if she dealt with the powerbrokers of politics. She'd been so furious about the man who'd hurt his young lover.

That had been astonishing, now that Eden thought about it. A rare lapse from Michelle, sharing even that little amount with her. She wondered if her boss regretted it. She'd never met someone like her before, with such high walls.

Well…maybe Francine. But, unlike with Michelle, Eden didn't much care what lay beyond them. Even if her father seemed to want to put all that evilness into context, Eden did not share his views. What a person *did* told you who they were. And Francine did nothing good in this world.

Not one damned thing.

In recent days, Eden had dug around the Bubba Bros a little but had turned up nothing as to their identities. It was a dead end and felt like a waste of resources to pursue them further.

She wondered if she should convey this to Michelle. Annoyance flitted into her at their argument and how her boss had made her feel small for asking what she wanted. Michelle acted as if no one dared question her, and here was Eden, some nothing from nowhere badgering her like a gnat?

At least that's how Michelle had made her feel.

Having said that, Eleanor Roosevelt was quite right when she'd said no one could make you feel anything without your consent.

Eden slumped back into her chair.

Whatever. She thumbed through her phone and decided to send Michelle the text to the next clue. She wouldn't put it up until this evening, but it wasn't like Michelle would know or care about the timing.

It wasn't like Michelle seemed to know or care much about Eden at all, now that she thought about it.

And that was an oddly deflating thought.

Michelle's phone pinged with an incoming text alert. Finally she'd get a response about getting the previous clue right. Michelle snatched up the device, only to find no personal comment from the woman at all. Just the next clue.

Which is what you wanted, a little voice inside her head pointed out acidly. *You didn't like her overfamiliarity. The way she always probed and challenged you with questions. You pulled back for a reason. Don't get peeved when she suddenly respects your boundaries now.*

Still, she was a bit miffed. Last time they'd texted, Lawless had made her laugh so loudly, she'd alarmed the driver. What had changed since then? Why was Lawless only now being sparse with her words— to the point of curt.

With a small cluck of annoyance at herself for caring, she studied the text.

Second-to-last clue: a king never seen alone.

Second-to-last. It would be over so soon. Michelle pushed that depressing thought away and studied the clue.

Nothing came to mind. She called up her mapping app to see if there were any obvious landmarks with royal names within view of Gemini Peaks.

Tilly bustled in and started doing paperwork in the filing cabinet.

A king never seen alone.

"—and told him he could take his refund in slices of cheese and leave."

Michelle's head snapped up. "I'm sorry, what?"

"Didn't think you were listening." She smiled. "Something on your mind?"

"A king never seen alone."

"Excuse me?"

"It's a clue." Michelle's mouth puckered. "I'm trying to work out what it means."

"Oh…Ms. Lawless's little scavenger hunt? Is that still going?"

"It's at the end now. Second-to-last clue."

"Have you looked up place names with 'king' in them?"

"Yes. And 'queen.' And various regents and royals."

"Have you asked Ms. Lawless for the answer?" Tilly looked amused.

Surprise filled her. "That is *not* how this works."

"It isn't?" Tilly cocked her head.

"No." Michelle bit off the word sharply. She wasn't about to explain how much satisfaction she gained from guessing every clue without crawling to Lawless for help. How she prided herself on nailing the answers in a blisteringly short amount of time.

"Do you want me to get Snakepit to hack into her computer and look for the answer?"

Okay, now Tilly was clearly mocking her. "I don't think that will be necessary." She hid her grin at the idea.

"You know, maybe you're being too literal." Tilly closed the filing cabinet with a clang. "Not all kings are people."

Michelle stared at her.

"King of the jungle, for instance. A lion?"

Ohhh!

Michelle was already bent over the keyboard before Tilly left the room.

Ten minutes later, she smugly fired off a text.

Lion's Lookout

According to a few news articles, it was also known as Lover's Lookout by locals. Where the teens would make out in cars at night. So…*never alone.*

Michelle waited impatiently for a reply. Or even an acknowledgment of her answer.

Nothing was forthcoming.

Oh, come on. That was unacceptable.

Well, it wasn't as if she needed the woman's commentary on how Michelle's mind worked. If she wanted that, she could go home and talk to her safta.

So…what do I want to do instead?

Phyllis Kensington was no longer on the table…so to speak. And Michelle had lost interest in any other paid…entertainment.

The rage room? She had no headache or stress to ease. And even TJ couldn't source and replenish mirrors this fast. She'd been there just two nights ago.

What do I most want to do?

The answer came alarmingly fast.

Talk to Eden Lawless, an annoying voice whispered in the back of her head. *Laugh at her antics. Preen when she compliments your clue-solving skills. Challenge her and be challenged. And...*

Let her ask me questions.

Michelle slammed that thought down cold.

No. Thanks. That ship had sailed.

Chapter 21
The Last Clue

BEFORE EDEN KNEW IT, IT was two days out from the election. The last clue would go up in a few moments, and the scavenger hunt's final answer tomorrow.

She enjoyed the sunset at Lover's Lookout, gazing down across all the beautiful rolling farmland that would soon be turned into a sea of solar panels if Francine had her way. The view was magic. Eden let the air fill her lungs. Memories came back of bringing her first girlfriend here, the dashing Diana who'd had the most luscious lips and a laugh so loud it was an attention-sucking vortex. She'd been fun and funny. Well, until dating Eden had been too hard after the mayor blacklisted her. She wondered briefly how Diana was doing these days.

In the distance, she could make out a car snaking its way up toward the lookout, about five minutes away, so she quickly posted her last clue before she had witnesses.

The final clue, the final sign, for now you've seen them all: the scales, the goat, the crab, the maiden, the bull, the ram, the water bearer, the archer, the fish, the twins, and the lion.

So, what remains in this zodiac wheel? What is left to find?

From that answer, seek the power of its place, the lair in which it rules. Soon you'll learn why you're on this chase and the secret of it all.

Satisfied, Eden stepped back to view the sign with a grin. Francine Wilson made a fitting Scorpio. Well, scorpion.

She texted the clue to Michelle. That done, she hightailed it out of there.

All Michelle sent back an hour later was: *nicely done.*

Because, yeah, of course the answer was obvious. As it would be to everyone tomorrow.

Especially the mayor.

Bubba was in the news the next day as the newspaper openly speculated about who else could have possibly named their beloved mayor a nasty scorpion.

What Eden found so satisfying was that everyone immediately knew to whom the clue referred. Who else had power and a vicious sting in her tail?

Bubba milked the news cycle for everything he was worth, bobbing up on a variety of TV news programs across the US to discuss the developing plot in the hunt. Each interview, he managed to get in that he was good at dealing with *cars—used, new—trucks*, much to the feigned horror of his interviewers.

Locally the debate centered on whether he was smart enough to have masterminded the stunt, not whether Francine was its subject.

Okay, this time I know it was you.

That text landed from an unknown number. At first, Eden thought it was the mayor. But it wasn't like Francine not to own her accusations. So…her dad?

And? Do you think it's not an apt title for Francine? Eden texted back.

I didn't say that. I just realized it was you. The hunt, all of it. It was very clever. Like you.

Yep, definitely her dad. Her phone pinged again.

And no, I'm not going to tell Francine—although my sources tell me you're her prime suspect. Be careful of cornered bears, honey. They have sharp claws.

Thanks Dad. I will. x

Francine clearly knew the scorpion clue was targeting her, because the next day dawned with the sound of hammering and trucks rumbling in Wingapo's town center.

Over breakfast, Melba reported from her gossiping network of yoga spies that scaffolding was going up all around City Hall.

Eden raced over there and stared with mounting frustration as an enormous temporary fence was constructed around the building.

Clearly Francine did not want anyone posting anything outside City Hall confirming she was the scorpion on the day before the election. She'd just spent thousands of taxpayer dollars to prevent a single piece of paper being stuck to her building's wall.

Crap. Nice play, Francine Wilson, because there went Eden's plans to do just that. She was half tempted to put her final answer on Francine's home, but her clue had clearly said the scorpion's place of power.

Double crap.

She strolled the perimeter as the chain-links went ever higher. Then—she paused, neck arching right back for a look.

"Barbed wire?" she called out to the fencing contractor rolling it out along the top. "Overkill much?"

"Mayor doesn't want any trouble before the election," the man said, giving her an eye roll and a grin. "A job's a job, right?"

Right.

There were no gaps in the fencing. No nearby trees for shimmying up and over. The fence was too thick for small wire cutters, and she'd be there all night if she needed a bolt cutter. Besides which, the moment her cutting tools severed any part of the fence, she'd have committed vandalism. Her contract clearly stated everything she did must be done *legally*.

So… Eden kicked at the dirt underfoot, wondering if maybe a bit of shallow digging could get her under it, but it was hard as rock. And even then, she'd probably be up for trespassing.

A guard suddenly appeared, eying her suspiciously. "Ma'am?" he said. "I need you to step back from City Hall for now unless you have official business inside."

"Why? It's public property."

"And I've got orders. No one's allowed to loiter or place any un-authorized signage on this building for the next forty-eight hours or they will be dealt with *immediately*." He turned away dismissively as a fencing contractor called to him.

All right, then, time to think laterally. Eden gazed at the surround-ing buildings. Her eye settled on an office facing City Hall. It was about four or five stories high and had a for-lease sign in one floor's window.

Eden grinned as an idea struck her.

She had to act quickly. The side of City Hall that faced the office building had yet to be fenced, so she bolted over to it. As furtively as she could, she paced the distance back to the office building.

Surely this was doable? Jotting down the rough distance in her phone, she pondered how to enact her plan. What she needed were allies who knew their stuff.

Eden didn't like to call Colin as a first resort because he was hell-ishly busy and it sucked always relying on your best friend's sort-of paramour. She didn't want him to feel put on the spot to help, even if she always paid him well. But this was an emergency.

Colin ran his own IT business that contracted out computer support to professional organizations. He specialized in clients who needed secrecy and discretion from the techs who fixed their equip-ment, so he had a number of contracts with political parties and vari-ous government departments. He knew a little bit about everything and everyone—especially in the political sphere.

He'd been in Eden's classes in college, which was how he'd met Aggie. So…he owed her. Not that she played that card *too* often.

"Eden," Colin sighed dramatically. "If this is about Aggie and me, can you leave it alone?"

It was kind of adorable how he had a one-track mind on the topic. "It may shock you to know, but I'm not calling to meddle in your love life for once, although Goddess knows someone should."

"Uh-huh," he said suspiciously. "So, it's work? Was the PAC stuff useful at all?"

"It was not what I expected," Eden said. "A guy like Bubba Nevada with a PAC."

"I've seen weirder stuff." He laughed. "But not often. Okay, what do you need this time?"

"Info. What's the maximum distance I could project something? Like photos with words on them? The words would have to be legible."

"You'd need a long-throw projector. How big is the viewing screen you're projecting it on?"

Eden regarded the wall of City Hall and counted the floors. "It's the side of a three-story building."

He chuckled. "Okay, big enough. And how far away do you want to project from?"

"Two hundred and fifty feet maximum? I'd be off the ground in an office building, two stories up."

"It's definitely doable. I presume there's a nice big window you can put the projector in? A window that *opens*."

Eden spun around and glanced up. Next to the *For Lease* sign, a window was partly opened. She exhaled in relief. "Yeah."

"Okay, I'll email you what you need to buy. I'll send you a link for the cheapest model; it won't break the bank, and it'll do the job."

"There's a small problem." She drew in a breath. "I need it today. Well, tonight."

"Of course you do." He laughed. "Where are you?"

"Wingapo?"

Silence.

More silence.

"Colin, don't you remember that lil ole place that you graduated from?"

"I remember it well. I was just thinking: You might be in luck. I have a buddy over in Hagerstown. I know he has the right gear because I've enjoyed a kick-ass outdoor movie night at his place. He could probably be convinced to rent his projector to you for the right price. Is it just for tonight?"

"Yep, a one-night spectacular. So, what's the right price?"

"Well, for a thousand-dollar-plus projector with a sweet seven thousand lumens..." He made mulling-over noises... "he'd probably expect at least a couple dozen Flying Dogs."

"Flying what?"

"Beer." Colin chuckled. "He loves the stuff."

"So, am I driving over and borrowing his projector, or...?"

"He'd never let it out of his sight. But he'd probably set his baby up and play the video for you."

"Okay, then I insist on paying him way more than a bunch of beer. I'll also throw in gas and any other expenses to get him here ASAP. Can I leave it with you to arrange? I have to go swing an office rental."

"You're going to rent an office for *one* night? I don't think it works that way."

"I know. And I'll be pretty pissed if they make me sign the lease for three months. But I'll do it if I have to."

Colin snorted. "Come on, you're Eden Lawless. I'm sure you'll sweet-talk the agent."

"Fingers crossed. Text me back about your friend, okay?"

"Roger that. His name's Rufus. I'll get back to you soon."

⊷⊙⊷

Two hours later, Eden was sweating as she left the realtor's office. They had hammered out quite the bargain. Eden had agreed to make a sizable donation to the agent's professional women's speaking group's annual fundraiser. In exchange, Eden had access to the office space for 48 hours and had to pay an enormous deposit. She supposed they'd both won; Eden hadn't had to sign a lease, but still... The agent had been a shark.

The only concession Eden had wrung out of her was that the woman absolutely could never divulge to anyone now or later who had rented the office space and she absolutely would not let anyone enter it without a search warrant during Eden's 48-hour tenancy.

Oddly enough, even that hadn't made the realtor blink.

Pure. Shark.

"Out of curiosity," Eden had asked the agent as they were finishing up, "what time do the nightclubs close around here?" She pointed to the one she could see three doors away.

"And by clubs you mean club," the woman said. "Midnight."

"Okay. Thanks."

A text from Colin pinged, confirming his buddy's interest.

Excellent.

Another hour later, Eden had reclined the seat in her van where it was parked around the corner from her temporary office. She was dealing with a little work and a couple of texts that had landed from old clients seeking her availability when a knock sounded.

A young man who was all beard and rumpled clothes and hair filled the passenger side of the window. "Hey," he mouthed and mimicked winding down the window.

She leaned over and inched the window down. "Yes?"

"Name's Rufus. Col sent me? Told me to look for the woman in a rainbow van." He gave her a cheery grin. "Said there might be beer in it for me?"

She laughed and unlocked the passenger door. "More than just beer. Get in."

He climbed inside and dumped a backpack on the floor. "Where do you want me to set up?" He looked around. "And what am I project-ing onto?"

"Up there is the source building." She pointed to the second-floor window of her leased office space. "Over there is the wall I want the projection to hit." She pointed to City Hall.

Rufus glanced between the two buildings. "Ah, you know there's a great big fence in front of the destination building, right?"

"I'm hoping the projection will be high enough to go over it?" Oh hell, *was* it? She wondered if she'd burned through a lot of money for nothing.

"Hope so," Rufus said. "Couldn't get the next floor up?"

"Not for lease."

"Mmm." He chewed his lip thoughtfully. "Well, okay. Guess we'll find out when we do a test run."

"No test runs. At all. It's showtime tonight for fifteen minutes and that's it."

He gave her a puzzled look. "*What?*"

"This isn't an authorized event," she clarified. "The mayor won't be happy." She waved at City Hall. "And I don't want to tip my hand by revealing my plans."

"Ah." Rufus ran a hand through his beard. "Well, that makes things more interesting. Okay, let me into the office, and I'll probably know anyway just from looking. In the meantime," he glanced at her earnestly, "I heard a rumor about beer."

Eden snorted. "Okay, I'll go find you some. Anything else?"

"Um… I work better with Doritos and pizza."

"You make it sound like it'll take you hours to set up."

"It's highly complicated tech."

"Don't you just set up the projector, plug it into power and a laptop? Then hit play on whatever app you use?" She lifted her eyebrows.

He blinked uncertainly at her slicing through his BS. "Uh…"

"Didn't Colin tell you we met in IT school?"

"Oh, right." He looked a bit sheepish. "Look, fine, it's not hard, but I'm hungry and the drive over took ages." He patted his stomach hopefully.

"Well, why didn't you say so?" She gave him the building's key. "Second floor. Office 2B. I'll be back with snacks. And I happen to know Hagerstown's only twenty miles away, so don't milk the thousand-mile-journey angle too hard, okay? Your credibility will be shot."

He chuckled. "Yeah, yeah, okay."

⬩━◦◦◦━⬩

Eden found Rufus playing a computer game when she returned, some end-of-the-world atrocity involving zombies or ghouls, and laid out an array of pizza, corn chips, and assorted sides on the IT-dude-approved food spectrum: one part grease, one part salt, one part crunch.

"Hey," he said. "Wondered when you'd get back. I'm even more starving now."

"Because of all the work you're doing?" Eden suggested as she unpacked the feast. "I don't think hunting zombie brains is helping the projector set up itself."

"Pfft," he said, "not much else I can do now without the files you want me to project. And Project Zomboid is grossly unappreciated for its story depth and problem solving." He reached for a paper napkin and piled it high with pizza. "Damn, this smells good."

It did…thanks to Jimmy's sinfully good cooking skills. Rufus made a good point. "Okay, you eat, I'll grab my laptop and upload my document to your computer."

She'd already worked out the wording for the projected slideshow, so it wouldn't take long to get everything prepped and ready.

Eden headed back to her van and went to unlock it. The van made no responding beep. Which meant she'd forgotten to lock it.

Damn it, Eden, get your head in the game!

She opened the door and reached under her front seat for her laptop. She came up empty.

Eden frowned. Then she pulled open the door fully, got on her hands and knees, and had a better hunt around.

Gone.

No! When was the last time she'd seen it? She'd been working on it just before Rufus had joined her. She'd put it under her seat when she'd left for the B&B to pick up his pizza. Then she'd been distracted chatting with Melba. She'd also done a little work while she waited for it to cook.

She'd brought the laptop inside with her—had she left it at the B&B?

Pulling out her phone, Eden called Melba to check her room on the off chance she'd left it there.

Melba returned to the phone after a few minutes. "I'm sorry, child, no laptop here."

"Damn it!" This was a disaster.

"Was…" Melba sounded hesitant, "…there anything on there that could cause you a problem?"

Oh. Oh hell. Good question.

She made a mental checklist of what she'd left on her laptop. It had all her recent jobs on it. Clients, privileged information... and...

The Fixers! Most of the information pertaining to Michelle and her company was on her phone, but...not all. She knew all too well that The Fixers valued their secrecy above all else. This could be *very* bad if someone got their hands on such sensitive information.

"I'm not sure," she replied to Melba.

A flash of dark blue caught her attention and she swiveled catching sight of a tall figure lounging on the other side of the street.

Eden locked eyes with a man she'd had far too many run-ins with over the years: Wingapo Police Chief Derrick Sharpe. He was so corrupt, he'd rough up his own grandmother if Francine told him to. Of course, Eden knew Sharpe better as the bullyboy who'd told her to leave Wingapo if she wanted her father, her ex, and her friends to all stay in continued good health.

The man folded his beefy, muscled arms and gave her the slowest of curling smiles which turned into a smirk.

Eden did not believe in coincidences. And it was vintage Sharpe to screw her over and then gloat about it. He never could resist a chance to remind people of his power.

"Never mind. Sorry to have bothered you," Eden said to Melba. "I'm pretty sure Chief Sharpe stole it."

"I don't imagine you'll be seeing it again anytime soon, then," Melba said, sounding sympathetic. "And no bother at all. I'm real sorry. And if there's anythin' me or Jimmy can do, you let me know."

"There is one thing. And I'll understand if you say no."

"Anythin'."

Eden detailed what she needed and the time she needed it. "I realize it's a bit late," she finished, biting her lip. She'd been planning on hiring a professional, but this would be much better. Eden could trust Melba and Jimmy, for a start.

Melba was immediately enthusiastic. "Well now," she said. "That actually sounds fun. And I can use it as a promotional opportunity. We'll be there with bells on, don't you worry."

Eden promised to pay her, then had to insist three times she meant it when Melba tried to offer her services for free, before finally winning and thanking her.

Then, heart in her throat, she texted Michelle.

Pretty sure the cops just stole my laptop. FYI they may have access to some info about your org. I can't remember exactly what I had on there but I keep a file on all my clients and jobs. I'm sorry.

A moment later her phone pinged.

Was the file encrypted?

Was Michelle nuts? Who routinely encrypts their client files?

People working for top secret organizations, obviously. *Shit.* This was so bad.

No. Sorry.

A beat passed, then Michelle texted: *At least tell me your laptop needed a password to open it?*

Yes, she replied. Eden felt a wash of relief she'd at least done that. But Aggie's name and date of birth wouldn't be hard to crack if anyone knew her. Of course, that would take time. Sharpe hadn't had it for long.

Was the address of our organization mentioned? And was it listed in your files as pertaining to the hunt? Is there a link between us at all?

Eden thought hard.

I think it's listed as just an address without a name. No, not mentioned with regards to the hunt.

I see. Leave it to me.

And that was it. No further comment appeared. Eden was tempted to text *sorry* again, but that seemed a bit redundant. One thing that came through loud and clear, however, was that Eden had disappointed her boss. Eden was an inconvenient mess that Michelle had to manage. And clean up.

This was terrible. With a sigh, she headed back to see Rufus and braced herself to rewrite her screed.

Rufus would just have to share his laptop. At least she'd saved a bunch of notes to the cloud.

"Sorry, buddy," she muttered when she reached his side. "The fictional apocalypse is going to have to wait. We have a real one to deal with."

Chapter 22
The Scorpion

A BRIGHT PURPLE VAN ROARED up Main Street, music blaring, at 11:30 p.m. and screeched to a halt not far from City Hall.

Eden spotted it from the office window and nudged a dozing Rufus awake. "Hey, get ready. Show's about to start."

Over all those wonderful B&B dinners, Eden had learned weeks ago that when Jimmy had been starting out in the cooking game, he'd tried running a food truck first. He gave it up when he'd struggled at interacting with crowds. They still had the van, and it was about to become the star of downtown Wingapo. Especially when the night-club's doors closed and patrons spilled out onto the street.

Melba Moore's soulful voice filled the air from the van's speakers. The other Melba leaped from the vehicle and rattled up the concession doors.

Eden had reached ground level, carefully locked the door to the office building, and bolted over to see her co-conspirators. She grinned at how conspicuous it all was. Exactly as intended.

"This looks great," she told Melba. "And smells even better! What's cooking?"

"Jimmy's special barbecue. And some extra cheesy potato skins. This is a great way to promote his menu and get folks talking about what a good cook my baby boy is."

"Ma," Jimmy hissed through the concession window, looking appalled. "I'm nineteen!"

"You'll always be my baby boy," she said, just as she always did.

He rolled his eyes and disappeared out the back.

Two security guards who had been stationed to watch the fencing made a beeline for the van. Eden gave Melba a pointed nod in their direction, then made herself scarce.

Returning to her office window, Eden was in time to see the exuberant woman below schmoozing the guards.

"Did I mention it's all free?" Melba announced cheerfully, loud enough for half the block to hear.

Even from up at her window seat, Eden could smell the wafting aromas.

"Think she'll have leftovers?" Rufus murmured, peering down.

"You're amazing," Eden glanced at him. "Are you never full?"

"You can smell that too, right?" he protested.

"I can." Eden smiled. It did smell sinfully good.

After fifteen minutes of nothing happening beyond downtown Wingapo filling with mouthwatering aromas and delightful music, the security guards stopped looking quite so suspicious, accepted paper plates of food, and wandered back down the road toward the padlocked main gate.

By now, young people were spilling out onto the street from the club, drawn to the loud R&B music and delicious smells.

"Beautiful young people!" Melba called out to them, her smile welcoming and bright. "Free food this evening! Courtesy of Melba C. Lotus's Spruce Treesort Bed and Breakfast! Come and try it out! My son Jimmy is the cook, so y'all better be loving it!"

Crowds began to head her way; obviously the word *free* was having a magical effect.

Melba continued to wave and call them over for the next fifteen minutes.

Brilliant woman. She was so good at this.

When three dozen people were buzzing around the food truck, and the guards had totally lost interest, Eden glanced at Rufus. "It's time. Hit it."

He turned to his equipment, tapped a key, and flicked a switch.

Instantly, a dazzling shard of light shot through the window and lit up an entire side of City Hall.

The crowd fell silent, everyone turning.

It was *perfect*. The size and shape…Only the tiniest line at the bottom of the viewing area skimmed the top of the barbed wire.

Rufus pressed play.

Get ready.

A new slide appeared.

You're just in time.

And then: *For the answer to the hunt.*

Immediately, excited gasps and murmuring could be heard. Dozens of phones were pulled out and held up to record.

The Wingapo Scavenger Hunt was designed to show you something…
All these beautiful places…

Pictures appeared of the billboard, the archery range, the rammed earth house, the water pipe, Mulligan's Farm, the fishing pond, and the view from Lion's Lookout…

ALL of these places will soon be covered over with solar panels.
The Wingapo government has pledged to approve a dozen solar plants.
On paper it sounds great.

A cartoon child punching the air appeared.

But in reality, there will be no more Mulligan's apples, or Bass Pond.
No archery ranges. Everywhere you've been, your view will be this.

An aerial shot appeared of thousands of solar panels.

The forest around the pipeline will be gone too.
The side of the highway into town?

The picture reappeared of the billboard.

Lined with panels.
To what end? Why will we lose so much of Wingapo's beauty?
For jobs? It will create about 30 jobs. Most will be non-local experts brought in.
You will lose a large part of Wingapo forever.
The character, gone.
The views, gone.
This is all part of Mayor Wilson's re-election campaign—the details are all on her website. If you read the small print.

A picture appeared of the small print. Then it zoomed in. And in again. And words appeared listing land redevelopment and acquisitions planned for the projects.

So, who is the scorpion of our scavenger hunt? Who has the power and a sting in her tail?

A picture of Francine appeared.

Think about what you will lose when you vote tomorrow.
Do not elect Francine Wilson. Say no to scorpions.

A link appeared to the scavenger hunt's website. As it did, Eden hit "Publish" on her updated web page. It now included all the solar plant information that Francine had buried. And the words: *Vote wisely. Say no to scorpions.*

It also included a video of what had just played on the side of City Hall.

Silence fell as the projection ended. Then a discontented murmur started through the crowd. The sound was odd. Not quite anger, not quite fear. Just...incredulity. Then chaos.

The two guards were staring up at the office, right toward Eden. Not that the men would be able to see anything beyond the white lamp.

"Shut it off," Eden said. "We need to get out of here now."

"Hells yeah," Rufus said urgently. "I've got my truck 'round the back. Already loaded my beers in there. Thanks for that." He was already unplugging his projector and wrapping it up. "Pleasure doing a special op with you. Colin said you're a blast. I see what he means."

He tossed his laptop and projector into his now bulging backpack, then looked around. His eye fell on piles of trash.

"No time," Eden said. "I'll clean up. You go. Now. Before those guards decide to investigate who just screwed over their boss."

Rufus bolted. Eden scooped up the trash, locked up, and then was hot on his heels.

He was gone by the time she made it to Gloria, but she saw his truck flash by. He leaned on his horn and gave her a grin.

That attracted the guards' attention, but they were having a nightmare of a time extracting themselves from the crowd suddenly pressing into them around Melba's van.

"Get your seconds here!" she was calling out, as she slid her gaze between the guards and Eden. "Over here, free food while you still can. Don't miss out, now!"

Timing! Eden could kiss her.

The crush of people was now entirely surrounding the two guards trying to push their way through.

Eden had sped all the way down Main Street by the time she spotted the guards in her rearview mirror banging on the main door to the office building.

Good luck with that. No other tenants were there at this time of night.

She'd made it. She couldn't believe it. Her final message was up, and no one had stopped her.

With elation, Eden stabbed her radio on, and laughed at the song that was playing. Then she howled out a jubilant chorus of "You Can't Always Get What You Want."

Like hell you can't.

———⋯———

Michelle paced her home in frustration, as she had done for hours. She drained her dirty martini—her gin concoction of choice whenever she was worked up—and resisted the urge to fire off another text.

The team would let her know when they knew something.

Every now and then, she'd watch the video Eden had just posted to her website, blasting the mayor for her invasive solar power plant expansions. It was effective, she had to admit. It got the point across without resorting to nastiness. People tended to switch off at nastiness. With any luck, by the time the polls closed tomorrow—she glanced at the time—correction, today, Mayor Wilson would be ousted.

A moment later, her phone pinged.

Retrieval successful

Where was it? Michelle texted back.

WP station

Michelle paused striding and raised her eyebrows. Her team had successfully broken into Wingapo's police station and retrieved Eden's laptop. Bold, even for them. She tapped a new text.

Any resistance?

No. Radio chatter says all cops sent to W border to stop target leaving. They went to bnb first, not there, so assumed her plan is to leave town

Michelle froze. Pissed-off police defending their attacked mayor were planning to prevent Lawless leaving town? She would be in a great deal of danger. Her heart began pounding.

Another ping sounded.

Based on police radio, they have plans to turn target into rectal paste

As she'd suspected. Michelle's lips thinned. She texted back: *You will ensure she gets out without issue. Whatever it takes, preferably with her being unaware. Any trouble, call me from the scene ASAP.*

Roger that

Michelle added: *btw any signs of intrusion or damage to laptop?*

No damage. Still locked, so maybe no intrusion

Not being unlocked now didn't mean anything, but her hopes rose a little. They had probably got to it in time.

All right, good. Update me on border situation when you arrive.

Michelle's pacing continued. She rarely involved herself directly in an operation, but this was a special case.

Lawless was new. Her first assignment. She needed extra oversight. And apparently an understanding about what a monumentally foolish idea it was to allow her laptop out of her sight when it contained details about The Fixers.

Thirty more minutes went by before her phone rang…an incoming video call from her operative.

"Ma'am," he said looking almost…sheepish? "Sorry to bother you, but we have a VIP here insistin' on speaking to my superior." He lowered his voice to a hiss. "She won't take no for an answer, and I'm not sure how hardball you want me to be with her."

"Put Mayor Wilson on," Michelle said dryly. Because who else would be senior enough and causing trouble on the border of Wingapo right now? She flicked her own video feed to black, leaving the audio on, and waited.

An angry brunette's face filled the screen. "Who is this?"

"Ah, Mayor Wilson. I'd say it's an honor, but you appear to be way-laying my men from their business."

"Who are you?" Wilson demanded again. She frowned at the screen. "I can't see your video."

"I can see you. Now, what seems to be the problem?"

"Your men just incapacitated all of my police officers and threatened to do the same to me!"

"Is that so?" Michelle studied the woman, curious as to how she had been able to terrify a whole town and rattle even the irrepressible Eden Lawless. "Might that have something to do with the fact your officers were blocking the road?"

"They're police! They're allowed! They were waiting for a fugitive."

"A...fugitive. And what has this fugitive been charged with?"

"Nothing yet." The vein on the mayor's forehead seemed to be popping.

"I'm sure you'll think of something creative," Michelle drawled. "But that won't be necessary."

"No? Who the hell do you think you are to assault my men?"

"We are an organization you never want to cross. We have the ear of people in power. We have resources. Money. Technology. We run this nation. We decide who gets in power and who stays in power. You do not cross us, understand?"

Wilson fell silent, but her impeccably arched eyebrows knitted together.

"Now, I need you to listen to me very closely," Michelle said, tone low and dangerous. "A vehicle is going to pass that way soon. I'm quite sure you know the one? It's painted like a hippie's LSD dream. You are going to let that vehicle through unmolested. If you or anyone you employ so much as stops it for a headlight check, I will add your name to my list. Trust me, you do *not* want to be on my list."

"How do you know Eden Lawless?" Wilson asked, and this time there was a faint hint of caution in her eyes.

"She has my protection."

"You did this? You sent her to screw me over? My election?"

"Now why would a DC powerbroker care in the least what you do in your backwater town?" Michelle asked.

"You're from DC?" Wilson said, eyes narrowing.

She looked like a cat on the hunt now. Searching for weaknesses.

"Who and where I'm from is none of your concern. But know this: if you touch one hair on Ms. Lawless's head, I will make you live to regret it. Am I clear?"

For the first time, the other woman looked unsettled. Even so, she muttered, "You could be bluffing."

"Look at your officers. Tell me, *how long* did it take my men to incapacitate them? Did they look like amateurs to you when they did it? Do you think they'd hesitate to do the same to you if I gave the order?"

Wilson glanced off screen, then back to Michelle. Her brows were a dark knot of confusion. "I agree you're professionals. But why do you care about Lawless? She's nothing. An annoying rabble rouser and a bleeding-heart liberal who screams about a new cause every day."

"That's just it, I don't care about her at all. However, she has my protection. And I do care when someone doesn't listen. This is your final warning: Back off. Allow Lawless to pass unimpeded."

The mayor bared her teeth. "I can't very well clear the road. My officers are all *unconscious!*"

"My team will assist them to an off-site location. You will leave now or join them if you resist. Be aware that my men will be guarding the road out of sight in case you decide to return with reinforcements."

Wilson hesitated.

"This is not a request. Leave. *Now.*"

The mayor swore under her breath and handed the phone back to the operative.

Michelle waited until she heard a car start up and drive off, then flicked video mode back on. "Send someone to follow her."

"Already happening. What do you want me to do with her thugs?"

Michelle gave a cool smile. "Drive them at least twenty miles away. Dump them there. Keep someone posted on the border road in case someone stops Lawless leaving. Once her vehicle has passed the border, alert me. Stay for an extra hour in case someone follows her, then head back to base. Bring me her laptop. We'll see if any of those graceless oafs breached it."

"Yes, ma'am."

She ended the call. All that was left was a text to Lawless. Then finally her heart would stop pounding.

Eden had floored it back to the B&B, dumped an impressive wad of cash on the table for Melba to find, and scrawled out a hasty but heartfelt letter of thanks.

Sure, The Fixers would pay the B&B's expenses, but Melba and Jimmy had earned a big bonus. Eden also left the key to the rented office space and asked Melba to return it to the realtor the next day, telling her she could also keep the cash deposit.

Then she grabbed a water bottle from the fridge, checked she had everything from her room, and sped out of there as fast as Gloria could go.

Eden was close to the outskirts of Wingapo when a text from Michelle came up on her phone. She immediately pulled over to check it. Her boss wouldn't be texting her at close to one in the morning for no reason.

Ms. Lawless, we've recovered your laptop. You'll find it at our offices in DC. Please report there to collect it.

Was it cracked? Eden tapped back fearfully.

Unlikely. Will confirm tomorrow with our team of experts.

Unlikely? Oh, thank goodness.

Just so you know, Michelle's next text said, *the laptop was indeed recovered at the police station.*

Those bastards, Eden thought. So, she hadn't been imagining Sharpe's gloating expression. Her phone chimed again.

You need to leave town ASAP. Police tend not to take well to break-ins at their own station. If you stay, you may be charged for what my team did. And I'd speculate the mayor will be after your blood soon enough anyway.

I understand, she texted back. *I'm already on my way out now. So far no cops anywhere around the border. That's a relief!*

Good.

And that was that.

It was kind of amazing how on top of everything Michelle was. The way she sent in security teams and kept track of employees. Even errant ones who fucked up as Eden had. It showed she was efficient. She was even up in the middle of the night coordinating a laptop retrieval effort. That was commitment to her company's secrecy.

Eden tossed the phone back on the passenger seat and then gunned it for the edge of town.

She'd half expected a police cordon waiting to stop her. Instead, she blew past the borders of Wingapo without incident and headed for home. No one even tried to stop her.

Huh. Unexpected.

Francine must be slipping.

<hr/>

The headline in the local paper's online edition on election day was about rabble rousers projecting conspiracy theories onto City Hall but wouldn't say what those "conspiracies" were. They couldn't. It would mean admitting their mayor's solar scheme might be ruinous for Wingapo County.

What the local reporters wrote or ignored didn't matter for once because the national media had no such reticence. They blasted all of it, everywhere: Eden's video, Francine's small print on solar plans, concerns over the environmental impact, and their view that the hunt had been one of the cleverest stunts to raise political awareness of an issue that they'd ever seen.

Footage of Bubba had wide circulation too. He grinned like a Cheshire cat when he posed for the cameras and said: "I might be the underdog candidate, but at least I'm not stupid enough to think covering every square inch of our beautiful county in solar panels is a good idea! As you all know, I'm good with Cars—Used, New—Trucks, so I know you'll vote for me!" And then he beamed for the cameras while shooting finger guns.

He was wrong. They didn't vote for him. They didn't vote for Francine either.

Doctor Ron's slightly startled expression at the news that he'd won, in a come-from-behind, poll-defying victory, was forever immortalized on the front page a day later.

His wife's long-suffering, pained expression said Sophia had pretty much expected exactly this, and there went her life. And didn't that just sum up everything?

Chapter 23

All Good Things

EDEN LAWLESS WAS BACK IN Michelle's office, this time looking less like a panda. More…well. Whatever a seasoned panda was. She'd come through, succeeded in her objectives, and had the look of someone still processing her victory.

Michelle would be lying if she said the sight of her employee didn't please her, even though Lawless had made even less of an effort to dress up this time. Seriously. Would it kill her to adopt corporate attire when meeting her CEO?

Well, *former* CEO now, wasn't it? In a few moments, the other woman's job would be officially concluded.

"Hey, that's new," Lawless said, twisting around in her chair and pointing to Michelle's latest acquisition on the wall. It was courtesy of a now highly remorseful Senator Cavaner. "Wait, is that a *Degas*?"

"You know art? Since when?" Michelle's lips tugged up.

"I can read the signature from here. And I know enough to spot that's not something you got from a shady dude in a back alley." Lawless grinned back at her.

Michelle's stupid, irritating heart decided it loved seeing the woman's grin. "It is indeed a Degas. And, no, I don't like ballet, if that's your next question."

"Must have cost a mint." Lawless stared at it in awe.

"Not really. I received it as a partial payment for services rendered."

"Partial…" Lawless's eyes went wide. "Just how much do you people charge?"

Michelle smirked. "It's a sliding scale depending on the client. Now then, to business…" She pushed a padded case across her desk. "Your laptop. It was found to have not been opened in the time it left your custody. However, next time use some real security on it. Our IT expert said a ten-year-old could have hacked it."

"Wingapo PD didn't."

"Proving only that they have technical savvy lower than a ten-year-old." Michelle leaned back in her chair, trying not to smile. "Also, maybe next time don't use your best friend's name and birth date as a password."

"You know my best friend's name and birth date?" Lawless stared at her in astonishment.

"We know everything." This time, she did smile. "Oh, and congratulations. I must say, Mayor Wilson's concession speech might have been the briefest in political history."

"Yeah." Lawless beamed. "Too funny. She just looked down the camera and snarled, 'Good luck, Ronald.' Not even his proper title. Didn't bother thanking her supporters."

"Perhaps she had none to thank."

Lawless laughed. "Goddess, you can be funny sometimes."

It was entrancing experiencing the full effect of the woman's personality again.

No…not entrancing! Jesus! Michelle couldn't roll her eyes hard enough at herself. *Focus. Finish the job, rubber-stamp her exit, move on.*

Michelle shuffled her papers. "Tilly would have collected your debit card and supplied you your final check on the way in, yes?"

"Yep. All sorted."

"The client was most grateful. She speaks highly of your creativity. Her words, not mine."

"She? The client's a woman?" Lawless peered at her, utterly lost. "Who? Wait, ages ago, when I first asked, you said you wouldn't confirm the client's identity even if I worked it out. Why are you dropping hints now?"

"Because the client was so pleased with your job, she asked me to give you her details so she can Skype with you and tell you herself. But please be aware the NDA still applies. You cannot share her name beyond this room. Now, the client is expecting your call any moment. So, on that score..." Michelle pushed over a scrap of paper. "Her Skype name and our temporary Wi-Fi login details. If you could take care of that now, that would be appreciated, so we can move on."

Michelle needn't have worried that Lawless would stand up the client. The look on the other woman's face was one of delighted intrigue.

She pulled her laptop out of the case, slid the scrap of paper close, and began tapping in the Wi-Fi password and client's Skype name—BlackeyedSusan.

A few moments later, the video call connected.

"Oh my goodness!" Lawless cried. "Mrs. Boone!"

Michelle fought back a laugh at the astonishment on her face at the sight of Dr. Ron's wife. Lawless truly was an open book.

"I'm well aware of who I am, young lady." The amusement was clear in her voice. Mrs. Boone continued, "Ms. Hastings suggested this might come as a shock."

"Just a little! I thought you hated politics! You didn't want to be a mayor's wife."

"And I still don't. But do you know what I hate even more? The solar plant listed for the field below our property. I have spent *decades* working on my garden so it'd be something beautiful to enjoy in my retirement with Ron. Goodness, I had all these grand plans of us sipping iced tea on our old wooden swing seat, looking over my black-eyed Susans and wild blue phlox in bloom, seeing in our twilight years. And Francine Wilson ruined that. I made so many entreaties to the mayor and planning authorities to prevent it, but no one was interested in listening."

"Francine's bribes talk loudly," Lawless said. "Goddess, I'm sorry."

"Forty years of work on my dream garden. Forty years!" Mrs. Boone's tone hardened. "So I took extreme measures."

"But how did a retired doctor's wife in Wingapo hear about The Fixers?"

"Your father is to thank for that. It turns out all his drinking wasn't for nothing."

Lawless's eyes narrowed.

"Sorry," Mrs. Boone murmured. "I didn't mean it quite like that. But as I understand it, he spent many an hour propped up at bars talking to strangers about his sad life. During one such bender, he met a political fellow from DC, in Wingapo for a weekend with his mistress. He'd used The Fixers before, I believe. Anyway, this fellow felt mighty sorry for your father and thought he was wanting someone to punish River for hurting him. He slid your father The Fixers' card."

"Punish Mom?" Lawless flicked a glance over to Michelle. "Would you..."

"No, never," Michelle said too quietly for Mrs. Boone to hear. "We don't take domestic cases. Nasty business."

"So," Mrs. Boone continued, "the fellow thought your father wanted to punish your mom for not taking him back. But your father wasn't interested. He was, as a matter of fact, so appalled anyone would infer from his drunken words that he wanted harm to come to his wife, that it shook him to the core. He was weeping when he talked to me the next day. I took the card off him, and he took himself to get help. And here we are."

"Sorry, what? Why was Dad crying on your shoulder?"

"He lives with us. He has the cottage at the back of our property."

"*Dr. Ron* is the medical colleague who took Dad in?"

"He is."

"Why didn't you say?" Lawless glanced to Michelle, but Mrs. Boone was the one who replied.

"I asked her not to. I didn't want you snooping too much around my husband due to your family connection in case it led you to working out I was the client. At that stage, I wanted no one to know. Especially not your father." She hesitated. "Due to his...issues...he has the potential to be indiscreet."

"So, Dad doesn't know you hired The Fixers. Does Dr. Ron?"

"Not even him. In fact, I have conveniently convinced my husband that running for mayor was his idea. He's so sweet, my Ronald. I knew people would love him and want him as their candidate."

"That explains some things." Lawless shook her head. "Wow, that's so out there."

"I'm just glad it's all worked out so well. Worth every dime. Now I get my beautiful garden and don't have to fret about what's coming." Mrs. Boone paused. "Thank you for that, Eden. You *do* look like him, you know. Your father. I thought that the moment I met you in Wingapo."

"It's the red hair, right?"

"That's a factor. He was so sad you two fell out. And I just wanted the chance to thank you personally for reconnecting with him. He has a spring in his step now that he hasn't had since River left."

"Oh, well, that's good." Lawless looked down at her hands. "I mean, nothing's really all worked out yet. We've just opened the lines of communication. It'll take time to trust him again."

"I know. Baby steps. But that's all I wanted to say. Thanks for completing your *secret mission* so well." Mrs. Boone chuckled before sobering. "And thanks for having the goodness in your heart to give a sorry man with his share of flaws another chance."

"It was my pleasure on the first part. You know my history with the mayor. Hell, everyone does. And I've always loved Dad, despite how bad he got. He frustrates me. And he makes me so mad, but it's always easier *and* harder to deal with stuff when love's involved, isn't it? So, we're working on it." She shrugged. "Like you say, baby steps."

Mrs. Boone clucked in agreement. "Well, that's it. I'll leave you to your day. Goodbye, dear."

The Skype call ended.

Lawless logged off and slapped her laptop closed. "Well, that was a hell of a thing," she murmured, sounding dazed as she slid the machine into her case. "I did *not* see that coming at all." She zipped it shut with a clicking whoosh.

"I must admit, neither did I when she first contacted us," Michelle said. "We do get all sorts of clients, with all sorts of motives. However, being able to enjoy your retirement years without looking at solar panels has to be a new one for us."

"I guess that's everything, then?" Lawless dug through a backpack she'd brought with her, and that dopey grin was back on her face.

"Yes," Michelle said uncertainly, wondering what the woman was looking for.

Lawless placed her phone on the desk, a battered thing that had been through the wars. "Do you know I had to beg your receptionist to let me hang onto this instead of locking it away? It was only by convincing her my phone was pivotal to our meeting that she let me keep it." Lawless hit a button.

Thin classical music came from the speakers. Well, more likely, speaker.

"What are you—" Michelle began to ask.

"—I had to Google classical music that says thanks and goodbye." Lawless glanced up. "I'm setting the mood for the gift-giving component of our meeting."

Michelle's brain began to gently melt down at the absurdity. "*Why am I being bestowed gifts at all? Not to mention a tinny version of* Vivaldi's *Four Seasons: Autumn?*"

"I want to thank you for getting my laptop back and being a good sport about it. I admit I half expected you to have deducted expenses from my final check for having to send in a team to extract it from the police chief's office."

"We look after our own here," Michelle said evenly, although it stung that Lawless thought her capable of ripping off an employee. Ironic that *that's* where she drew the line. Of all the awful things her organization had done to people, here Michelle was, most offended by the charge of possible "wage thief." "Those who do well are properly compensated. And you, Ms. Lawless, did well."

"Sorry, I seem to have ruined the mood."

There was *no* mood! Michelle was about to say as much when Lawless dug deep into her bag and plucked out a mini bottle of champagne. It was like something one would find in a hotel room bar fridge, only the label was one she recognized as being roughly comparable to swilling urine.

She regarded the bottle in mute horror. If Lawless thought Michelle was going to indulge her by toasting her success with *that*, she would be sorely disappointed.

Lawless burst out laughing. "Your face! It was so worth it. Don't worry, it's a gag gift. I kept telling the booze shop guy I needed the *worst* bottle he had. He thought I was crazy but said this by far was the lousiest champagne he knows."

"He's quite correct." Michelle bared her lips. "I wouldn't even use that for drain cleaner. But why are you throwing good money away on bad champagne?"

"Because it's funny. I really wanted to see your expression and whether you'd throw me out the window or not. Hannah said you were a collector and really picky about your bubbles, and I figure, if I can't afford the very best, I can at least get you the very worst." She grinned at her own insane logic.

"I'm not sure you want to be raising the topic of your collusion with my grandmother," Michelle warned.

"I hear you," Lawless said seriously, raising her hands, "and I did consider the risk. But since we won't see each other again, I figured it was worth it for a farewell to remember. Besides, that way you won't forget me in a hurry either!"

As if I'd forget my first and last panda employee.

"So, being serious now, I also got you this." Lawless slid on the table a box of Swiss 95 percent cocoa chocolate.

Michelle's mouth watered, and she noted the brand was one she approved of a great deal. "Well, that's an improvement. And I appreciate the thought, but it's really unnecessary."

Lawless shrugged. "I disagree. See, it's like this: Kevin needs a special someone. I spent months working out lists of potentials, their likes and dislikes, not to mention how far away they are, so Aggie can just look down the list, examine the photos, and choose the best one."

Michelle stared at her in complete confusion. "Who on earth is Kevin? And why are you telling me about your matchmaking efforts regarding this individual?"

"Kevin's a guinea pig," Lawless said, as though that should be obvious. "A one-eyed handsome dude we sprung from an animal testing lab a few years back." Lawless flicked through her phone and held up a photo of a tan and white guinea pig that was indeed impressive if you liked that sort of thing. "He's Insta famous and utterly adored by his favorite human, Aggie, but we're both worried he's lonely for company since his last friend curled up her little toes. I've been researching a companion for him as part of my birthday present for Aggie."

Michelle rubbed her temple in exasperation. "I dread to ask why you are informing the CEO of The Fixers of *any* of this."

"Because the master list of guinea pigs and their sellers around DC that I spent *three months compiling* is *on* my laptop. My whole life is on this laptop." She patted it. "Along with all my work, all my clients, all my life's research. Plus, twenty percent of a bad lesbian sci-fi thriller I wrote when I was sixteen which I claim I keep for sentimental value but secretly think one day I'll finish. A whole ton of music. And you *rescued* it. All of it. From the actual heart of darkness of Wingapo. *I know, I know*, you were protecting your organization's secrecy, but you have also given me back my whole life. So: bad champagne, good chocolate, and tinny classical music is the very least I can do." Lawless added in a heartfelt tone, "Thank you, Michelle."

Finally, it made sense. As much as things could make sense in the brain of Eden Lawless. "Well, it *is* what we do. But I will enjoy the chocolate, at least." Extending her index finger, she poked the hideous bottle back toward Lawless. "May I suggest you use the so-called champagne for engine cleaner. It probably would cut right through the grease like acid. Grace will never run better." She smiled.

Eden threw back her head and laughed. "Good one. And it's Gloria. As in Steinem." She clambered to her feet. "Well, I better hit the road."

Michelle's heart sank.

Don't go.

Her grandmother's words flooded her mind. She could form a friendship with an ex-employee, couldn't she?

Except Michelle didn't really form friendships with anyone. She couldn't talk about what she did for a living with most people; they'd run from her if they knew. And she couldn't befriend any underling when she was the CEO. That was unacceptable. So, no, friendship was impossible.

That decided, before she knew it, Michelle was standing too. It took a moment to realize the woman was now standing in front of her, laptop bag slung over one shoulder, and giving her an altogether too soft look.

No one ever looked at her that fondly, except her safta. Michelle was quite sure it was undeserved, but still. It was…unexpectedly nice. Warmth filled her chest. She'd miss it.

I will not, her brain protested.

Who was she kidding? She would. But the Eden Lawless experience was officially over.

"It's been really great working with you," Lawless was saying.

Why was she standing so close? Michelle blinked in surprise. When had she moved?

"I truly am sorry for making you send in a team for my laptop," she continued. "I also feel awful about the whole business with Hannah. I just found you too interesting not to ask about. I loved your safta. Please give her my best. And, hey, take care of yourself too, okay?"

Lawless swayed in, and suddenly, engulfing arms surrounded Michelle as that unmistakable voice whispered into her ear, "I'll miss you, Michelle."

Michelle was so startled she didn't so much as twitch. Her heart sped up like it was planning to launch itself into space.

Then Lawless was stepping back, her grin turning shy, cheeks pinkening. "Oh dear." She chuckled. "Halfway into that I remembered that you're not like all my protester friends and might not like being hugged. But see, I was committed by then. Couldn't have done a last-minute pull-back move without looking completely uncool." She grinned and grabbed her phone, hitting stop on the music playback.

The office fell eerily silent without Vivaldi.

Michelle stared unblinkingly back at her. *What just happened?* She'd just been *bodily seized* and pulled against this woman's shape and warmth as if that were a *totally acceptable* thing to do! And, God, Michelle wanted her to do it again. Lawless's body had been soft, her embracing arms so gentle. She smelled of apple shampoo and fresh cotton, not a hint of perfume or artificial scents.

"You okay there, Michelle?" Lawless asked after a moment, eyes twinkling.

"That was *not* appropriate," she whispered.

Lawless gave her a sheepish look. "Ah. See, it *is* my standard fare-well for one and all. Sorry for overstepping. I guess that was some lasting last impression I just made." She laughed in what seemed to be embarrassment. "Oops. Anyway, have a great life, Michelle." Lawless turned to leave.

"Wait!" Michelle said sharply. "I mean. I...there was one other piece of business."

Lawless turned back and frowned. "There was?" She hitched her laptop case strap higher on her shoulder.

"I've been considering something. You appear to have a skill set none of my other operatives possess."

"I do?"

Michelle inhaled. *What are you doing! Say goodbye. Let her go. Make her go!* "You have a flair for creativity that's not common. The problem-solving is one thing. I understand you were stymied by that fence going up around City Hall. So you came up with a solution. But then to work out a way to have an audience, so there'd be people to be talking it up online, people the news services could quote, was quite clever. You added an atmosphere. And you did all of this while without your primary work tool." She waved at the laptop. "So, Ms. Lawless, would you like to work for me?"

"For...you?" Lawless clarified. "Specifically?"

"I meant The Fixers, of course. I have a few other jobs in the pipe-line that might be right up your alley. And because they're local this time, I can even give you a desk so you're not forced to work from a bed and breakfast or your van."

"I..." Lawless looked as if Michelle had just hit her over the head.

Dear God, she isn't going to say no, is she?

Michelle had just metaphorically flung herself in front of this woman and all but begged. Her jaw ground at the thought that she was about to be humiliated. Even so, she felt the need to sell her offer. "The remuneration will be ample. Plus, all benefits—health, dental, and so on. You'd be properly looked after."

Why did I say that?

"By the organization," Michelle added quickly. "And while you're working for us, IT will upgrade you to a far better device so you can be properly protected in the event you lose your laptop again." *Ugh.* Could she *sound* more desperate? Her brain was already screaming at her for this ridiculous, half-baked plan to keep Lawless around.

"I didn't *lose it* the first time," she noted dryly. "Wingapo's chief of police broke into my van and stole it."

"Yes, of course." Michelle agreed, now hating everything about this conversation. "Well? Want some regular work for once?" *Oh, that just sounded catty.* She offered a flash of a smile, hoping to lighten her remark.

"Do I get a view?" Lawless asked, and that cheeky, dimpled grin made a reappearance.

A view? Of all the… Employees who'd worked here for *years* had never acquired a desk with a view!

"Of course," Michelle said. Her brain howled even louder.

"Do you…understand I've never worked in an office before?" Lawless asked, suddenly looking less sure of herself. "I may make mistakes. Maybe I should think it over."

"Offices are simply buildings, Ms. Lawless. I assume your quick mind can learn its inner workings in much the same way you can read a protest or cause. Surely you're not saying you're daunted by the fact my workplace has four walls?"

"I didn't say I was daunted." Lawless tilted her head. "I guess I can give it a crack. I'm sure it'll be a learning curve, but it might be kind of cool to try something new. Just to say I've done it once."

"*Cool*," Michelle mused. "I don't think anyone's ever described my organization that way before. I'm gathering, though, you're willing to take on the challenge? You do strike me as the sort who thrives on a challenge." Her gaze skidded up and down Lawless's form.

Lawless caught it and lifted her eyebrows in a matching challenge. "Well, okay, then," she said, sounding decided. "I really like the idea of doing more good. There's enough evil in the world already. Sign me up. We'll see how it goes, okay?"

Michelle's plastered-on smile faltered. *More* good things? She truly thought Michelle and The Fixers did good. Now would be the perfect time to set her straight. To explain that ninety percent of the time The Fixers did bad things. Five percent of the time, they did pure evil.

And that was because 100 percent of the time, they fulfilled the whims and wishes of the rich and powerful and rarely did that coincide with doing good things.

Tell her.

"Welcome aboard," Michelle said smartly. "You start Monday."

Lawless's smile was bright enough to light a galaxy.

"Oh, and Ms. Lawless?" Michelle said sternly. "There'll be no more of that..." she waved at her. "Goodbye hugging business. Or *any* hugging at all. Understood?"

"Yes, Michelle." Lawless's eyes twinkled. "No more hugging. That goes for you too."

Michelle's eyes narrowed into warning slits.

In the face of her volcanic levels of indignation, Lawless merely chuckled.

END BOOK ONE
The story concludes in *Chaos Agent*

Other Books from
Ylva Publishing

www.ylva-publishing.com

The Red Files
(On the Record series – Book 1)

Lee Winter

ISBN: 978-3-96324-534-3
Length: 304 pages (103,000 words)

Ambitious journalist Lauren King is stuck reporting on the vapid LA social scene's gala events while sparring with her rival—icy ex-Washington correspondent Catherine Ayers. Then a curious story unfolds before their eyes, involving a business launch, thirty-four prostitutes, and a pallet of missing pink champagne. Can the warring pair join together to unravel an incredible story?

Rival reporters team up for the story of their careers in this lesbian romantic suspense filled with humor, twists, and one fierce ice queen.

Under Your Skin
(On the Record series – Book 2)

Lee Winter

ISBN: 978-3-96324-026-3
Length: 332 pages (111,000 words)

What do a food-delivery robot, a face from the past, and plans to microchip veterans have in common? Caustic DC bureau chief Catherine Ayers would love to know but she and Lauren King are busy wedding planning in Iowa. That means a lot of beefy brothers, a haughty cat, and a sharp-tongued Meemaw. But she's sure she can play nice. Well, pretty sure.

Ice queen Ayers and Iowan girl King are back chasing a crazy story and planning one big fat wedding in this lesbian romance sequel to The Red Files.

A Curious Woman
Jess Lea

ISBN: 978-3-96324-160-4
Length: 283 pages (100,000 words)

Bess has moved to a coastal town where she has a job at a hip gallery, some territorial chickens, and a lot of self-help books. She's also at war with Margaret, who runs the local museum with an iron fist. When they're both implicated in a senseless murder, can they work together to expose the truth?

A funny, fabulous, cozy mystery filled with quirkiness and a sweet serve of lesbian romance.

Under a Falling Star
Jae

ISBN: 978-3-95533-238-9
Length: 369 pages (91,000 words)

Falling stars are supposed to be a lucky sign, but not for Austen. The first assignment in her new job—decorating the Christmas tree in the lobby—results in a trip to the ER after Dee, the company's COO, gets hit by the star-shaped tree topper. There's an instant attraction between them, but Dee is determined not to act on it, especially since Austen has no idea that Dee is her boss.

About Lee Winter

Lee Winter is an award-winning veteran newspaper journalist who has lived in almost every Australian state, covering courts, crime, news, features, and humour writing. Now a full-time author and part-time editor, Lee is also a 2015 and 2016 Lambda Literary Award finalist and has won several Golden Crown Literary Awards. She lives in Western Australia with her long-time girlfriend, where she spends much time ruminating on her garden, US politics, and shiny, new gadgets.

CONNECT WITH LEE

Website: www.leewinterauthor.com

The Fixer
© 2023 by Lee Winter

ISBN: 978-3-96324-746-0

Available in e-book and paperback formats.

Published by Ylva Publishing, legal entity of Ylva Verlag, e.Kfr.

Ylva Verlag, e.Kfr.
Owner: Astrid Ohletz
Am Kirschgarten 2
65830 Kriftel
Germany

www.ylva-publishing.com

First edition: 2023

Credits
Edited by Alissa McGowan and Michelle Aguilar
Cover Design and Print Layout by Streetlight Graphics